A BALL OF MALT

AND

MADAME BUTTERFLY

A BALL OF MALT

AND

MADAME BUTTERFLY

A Dozen Stories by

BENEDICT KIELY

LONDON
VICTOR GOLLANCZ LTD
1973

ISBN 0 575 01663 9

HYNDBURN
ACCRINGTON

ACKNOWLEDGEMENTS

The first four stories have appeared in *The New Yorker*;
WILD ROVER NO MORE in *The Northwest Review*; A BOTTLE OF
BROWN SHERRY and A BALL OF MALT AND MADAME BUTTERFLY in
The Kenyon Review and the last-named in *Penguin Modern Stories*;
GOD'S OWN COUNTRY in *Winter's Tales From Ireland*; THE GREEN
LANES in *Audience*; THE WEAVERS AT THE MILL in the *Kilkenny
Magazine*; and DOWN THEN BY DERRY in the *Dublin Magazine*.
To the editors I send the customary thanks and acknowledge-
ments.

01591390

Fy/CL

MADE AND PRINTED IN GREAT BRITAIN BY
THE GARDEN CITY PRESS LIMITED
LETCHWORTH, HERTFORDSHIRE
SG6 1JS

CONTENTS

For Arthur Doran
of Mourne

A GREAT GOD'S ANGEL STANDING

Pascal Stakelum, the notorious rural rake, and
Father Paul, the ageing Catholic curate of Lislap, met the
two soldiers from Devon by the bridge over the Camowen
River and right beside the lunatic asylum. It was a day of
splitting sunshine in the year of the Battle of Dunkirk. Pascal
and the priest were going to visit the lunatic asylum, Father
Paul to hear confessions, Pascal to bear him company and to
sit at a sealed distance while the inmates cudgelled what wits
they had and told their sins. The two soldiers, in battledress
and with heavy packs on their backs, were on their way home
from Dunkirk, not home to Devon exactly but to Sixmilecross, to the house of two sisters they had married in a hurry
before they set off for France. It was, as you may have guessed,
six miles from our garrison town of Lislap to the crossroads
village where the two sisters lived, and it was a very warm
day. So every one of the four, two in thick khaki, two in dull
black, was glad to stop and stand at ease and look at the
smooth gliding of the cool Camowen.

The bridge they rested on was of a brownish grey stone,
three full sweeping arches and, to the sides, two tiny niggardly
arches. In a blue sky a few white clouds idled before a light
wind, and beyond a wood at an upstream bend of the river a
two-horse mowing-machine ripped and rattled in meadow
grass. The stone of the bridge was cut from the same quarry as
the stone in the high long wall that circled the lunatic asylum
and went for a good half-mile parallel with the right bank of
the river.

—In France it was hot, said the first soldier.

—He means the weather was hot, said the second soldier.

The four men, priest and rake and soldiers two, laughed at

that : not, Pascal says, much of a laugh, not sincere, no heartiness in it.

—Hot as hell, said the second soldier. Even the rivers was hot.

—Boiling, said the first soldier. That canal at Lille was as hot as a hot bath.

—Ruddy mix-up, said the second soldier. The Guards, they fired at the Fusiliers, and the Fusiliers, they fired at the Guards. Nobody knew who was what. Ruddy mix-up.

They took the cigarettes Pascal offered.

—Boiling hot and thirsty, said the second soldier. Never knew such thirst.

Father Paul said : You could have done with some Devon cider.

—Zider, said the first soldier. There were zomething.

—Zomerzet you are, said the second soldier.

They all laughed again. This time it was a real laugh.

The Camowen water where it widened over gravel to go under the five stone arches was clear and cool as a mountain rockspring. Upstream, trout rings came as regularly as the ticks of a clock.

The two soldiers accepted two more cigarettes. They tucked them into the breast-pockets of their battledress. They hitched their packs, shook hands several times and knelt on the motorless roadway for Father Paul's blessing. They were not themselves Arcees, they said, but in camp in Aldershot in England they had been matey with an Arcee padre, and they knew the drill. Blessed after battle, they stood up, dusted their knees as carefully as if they'd never heard of mud or blood and, turning often to wave back, walked on towards the two sisters of Sixmilecross.

—Virginia, Father Paul said, was the best place I ever saw for cider.

Just to annoy him, Pascal said : Virginia, County Cavan, Ireland.

They were walking together on a narrow footwalk in the shadow of the asylum wall.

8

—Virginia, U.S.A., Paul said. The Old Dominion. Very well you know what Virginia I mean. They had great apple orchards there, and fine cider presses, around a little town called Fincastle under the shadow of the Blue Ridge Mountains. That was great country, and pleasant people and fine horses, when I was a young man on the American mission.

It was a period out of his lost youth that Paul frequently talked about.

In those days of his strange friendship with Pascal he was thin and long-faced and stoop-shouldered with the straining indignant stoop that is forced on tall people when the years challenge the power to hold the head so high. That day the sun had sucked a little moisture out of his pale cheeks. He had taken off his heavy black hat to give the light breeze a chance to ruffle and cool his thin grey hair, but the red line the hat rim had made was still to be seen and, above the red line, a sullen concentration of drops of sweat. He was though, as Pascal so often said, the remains of a mighty handsome man and with such dignity, too, and stern faith and such an eloquent way in the pulpit that it was a mystery to all of us what the bishop of the diocese had against him that he had never given him the honour, glory and profit of a parish of his own.

—In the mood those two boyos are in, Pascal said, it will take them no time at all walking to the sisters at Sixmilecross.

That was the way Pascal, in accordance with his animal nature, thought; and Sixmilecross was a village in which, as in every other village in our parts, Pascal had had some of the rural adventures that got him his dubious reputation, and that made us all marvel when we'd see a character like him walking in the company of a priest. In Burma, I once heard an old sweat say, adulterers kill a pig to atone for their crime, so it was only apt and proper, and even meet and just, that Pascal should be a pork butcher. When he went a-wooing in country places he'd never walk too far from his rattly old Morris Cowley without bringing with him a tyre lever or starting handle, for country girls were hell for having truculent brothers and if they didn't have brothers they had worse and

9

far and away worse, male cousins, and neither brothers nor male cousins, least of all the male cousins, had any fancy for Pascal rooting and snorting about on the fringes of the family. That's Pascal, for you. But at the moment, Paul is speaking.

—A man hungers to get home, he said. The men from Devon won't count the time or the number of paces. Time, what's time? They've come a long walk from the dreadful gates of eternity. Once I told you, Pascal boy, you were such a rake and run-the-roads you'd have to live to be ninety, to expiate here on this earth and so dodge the devil.

Complacently Pascal said : The good die young.

—Ninety's a long time, Father Paul said. But what's time? Here in this part of my parish . . .

They were walking in at the wide gateway. He waved his black wide-brimmed hat in a circle comprehending the whole place, as big almost as the garrison town itself, for all the crazy people of two counties, or those of them that had been detected and diagnosed, were housed there.

—This part of my parish, he said. As much happiness or unhappiness as in any other part of the parish. But one thing that doesn't matter here is time. As far as most of them know, time and eternity are the same thing.

They walked along a serpentine avenue, up sloping lawns to the main door. The stone in the walls of the high building was cut from the same quarry as the stone that bridged the river, as the stone in the encircling wall. The stone floor in the long cool corridor rang under their feet. They followed a porter along that corridor to a wide bright hospital ward. Unshaven men in grey shirts sat up in bed and looked at them with quick bright questioning eyes. The shining nervous curiosity of the ones who sat up disturbed Pascal. He preferred to look at the others who lay quietly in bed and stared steadily at points on the ceiling or on the opposite wall, stared steadily but seemed to see neither the ceiling nor the opposite wall, and sometimes mumbled to nobody words that had no meaning. A few men in grey suits moved aimlessly about the floor or sat to talk with some of the bright curious men in the beds.

Beside the doorway a keeper in blue uniform dotted with brass buttons sat and smoked and read a newspaper, raised his head and nodded to the priest, then returned to his pipe and his newspaper.

Father Paul moved from bed to bed, his purple stole about his neck. The murmur of his voice, particularly when he was at the Latin, was distinctly audible. His raised hand sawed the air in absolution and blessing. Once in a while he said something in English in a louder voice and then the man he was with would laugh, and the priest would laugh, and the man in the next bed, if he was a bright-eyed man, would laugh, and another bright-eyed man several beds away would start laughing and be unable to stop, and a ripple of laughter would run around the room touching everybody except the staring mumbling men and the keeper who sat by the door.

Pascal sat beside an empty bed and read a paperbacked book about a doctor in Germany who was, or said he thought he was, two men, and had murdered his wife, who had been a showgirl, by bathing her beautiful body in nitric acid. That sinful crazy waste of good material swamped Pascal in an absorbing melancholy so that he didn't for a few moments even notice the thin hand gripping his thigh. There, kneeling at his feet, was a man in grey clothes, misled into thinking Pascal was a priest because Pascal wore, as did the gay young men of that place and period, a black suit with, though, extremely wide and unclerical trousers. Pascal studied, with recognition, the inmate's grey jacket, the scarce grey hair, the spotted dirty scalp. The kneeling man said: Bless me, father, for I have sinned.

—Get up to hell Jock Sharkey, Pascal said. I'm no priest. You're crazy.

He was, he says, crimson in the face with embarrassment. The keeper was peeking over his newspaper, laughing, saying Jock sure was crazy and that, in fact, was why he was where he was. The keeper also blew smoke-rings from thick laughing lips, an irritating fellow. He said: Fire away, Pascal. It'll keep him quiet. I hear him two or three times a week.

—It wouldn't be right, Pascal said.

He had theological scruples, the only kind he could afford.

Only once in my life, he was to say afterwards, did a man ever ask me to listen to him confessing his sins and, fair enough, the place should be a lunatic asylum and the man, poor Jock Sharkey, that was put away for chasing women, not that he ever overtook them or did anybody any harm. They walked quick, he walked quick. They walked slow, he walked slow. He was just simply fascinated, the poor gormless bastard, by the sound of their feet, the hobbled trot, the high heels, you know, clickety-click, thigh brushing thigh. Poor Jock.

—What he'll tell you, said the keeper, is neither right nor wrong. Who'd anyway be better judge than yourself, Pascal? Even Father Paul doesn't know one half of what you know. You, now, would know about things Paul never heard tell of.

The man on his knees said : I suppose you'll put me out of the confession box, father. I'm a terrible sinner. I wasn't at mass or meeting since the last mission.

—Why was that? said Pascal the priest.

—The place I'm working in, they won't let me go to mass.

—Then it's not your fault, said Pascal. No sin. Grievous matter, perfect knowledge, full consent.

He did, he said afterwards, remember from his schooldays that impressive fragment of the penny catechism of Christian doctrine : the stud-book, the form-book, the rules for the big race from here to eternity.

—But when I go to confession, father, I've a bad memory for my sins. Will you curse me, father, if I forget some of them?

—By no means, Jock. Just recite what you remember.

The keeper, more offensive as his enjoyment increased, said that Pascal wouldn't know how to curse, that he didn't know the language. The head of the kneeling man nodded backwards and forwards while he mumbled the rhythmical words of some prayer or prayers of his childhood. Now and again the names of saints came clearly out of the confused unintelligible mumble, like bubbles rising from a marshy bottom to the surface of a slow stream. Then he repeated carefully, like a child reciting, these words from an old rebel song : I cursed three times since last Easter Day. At mass-time once I went to play.

Pascal was seldom given to visions except in one particular direction, yet he says that at that moment he did see, from his memory of school historical pageants, the rebel Irish boy, kneeling in all innocence or ignorance at the feet of the brutal red-coated captain whose red coat was, for the occasion, covered by the soutane of the murdered rebel priest.

The keeper said : You should sing that, Jock.

—I passed the churchyard one day in haste, Jock said, and forgot to pray for my mother's rest.

—You're sure of heaven, said the keeper, if that's the sum total of your sins. The Reverend Stakelum himself, or even Father Paul, won't get off so easy.

The penitent looked up at Pascal and Pascal looked down at stubbly chin, hollow jaws, sorrowful brown eyes. Poor Jock, Pascal thought, they put you away just for doing what I spend all my spare time, and more besides, at : to wit, chasing the girls. Only you never even seemed to want to catch up with them.

For poor Jock was never more than what we called a sort of a mystery man, terrifying the girls, or so they claimed, by his nightly wanderings along dark roads, his sudden sprints that ended as sharply and pointlessly as they began, his shouted meaningless words provoked perhaps by a whiff of perfume in his nostrils or by that provocative tap-tippity-tap of high hard heels on the metalled surface of the road. A child might awaken in the night and cry that there was a man's face at the window. A girl might run home breathless and say that Jock had followed her for half a mile, suiting his pace to hers, like a ghost or a madman. He couldn't be a ghost, although he was as thin and as harmless as any ghost. So we put him away for a madman.

He stared long and hard at Pascal. His thin right hand tightly grasped Pascal's knee.

—David Stakelum's son, he said. I'd know you anywhere on your father. Thank God to see you in the black clothes. Your father was a decent man and you'll give me the blessing of a decent man's son.

He bowed his head and joined his hands. Behind the newspaper the keeper was gurgling. Pascal said afterwards that his father wouldn't be too pleased to think that his hell's own special hell-raker of a son bore him such a resemblance that even a crazy man could see it. But if his blessing would help to make Jock content then Jock was welcome to it. So he cut the sign of the cross over the old crazy dirty head. He touched with the tips of the fingers of both hands the bald patch on the dome. He held out those fingers to be kissed. The most fervent young priest fresh from the holy oil couldn't have done a better job. Pascal had so often studied the simple style of Father Paul. The keeper was so impressed that he folded the newspaper and sat serious and quiet.

Father Paul walked slowly towards them, along the narrow passage between the two rows of beds. Walking with him came a fat red-faced grey-headed inmate. The fat inmate talked solemnly, gestured stiffly with his right hand. The priest listened, or pretended to listen, turning his head sideways, stretching his neck, emphasising the stoop in his shoulders. He said : Mr. Simon, you haven't met my young friend, Pascal.

The fat man smiled benevolently at Pascal but went on talking to the priest. As you know, sir, I am not of the Roman Catholic persuasion, yet I have always been intrigued by the theory and practice of auricular confession. The soul of man, being walled around and shut in as it is, demands some outlet for the thoughts and desires that accumulate therein.

He had, Pascal says, a fruity pansy voice.

—The child, he said, runs to its mother with its little tale of sorrow. Friend seeks out friend. In silence and secrecy souls are interchanged.

14

It was exactly, Pascal was to say, as if the sentences had been written on the air in the loops and lines of copper-plate. You could not only hear but see the man's talk : A Wesleyan I was born, sir, and so remain. But always have I envied you Roman Catholics the benefits of the confessional, the ease that open confession brings to the soul. What is the Latin phrase, sir?

Paul said : Ad quietam conscientiam.

—Ad quietam conscientiam, Simon repeated. There is peace in every single syllable. There is much wisdom in your creed, sir. Wesley knew that. You have observed the spiritual similarity between Wesley and Ignatius of Loyola.

The keeper said : Simon, Doctor Murdy's looking for you. Where in hell were you?

—He asks me where I have been, sir. Where in hell.

Father Paul said : He means no harm, Simon. Just his manner of speaking.

Simon was still smiling. From elbow to bent wrist and dangling hand, his right arm was up like a question mark. He said to Father Paul : Surveillance, sir, is a stupid thing. It can accomplish nothing, discover nothing. If I were to tell this fellow where I had been, how could he understand? On this earth I have been, and beyond this earth.

He shook hands with the priest but not with Pascal nor the keeper nor Jock Sharkey. He walked with dignity past the keeper and back down the ward.

—There goes a travelled man, Pascal said.

Father Paul was folding his purple stole. He said : There are times when religion can be a straitjacket.

—It's not Simon's time yet for the straitjacket, the keeper said. When the fit takes him he'll brain the nearest neighbour with the first handy weapon.

At the far end of the ward where Simon had paused for a moment, there was a sudden noise and a scuffling. The keeper said : Too much learning is the divil.

He thumped down the passage between the beds.

—Now for the ladies, Father Paul said. You'll be at home there, Pascal, They say all over the town that no man living has an easier way with the ladies.

Pascal was to report to myself and a few others that if Paul had wanted to preach him a sermon to make his blood run cold and to put him off the women for the rest of his life, he couldn't have gone about it in a better way.

Is it true that, as the poet said, you never knew a holy man but had a wicked man for his comrade and heart's darling? Was it part of Paul's plan to pick Pascal as his escort and so to make an honest boy out of him or, at least, to cut in on the time that he would otherwise spend rummaging and ruining the girls of town and country? The thing about Pascal was that, away from the companionship of Paul, he thought of nothing but women when, of course, he wasn't butchering pork, and perhaps he thought of women even then. Like many another who is that way afflicted he wasn't big, violent, handsome, red-faced or blustering. No, he went about his business in a quiet way. His hair was sparse, of a nondescript colour, flatly combed and showing specks of dandruff. He wore horn-rimmed spectacles. He was one of those white-faced fellows who would, softly and secretly and saying nothing about it to their best friends, take advantage of their own grandmothers. The women were mad about him. They must have been. He kept himself in fettle and trim for his chosen vocation. When the two soldiers and Paul were, in the sunshine on the Camowen Bridge, talking of Devon cider, Pascal was thinking, he says, of sherry and raw eggs, and oysters, porter and paprika pepper.

On the day of Paul's funeral he said to me : A decent man and I liked him. But, my God, he had a deplorable set against the women or anybody that fancied the women.

—Except myself, he said. For some reason or other he put up with me.

—That day at the female ward, he said, at the geriatrics you call 'em, I cheated him, right under his nose, God forgive me. And may Paul himself forgive me, since he knows it all now.

Pascal stood at the threshold of this female ward while Father Paul, purple stole again around his neck, moved, listening and forgiving with God's forgiveness, from bed to bed. Pascal wasn't much of a theologian, yet looking at the females in that female ward he reckoned that it was God, not the females, who needed forgiveness. They were all old females, very old females, and as such didn't interest Pascal. He had nothing, though, against old age as long as it left him alone. His father's mother was an attractive, chubby, silver-haired female, sweet as an apple forgotten and left behind on a rack in a pantry, wrinkled, going dry, yet still sweet beyond description. But these sad old females, a whole wardful of them, were also mad and misshapen, some babbling like raucous birds, some silently slavering.

He couldn't make up his mind whether to enter the ward and sit down or to walk up and down the cool echoing corridor. He always felt a fool when walking up and down like a sentry, but then he also felt a fool when standing or sitting still. He was just a little afraid of those caricatures of women. This was the first time he had ever been afraid of women, and afraid to admit to himself that these creatures were made in exactly the same way as women he had known. He was afraid that if he went into the ward and sat down he would see them in even greater detail than he now did from the threshold. He was young. Outside the sun was shining, the Camowen sparkling under the sun, the meadow grass falling like green silk to make beds for country lovers. But here all flesh was grass and favour was deceitful and beauty was vain. It was bad enough looking at the men. To think what the mind could do to the body. But it was hell upon earth looking at the women. Jock Sharkey, like a million lovers and a thousand poets, had gone mad for beauty. This, in the ward before him, was what could happen to beauty.

He stepped, shuddering, back into the corridor and collided with a tall nurse. He apologised. He smelled freshly-ironed, starched linen and disinfectant, a provoking smell. A quick flurried glance showed him a strong handsome face, rather boyish, brick-red hair bursting out over the forehead where the nurse's veil had failed to restrain it. He apologised. He was still rattled by his vision in the ward. Contrary to his opportunist instinct he was even about to step out of the way. But the nurse didn't pass. She said : It is you, Pascal Stakelum, isn't it? Did they lock you up at last? A hundred thousand welcomes.

He had to do some rapid thinking before he remembered. There were so many faces in his memory and he was still confused, still a little frightened, by those faces in the ward. She didn't try to help. She stood, feet apart and solidly planted, and grinned at him, too boyish for a young woman but still fetching. She was, if anything, taller than he was. Her brother, then he remembered, had gone to school with us, a big fellow, as dark as she was red, very clever but capricious, making a mockery of things that he alone, perhaps, of all of us could understand and, in the end, throwing the whole thing up and running away and joining the Royal Air Force. So the first thing Pascal said, to show that he knew who she was, was to ask about the brother, and when would he be coming home. She said : He won't be coming home.

—Why for not?

She said he had been killed at Dunkirk.

Coming right after the prospect of the mad old women, that was a bit of a blow in the face, but at least, he told himself, clean death in battle was not madness, deformity, decay; and the moment gave Pascal the chance to sympathise, to get closer to her. He held her hands. He said he was sorry. He said he had always liked her brother. He had, too. They had, indeed, been quite friendly.

She said : It's war. He would always do things his own way.

She seemed proud of her brother, or just proud of having a brother dead at Dunkirk.

—This is no place to talk, Pascal said. And I'm with Father Paul. Meet me this evening at the Crevenagh Bridge.

18

That was the old humpy seventeenth-century bridge on the way to a leafy network of lovers' lanes and deep secret bushy ditches.

—Not this evening, she said. I'm on duty. But tomorrow.

—Eight o'clock on the dot, said Pascal.

That was his usual time during the summer months and the long warm evenings. And he was very punctual.

She walked away from him and towards Father Paul. He looked after her, no longer seeing the rest of the ward. She was a tall strong girl, stepping with decision and a great swing. Jock Sharkey would have followed her to the moon.

Father Paul, the shriving done, was again folding his stole. He joked with a group of old ladies. He told one of them that on his next visit he would bring her a skipping rope. He told another one he would bring her a powderpuff. He distributed handfuls of caramels to the whole crew. They cackled with merriment. They loved him. That was one bond between Pascal and himself. The women loved them both.

—But if he meant to preach to me that time, Pascal said to us, by bringing me to that chamber of horrors, I had the laugh on him.

In the sunshine on the lawn outside, the superintending doctor stood with his wife and his dogs, three Irish setters, one male, two female. The doctor and his wife stood, that is, and the setters ran round and round in erratic widening circles.

Those smart-stepping Devon men were by now approaching Sixmilecross, and the two sisters, and rest after battle and port after stormy seas.

The doctor was a handsome cheery fellow, even if he was bald. He wore bright yellow, hand-made shoes, Harris tweed trousers and a high-necked Aran sweater. The wife was small and dainty and crisp as a nut, and a new wife; and the two of them, not to speak of the three setters, were as happy as children. They talked—the doctor, the woman, Paul and Pascal—about the war, and about the two soldiers from Devon and their two women in Sixmilecross. Then Father Paul wished the doctor and his wife many happy days, and he and Pascal stepped off towards the town. At the gateway they met a group of thirty or forty uniformed inmates returning, under supervision, from a country walk. One of them was gnawing a raw turnip with which, ceasing to gnaw, he took aim at Pascal and let fly. Pascal fielded the missile expertly—in his schooldays he had been a sound midfield man—and restored it to the inmate who was still chewing and looking quite amazed at his own deed. All this, to the great amusement of the whole party, inmates and three keepers. But, oddly enough, Paul didn't join in the merriment. He stood, silent and abstracted, on the grass at the side of the driveway. He looked at the sky. His lips moved as though he were praying, or talking to himself.

Pascal gave away what cigarettes he had left to the hiking party and he and the priest walked on, Paul very silent, over the Camowen. When they were halfways to the town, Paul said : Some men can't live long without a woman.

Pascal said nothing. He remembered that there was a story that Paul had once beaten a loving couple out of the hedge with a blackthorn stick. He remembered that Paul came from a stern mountainy part of the country where there had been a priest in every generation in every family for three hundred years. He thought of the red nurse and the hedge ahead of her. So he said nothing.

—That new wife of his, Paul said, was American. Did you notice?

—She dressed American, Pascal said. But she had no accent.

—She comes from a part of the States and from a class in society where they don't much have an accent, Paul said. At least not what you in your ignorance would call an American accent.

Pascal said : The Old Dominion.

—You're learning fast, Paul said.

The town was before them.

—Three wives he had, Paul said. One dead. Irish. One divorced. English. And now a brand new one from Virginia. Some men can't go without.

Pascal made no comment. He contented himself with envying the bald doctor his international experience. He resolved to travel.

—Most men, said Paul, aren't happy unless they're tangled up with a woman. The impure touch. But the French are the worst. Their blood boiling with wine. From childhood. How could they keep pure?

Pascal hadn't the remotest idea. So he made no comment. He didn't know much about the French but he reckoned that just at that moment in history they had enough and to spare on their plates without also having to worry about purity.

—But pleasures are like poppies spread, Paul said.

He was a great man always to quote the more moralising portions of Robert Burns. Pascal heard him out: You seize the flower, it's bloom is shed. Or like the snow falls in the river—a moment white, then melts forever. Or like the borealis race, that flit ere you can point their place. Or like the rainbow's lovely form, evanishing amid the storm.

—Burns, said Father Paul, well knew what he was talking about. Those, Pascal, are the words of wisdom gained through sad and sordid experience.

Pascal agreed. He was remembering the nurse's dead brother who had been a genius at poetry. He could write parodies on anything that any poet had ever written.

When Pascal met the nurse at the Crevenagh Bridge on the following evening she was, of course, in mourning. But the black cloth went very well with that brilliant red hair. Or like the rainbow's lovely form. There was something about it, too, that was odd and exciting, like being out, he said, with a young nun. Yet, apart from the colour of her clothes, she was no nun. Although, come to think of it, who except God knows what nuns are really like?

Pascal, as we know, was also in black but he had no reason to be in mourning. It had rained, just enough to wet the pitch. Otherwise the evening went according to Operation Pascal. When he had first attacked with the knee for the warming-up process he then withdrew the knee and substituted the hand, lowering it through the band of her skirt, allowing it to linger for a playful moment at the bunker of the belly button. Thereafter he seemed to be hours, like fishermen hauling a net, pulling a silky slip out of the way before the rummaging hand, now living a life of its own, could negotiate the passage into her warm drawers. Pascal didn't know why he hadn't made the easier and more orthodox approach by laying the girl low to begin with and then raising skirt and slip, except it was that they were standing up at the time, leaning against a sycamore tree. The rain had passed but the ground was wet, and to begin his wooing by spreading his trenchcoat (Many's the fine rump, he boasted, that trenchcoat had kept dry, even when the snow was on the ground.) on the grass, seemed much too formal. Pascal Stakelum's days, or evenings or nights, were complex with such problems.

Later came the formal ceremonious spreading of the trenchcoat on a protective mattress of old newspapers, and the assuming by both parties, of the horizontal. By that time the big red girl was so lively that he swore she'd have shaken Gordon Richards, the King of them All, out of the saddle. She kept laughing and talking, too, so as to be audible, he reckoned, thirty yards away but fortunately he had chosen for the grand manoeuvre a secluded corner of the network of lanes and ditches. He had a veteran's knowledge of the terrain and he was nothing if not discreet.

He was not unmindful of the brother dead in faraway France. But then the brother had been such an odd fellow that even in Pascal's tusselling with his strong red sister he might have found matter for amusement and mockery. As Pascal bounced on top of her, gradually subduing her wildness to the rhythmic control of bridle and straddle and, in the end, to the britchen of his hands under her buttocks, he could hear her brother's voice beginning the schoolboy mockery of Shelley's soaring skylark : Hell to thee, blithe spirit. Pascal and the splendid panting red girl moved together to the poet's metre.

That was one brother Pascal did not have to guard against with starting handle or tyre lever. Working like a galley slave under the dripping sycamore he was in no fear of ambush.

Paul got his parish in the end, the reward of a well-spent life, he said wryly. He died suddenly in it before he was there for six months. That parish was sixty miles away from Lislap, in sleepy grass-meadow country where the slow River Bann drifts northwards out of the great lake. Pascal missed Paul's constant companionship more than he or anybody else would have believed possible and began, particularly after Paul's sudden death, to drink more than he had ever done before, and went less with the girls, which puzzled him as much as it did us. It worried him, too : for in the house of parliament or public house that we specially favoured, he asked me one day was he growing old before his time because he was growing fonder of drink and could now pass a strange woman on the street without wondering who and what she was.

—You're better off, Pascal, I said. What were you ever doing anyway but breaking them in for other men? You never stayed long enough with any one woman to be able in the long run to tell her apart from any other woman.

He was more hurt than I had imagined he would be. But he sadly agreed with me, and said that some day he hoped to find one real true woman with whom he could settle down.

—Like with poor Paul that's gone, he said. Some one woman that a man could remember to the last moment of his life.

—No, I'm not crazy, he said. Two days before his death I was with Paul in his parish, as you know. We went walking this evening after rain, by the banks of a small river in that heavy-grass country. That was the last walk we had together. The boreen we were on went parallel with the river bank. We met an old man, an old bewhiskered codger, hobbling on a stick. So Paul introduced us and said to Methusaleh : What now do you think of my young friend from the big garrison town of Lislap?

—The old fellow, said Pascal, looked me up and looked me

23

down. Real cunning country eyes. Daresay he could see through me as if I was a sheet of thin cellophane. But he lied. He said : Your reverence, he looks to me like a fine clean young man.

—That was an accurate description of me, Pascal Stakelum, known far and wide.

Pascal brooded. He said : A fine clean young man.

—Then that evening, he said, we sat for ages after dinner, before we knelt down to say the holy rosary with those two dry sticks of female cousins that did the housekeeping for him. One quick look at either of them would put you off women for time and eternity. There's an unnerving silence in the houses that priests live in : the little altar on the landing, you know, where they keep the sacrament for sick calls at night. Imagine, if you can, the likes of me on my bended knees before it, wondering would I ever remember the words when it came my turn to lead the prayers. But I staggered it. Closed my eyes, you might say, and took a run and jump at it, and landed on the other side word perfect. It would have been embarrassing for Paul if I hadn't been able to remember the words of the Paterandave in the presence of those two stern cousins. One evening one of them sat down opposite me in a low armchair and crossed her legs, poor thing, and before I could look elsewhere I had a view of a pair of long bloomers, passion-killllers, that were a holy fright. You wouldn't see the equal of them in the chamber of horrors. Six feet long and coloured grey and elastic below the knee. But when the two cousins were off to bed, and good luck to them, we sat and talked until all hours, and out came the bottle of Jameson, and Paul's tongue loosened. It could be that he said more than he meant to say : oh, mostly about Virginia and the Blue Ridge Mountains and the lovely people who always asked the departing stranger to come back again. Cider presses near Fincastle. Apple orchards. Dogwood trees in blossom. He went on like that for a long time. Then he got up, rooted among his books, came back with this one book covered in a sort of soft brown velvet with gold lettering and designs on the cover

24

and, inside, coloured pictures and the fanciest printing you ever saw, in red and in black. He said to me : Here's a book, Pascal, you might keep as a memory of me when I'm gone.

—So I laughed at him, making light of his gloomy face, trying to jolly him up, you know. I said : Where, now, would you be thinking of going?

—Where all men go sooner or later, he said.

—That was the end of my laughing. That's no way for a man to talk, even if he has a premonition.

—Keep the book as a token, Paul said to me. You were never much for the poetry, I know. But your wife when you find her might be, or, perhaps, some of your children. You've a long road ahead of you yet, Pascal, all the way to ninety, and poetry can lighten the burden. That book was given to me long ago by the dearest friend I ever had. Until I met yourself, he said. Long ago in a distant country and the wench is dead.

—Those were the last words I ever heard Paul speak, excepting the Latin of the mass next morning, for my bus passed the church gate before the mass was rightly over, and I had to run for it. But bloody odd words they were to come from Paul.

—Common enough words, I said. Anybody could have said them.

—But you didn't see the book, Pascal said. I'll show it to you.

He did, too, a week later. It was an exquisite little edition, lost on Pascal, I thought with some jealousy, both as to the perfection of the bookmaker's art and as to the text, which was William Morris telling us, there in a public house in Lislap, how Queen Guenevere had defended herself against the lies of Sir Gauwaine, and a charge of unchastity. Fondling the book, I was not above thinking how much more suitable than Pascal I would have been as a companion for old Paul. So that I felt more than a little ashamed when Pascal displayed to me with what care he had read the poem, underlining here and there in red ink to match the rubric of the capitals and the running titles on the tops of the pages. It was, almost certainly, the only poem to which he had ever paid any particular attention, with the possible exception of that bouncing parody on Shelley's skylark.

—It's like a miniature mass book, he said. Red and black. Only it was by no means intended for using at the mass. See here.

He read and pointed with his finger as he read: She threw her wet hair backward from her brow, her hand close to her mouth touching her cheek.

—Coming from the swimming-pool, Pascal said, when the dogwoods were in blossom. You never knew that Paul was a champion swimmer in his youth. Swimming's like tennis. Brings out the woman in a woman. Arms wide, flung-out, breasts up. Oh, there were a lot of aspects to Paul. And listen to this: Yet felt her cheek burned so, she must a little touch it. Like one lame she walked away from Gauwaine.

—Time and again, Pascal said, he had heard it said that lame women had the name for being hot. Once he had seen on the quays of Dublin a one-legged prositute. The thought had ever afterwards filled him with curiosity, although at the time he wouldn't have risked touching her for all the diamonds in Kimberley.

—And her great eyes began again to fill, he read, though still she stood right up.

That red nurse, he remembered, had had great blue eyes, looking up at him like headlamps seen through mist.

—But the queen in this poem, he said, was a queen and no mistake. And in the summer it says that she grew white with flame, white like the dogwood blossoms and all for this Launcelot fellow, lucky Launcelot, and such a pansy name. One day, she says, she was half-mad with beauty and went without her ladies all alone in a quiet garden walled round every way, just like the looney bin where I met that nurse. And both their mouths, it says, went wandering in one way and, aching sorely, met among the leaves. Warm, boy, warm. Then there's odd stuff here about a great God's angel standing at the foot of the bed, his wings dyed with colours not known on earth, and asking the guy or girl in the bed, the angel has

26

two cloths, you see, one blue, one red, asking them, or him or her, to guess which cloth is heaven and which is hell. The blue one turns out to be hell. That puzzles me.

It puzzled both of us.

—But you must admit, said Pascal, that it was a rare book for a young one to be giving a young priest, and writing on it, look here, for Paul with a heart's love, by the Peaks of Otter in Virginia, on a day of sunshine never to be forgotten, from Elsie Cameron. Usually the women give breviaries to the priests, or chalices, or amices, or albs, or black pullovers. She must have been a rare one, Elsie Cameron. Would you say now that she might have had a slight limp? It's a Scottish name. Paul was forever talking about what he called the Scots Irish in Virginia and the fine people they were. All I know is that Scottish women are reputed to be very hot. They're all Protestants and don't have to go to confession.

Pascal had known a man who worked in Edinburgh who said that all you had to do to set a Scotswoman off was to show her the Forth Bridge, the wide open legs of it. That man had said that the Forth Bridge had never failed him.

When I said to Pascal that all this about Paul could have been as innocent as a rose, he said he was well aware of that : he wasn't claiming that Paul had done the dirty on the girl and left her to mourn out her life by the banks of the James River. But that it may all have been innocent for Paul and Elsie only made it the more mournful for Pascal. Fond memories and memories, and all about something that never happened.

—Any day henceforth, Pascal said, I'll go on a journey just to see for myself those Blue Ridge Mountains. Were they ever as blue as Paul thought they were? Cider's the same lousy drink the world over. What better could the orchards or women have been in Virginia than in Armagh? You see he was an imaginative man was old Paul, a touch of the poet, and soft as putty and sentimental away behind that granite mountainy face. Things hurt him, too. He told me once that one day walking he met that mad Maguire one from Cranny, the one with the seven children and no husband, and tried to talk reason to her, and she used language to him the like of which he had never heard, and he turned away with tears in his eyes. He said he saw all women degraded and the Mother of God sorrowful in Nancy Maguire who was as bad as she was mad. An odd thought. He should have taken the stick to her the way I once heard he did to a loving couple he found under the hedge.

But pleasures are like poppies spread, as Paul would say, walking the roads with Pascal ad quietam conscientiam, looking at mad Nancy and listening to her oaths, seeing Elsie Cameron under the apple trees under the Blue Mountains in faraway Virginia. Once I wrote a story about him and it was printed in a small little-known and now defunct magazine. That story was all about the nobility of him and the way he used to chant the words of Burns; and then about how he died.

He came home to his parochial house that morning after reading the mass and sat down, one of the cousins said, at the breakfast table, and sat there for a long time silent, looking straight ahead. That wasn't like him. She asked him was he well. He didn't answer. She left the room to consult her sister who was fussing about in the kitchen. When she came back he had rested his head down on the table and was dead.

Looking straight ahead to Fincastle, Virginia, and seeing a woman white with flame when the dogwood blossomed, seeing the tall angel whose wings were the rainbow and who held heaven, a red cloth, in one hand, and hell, a blue cloth, in the other.

There was no place in that story of mine for Pascal Stakelum, the rural rake.

THE LITTLE WRENS AND ROBINS

Cousin Ellen wrote poetry for the local papers and was the greatest nonstop talker you, or anybody else, ever listened to. The poetry was of three varieties : religious poetry, love poetry and nature poetry that went like this, the nature poetry, I mean :

> *Farewell to the dreary Winter,*
> *Welcome to the days of Spring*
> *When the trees put on their coats of green,*
> *And the birds with joy will sing.*
> *The daffodils put on their gowns,*
> *How proudly they stand up,*
> *To shake their dewy golden coats*
> *On the smiling buttercups.*

After reading the poem of which that was the opening stanza, I was ever afterwards somewhat in awe of Cousin Ellen : her daring in rhyming only one little up with all those buttercups, her vision of the daffodils as tall fashion models swaying and pirouetting in extravagant golden gowns, of the smirking of those sly little gnomes and peeping-toms, the buttercups, who were so delighted that the stately ladies should shake the dew of their coats to be caught in and savoured from the yellow cups. No one could deny that Cousin Ellen had a poetic mind and a special vision, except my father who loved quietude, and long calm silent days, and a garden growing, and who was driven out of all patience by Ellen's ceaseless clickety-clack when, once a month, she travelled twenty-five miles by train from Hazelhatch to visit us.

—And Uncle Tommy, did you hear that Peter McQuade of

Lettergesh sold that bay mare he had at an unimaginable high price, I don't know what the exact sum was, but it was, I hear, absolutely over the moon and out of sight, he ran her at the Maze Races and won all before her and he brought her south to the Curragh of Kildare, and some rich American saw her and brought her on the spot and flew off with her to Hialeah in Florida, that was a travelled mare, they say Florida's lovely, America that's where the money is, not that money's everything if you haven't happiness, get out there to America, Ben boy, before it's too late, as I left it too late and this, Aunt Sara, is an American fashion magazine I brought for you to look over, the styles will absolutely blind you, you should have been at Hazelhatch last Sunday when the Reverend Dr. Derwent preached the most divine sermon about the Sacred Heart, I wrote a poem in my head on the way home from church and sent him an autographed copy, you see he clips every one of my poems out of the papers and pastes them into one big book, he says that he'll be the first person ever to possess my collected works, he's just divinely handsome, too handsome for a priest as they say although personally I see no harm at all in a priest being handsome, Our Divine Lord himself was the handsomest person that ever lived and exactly six feet in height, and very much the favourite man of the bishop at the present moment, he's leading the diocesan pilgrimage to Lourdes, Fatima, Rome and home by Lisieux this year, an all-rounder, and I have every intention of going, I never saw Lisieux and I have always adored Saint Thérèse, they may call her a little flower but she was in her own quiet way a warrior, as Dr. Derwent says, and she wrote the divinest book, solid as a rock just like Mamma who's in the best of health, nothing shakes her, all plans to make the business prosper, we're expecting such a passing rush of tourists this year on the way to West Donegal, they all stop to stock up with food and drink at Hazelhatch Inn, that old picturesque thatch and the diamond-paned latticed windows, particularly those high cosy dormers, catch the eye, you'd be amazed the number of people who stop to take pictures and then come in and buy, beauty and business mixed ...

Like Molly Bloom she was no great believer in punctuation which is really only a pausing for breath, and Cousin Ellen's breath always seemed as if it would last for hours. My father said that after half-an-hour or less of her monologue, in which she needed no assistance except seemingly attentive faces, he always felt that he was drowning in a warm slow stream, drifting slowly, sinking slowly, brain and body numb, faraway bells in his ears, comfortable, but teetotally helpless. That talk, he claimed, threatened the manhood in a man, which was why all men had escaped, while there was still time, from Cousin Ellen, except Dr. Derwent who was sworn celibate and thus safe, and except for one other wretch whom she talked into matrimony and who lasted for a year and then vanished mysteriously : dead by asphyxiation, my father said, and buried secretly under the apple trees at the back of the old house at Hazelhatch.

Those were lovely apple trees.

Drowning in what deep waters of constant talk was I, the Saturday I walked her through the marketing crowds in from the country, from brown mountains and green river valleys, to our town? We went along John Street and High Street and Market Street, by the Catholic church with the high limping spires that could be seen for miles, by the eighteenth-century courthouse with Doric columns that was once admired by no less a person than Tyrone Guthrie who said that if you tilted the long sweep of High Street and Market Street the other way, the courthouse steps would be the perfect stage on which to produce a Passion Play. Church and courthouse were our architectural prides. Cousin Ellen, as far as I can remember from my drowning swoon, talked about love. Being all of eighteen I was still interested.

—Your sister, Dymphna, in Dublin, she said, is very happy, Edward and myself called to see her two months ago, not rich but happy and happiness is all, I said to her if only Edward and myself can be as happy as yourself and your husband, you know, Ben, Edward and myself are to be wedded shortly and I do hope everything turns out for the best, and I hope that suitcase isn't too heavy, but oh you're so young and strong and athletic, and they really shouldn't allow these fruit-stalls on the open street any more, not with modern traffic and all that, although you have to admit that they're most colourful and picturesque but they really belong to the Middle Ages, and see me safely now on to the bus for Dromore, the crowd here is just fearful, and oh this letter I forgot, do drop it in the post office for me, it's for Edward, love is all, just a perfect understanding between people and when human love fails there is always the love of the Sacred Heart which I wrote in a poem that Dr. Derwent read out from the pulpit, there is nothing on earth we may cling to, all things are fleeting here, the pleasures we so oft have hunted, the friends we've loved so dear . . .

Then off she went not, as it happened, to Dromore where she had wanted to visit some other relatives, but to Drumquin, because in the confusion into which she had talked me, I deposited herself and her suitcase on the wrong bus. To the casual observer there isn't much difference between Drumquin and Dromore, but one is twenty miles from the other, and it's a bind to be in one when you want to be in the other. But Cousin Ellen found some obliging commercial traveller who drove her to Dromore, and God help him if he had to listen to her for the time it took to drive twenty miles. She wrote me a most amusing letter about it all. She was easier to read than to listen to. The accident about the buses had really tickled her, she said, for life was just like that : you headed off for somewhere and ended up somewhere else. She bore no grudge and we would be better friends than ever, wouldn't we? We were, too.

About that time I headed off for Dublin to go through the motions of a university education, and didn't see Cousin Ellen again, although we constantly exchanged letters, until the husband had come and gone, and she herself was in hospital close to Hazelhatch with some rare ailment that was to stop her talk forever, and her poetry.

The letter to Edward that that day she gave me to post I found two weeks later when, pike-fishing on the Drumragh River, I had a little leisure and used it to clear out my pockets. Since it then seemed too late to send it to where it should have gone I tore it up into tiny pieces and cast it on the running water. My mother always said that you should never burn letters from friends or, indeed, anything that had to do with friendship. Fire destroyed. Water did not. So she was constantly making confetti out of letters and flushing them down the john.

The deep pike-water of the Drumragh, still patterned with froth from the falls at Porter's Bridge, bore away northwards the words of love that Ellen had meant for Edward. Life, she might have said had she then known, was also like that. Our friendship, at any rate, remained unaltered. After all, she was the only other writer in the family.

> *Ah, yes! And the tiny little lambs,*
> *They, too, will play and skip*
> *In the fields just decorated*
> *With the daisy and cowslip.*
> *The blackbird and the thrushes*
> *They are glad to see you here,*
> *The little wrens and robins*
> *To all you bring good cheer.*

She was, as you may remember, addressing the Spring. Her favourite picture hung on a wall of the old oak-timbered country kitchen at Hazelhatch. It was called : Springtime on an Ayrshire hillside, or, the Muse of Poetry descends to Robert Burns while at the plough.

But those words were a paltry effort to describe that picture and, out of respect for the memories of Burns and Cousin Ellen and, of course, of the Muse, I will try to do better.

The poet in the picture wears the height of style : a blue

tailed-coat, knee-breeches a little off-white, strong woollen stockings and stout buckled shoes. He has taken one hand, the right, from the plough and is using that hand to raise with a sweep a tall hat of a type that in nobler times may have been general issue for ploughmen, or poets. His profile is noble, his head held high to escape extinction in an ample cravat. He salutes a plump girl in a white revealing nightgown sort of costume of the period, perhaps, of the French Director- ate, and who is standing on a cloud about two feet above the backs of two patient and unnoticing horses. The girl on the cloud carries a wreath and it is clearly her intention to put the wreath where the tall hat has been. In the bottom left-hand corner a fieldmouse is playing the part of a wee sleekit cowering timorous beastie yet is clearly, to judge from the glint in her eyes, an intent observer of the coronation ceremony and, in the words of another poet, is confidently aware that a mouse is miracle enough to stagger sextillions of infidels. In the back- ground, for it is spring in Ayrshire and a little late for plough- ing the birds are plentiful on the branches and in a pale blue sky.

That picture, I feel, had its influence on Ellen :

> *The man whose work is in the field*
> *From you his joy can't hide,*
> *As he treads along at break of day*
> *With two horses by his side.*
> *He whistles all along his way*
> *And merrily will sing.*
> *This is a birthday once again,*
> *Each morning of the Spring.*

That picture, too, is always very much present to me. When the Empress of Hazelhatch, as my youngest sister called Ellen's mother, our grass-widowed aunt by marriage, died, and Hazel- hatch passed into the hands of strangers, she left me the picture. Ellen and myself, she said, had liked it, and each other. Was the old lady remembering, too, one sad lulled day of

34

sunshine when we sat in the kitchen at Hazelhatch and looked at the picture and she told me what I had already partly guessed that morning, that Ellen would die in hospital?

All around us in the old kitchen were cases of brown stout just freshly bottled in a careful and religious ritual at which I had been allowed to assist, along with a new girl who was there, from the County Mayo, to work in the bar and grocery and learn the trade. A long procession of girls had come and gone and benefited, perhaps, from the strict wisdom of the Empress, even if they had most certainly sighed and writhed and groaned under her discipline. She still decanted her own port, a good Graham, black as your boot—and solid, but that decanting she did on her own, no assistants, no encouragement even to spectators. Certain things were just too sacred.

That port was famous.

—It fixed her marriage, my father said, good and proper. Your good mother's brother could think of nothing but port and running horses. Never left the bar except to go to Punchestown or the Maze or Strathroy Holm or Galway or Gowran Park or Tramore or Bellewstown Hill or the Curragh itself, or the horsefairs of Ballinasloe or Cahirmee. When he ran away to the States and never came back he was both bow-legged and purple in the face.

—He couldn't come back, said my mother.

She felt very sore about the whole story. He had been her favourite brother. She explained : He went to Canada, not the States, and then jumped the line at Buffalo and could never again get his papers in order. He got in but couldn't get out. There were hundreds like him.

—I often wondered why he ran away, said that youngest sister with the thin face and the dark hair and the whiplash of a tongue. Then I met the Empress of Hazelhatch with her long black gown and her hair mounted high on a Spanish comb, and dyed horse-chestnut as sure as God, and her pince-nez, sitting behind the bar all right to speak to the better sort of people, but never demeaning herself by serving a customer, and I knew then why he would run to Alberta, or farther if he

35

could get without beginning to come home again round the world.

Because that sister was herself an embryo empress she was never happy at Hazelhatch. For myself, as easy-going as my father or a wag-by-the-wall clock, I loved my visits to the place, the picture of the poet, the strong drone of the old lady's voice, the odour of good groceries and booze, the glow of old oak, the high bedroom with slanted ceiling and dormer window and an angled criss-crossed vision of the road west to Mount Errigal and the Rosses and the ocean, the apples in the orchard, the procession of young, discontented and frequently sportive girls. Memories of those visits stay with me, stilled, separated from all else, not frayed by time. That particular day the Empress said to me : How did Ellen look when you saw her this morning?

Nobody except her mother could have considered or enquired how Ellen looked. She talked so much you didn't see. So, to answer, I had to think back painstakingly. That was all the more difficult to do because we had left the kitchen and gone, rather sadly, out to the orchard where it seemed unkind and even sinful to think how somebody looked who was going to die, and who had loved that orchard.

> *Oft times I sit and think,*
> *And wonder if God sends*
> *This season, Spring, so beautiful*
> *To all his city friends.*
> *Ah no! there are no green fields*
> *There are no little lambs to play...*

For one thing, that morning Ellen had not been in the least like the Muse of Poetry descending to salute Robert Burns at the plough. She had always dressed modestly, mostly in browns or mother-of-god blues with the breast-bone well covered in white frills and lace and such; and there had never been a pick on her bones. Never before had I noticed that she was so freckled, scores of tiny dark-brown freckles around her eyes

36

and down the slopes of her nose. The paleness of her ailing face, perhaps, made them more than ever noticeable. Freckled people are always great talkers and even illness could not stop her tongue : only death or the last gaspings that preceded it.

—It must be heavenly for you, she said, to feel that you are really and truly walking the paths of learning, and in a city that has been ennobled by the footsteps of so many great scholars and poets, how I envy you, I always so wanted to get to the university, but when I'm up and about again and out of this bed I promise you a visit in Dublin and you must show me all the sights and famous places, promise, you'll find my mother very quiet and brooding these days, I can't think what's wrong with her, but sometimes she gets like that, it may be that the new girl and herself do not get on so well, a strange girl from the County Mayo, a great singer, she came to see me several times, and sometimes I think she resembles me, she wants to sing just as I write poems, a lovely voice, too, but it's so sad, such clean regular features and an exquisite head of dark hair, but that purple discolouration on one side of her face, God help her, she would have to sing always with one side of her face away from the audience ...

Because there was winter and the end of things in the room, even if it was high summer outside the window, I told her about the letter forgotten, then torn into fragments and sent sailing on the Drumragh. I told her about my mother and her opinions on fire and water. She said that, perhaps, it would have been better for both of them, meaning the vanished husband and herself, if it had ended the way the letter did : gone peacefully on the easy water. She said my mother had always been kind. She stepped out of bed and walked with me as far as the door of the room. She wore a heavy blue dressing-gown. She kissed me. We never met again.

> *Ah no! there are no green fields,*
> *There are no little lambs to play,*
> *But walk out in the country*
> *On any fine spring day ...*

37

So I in the orchard, all alone and sad, am fixing a puncture in the back wheel of the lofty ancient bicycle on which the Empress of Hazelhatch is wont to cruise forth in deep-green drowsy summers, her skirts high above the dust, her head high above the hedges, surveying the labour of the fields, occasionally saluting the workers. To me, and softly singing to herself for she is proud of her voice and the old lady flatters her about it, comes the Mayo girl with the face, flawless and faultless in shape but discoloured on the left cheek. She stands beside me, at my left hand. Our hands touch as we run the bicycle tube through a basin of water so as to raise a bubble and locate the puncture. The birds in the orchard trees are silent because it is the sultry month of least song. But the girl for a while sings in a sort of sweet whisper about, of all things, moonlight in Mayo. Then she says: It isn't my day off, and I want to get to Strabane.

—Why?

—What do you think? A fella.

—Ask her for the evening off.

—She's hell on fellas. You ask her. She'd grant you anything.

—I'm a fella.

—You're the white-headed boy around here. Say you want to take me to the pictures.

—What picture?

—Any picture. No picture.

> *But walk out in the country*
> *On any fine spring day.*
> *And there you'll find what art can't paint*
> *Nature's gifts so fair:*
> *The trees, the flowers, the streamlets*
> *And the many birds so rare.*

The road is dusty and the hedges high. Had Ellen never written a poem about summer? The girl sings as she walks. It is four miles to the village of Lifford, old houses shaggy with flowering creepers, then across the great bridge where the Mourne River, containing the water of the Drumragh, from Tyrone, meets the Finn River from Donegal to form, between them, the spreading Foyle; then half a mile across level water-meadows to the town of Strabane. She sings about the bird in the gilded cage. But walking through Lifford, curious faces looking out over half-doors, she stops singing and says: Mrs. Lagan is dying, isn't she?

Ellen's married name takes me by surprise. She says: You needn't talk about it if you don't want to. It's just that I like her.

—So do I.

—She's very clever. She's a great poet.

—Not exactly great.

—She gets printed.

—In local papers.

—Nevertheless.

We lean on the bridge and watch the mingling of the Mourne and the Finn, and the wagtails darting and diving over a shining triangle of sand and gravel. She says: The old lady is kindly but very strict. Mrs. Lagan is generous but very sad. They say there never was a man, but one, who could listen to her or talk her down. She should have lived in a world where men talked more.

—Like where?

—New York or Dublin or London or Milan. Big singing cities. Her soul's mate was a flowery preaching priest. They should have been allowed to marry, the old lady says. They'd have made a perfect couple. She'd have made a perfect minister's wife. Did you ever look at a minister's wife? They're all like that. All poetry and bazaars.

—She could have preached better than anyone.

We follow the level road across the water-meadows. There is a raised footwalk designed to keep pedestrians dry-shod in time of flood. The clock has stopped forever on that still day in Strabane. She says: She likes me to sing when I go to see her.

She sings : Ah, sweet mystery of life at last I've found you. When she has finished singing I declaim :

You may have your city pleasures
And its praises you may sing,
But there's naught on earth that can compare
With the country's dales in spring.

—What's that?

—The voice of Cousin Ellen.

—I could sing that.

She sings it to a slow sweet tune I never heard before or since. Under the apple trees had Ellen's poetic soul taken possession of the girl?

We sit on the quiet river bank to pass the time until my train departs for Dublin or until her fella arrives. She sits at my left hand. When I hold her chin and try to turn her lips towards me she stiffens her neck, then looks away towards the town. So, when I hear the train whistle, I leave her unkissed there by the Mourne River, waiting for the fella. Often afterwards in Dublin I wonder what song she sings for him, what side of her face does she turn towards him.

A ROOM IN LINDEN

O N E D A Y I N the dark maze of the yew-hedges Sister Lua, who has arthritis, looks up at him from her wheelchair which he's pushing, and says: Tell me the truth. Don't be modest about it. Are you Nanky Poo?

Since he is a bookish young man it is an exciting thing for him to have history living along the corridor. The poet he's reading just before he leaves his room writes that there's a wind blowing, cold through the corridor, a death-wind, the flapping of defeated wings from meadows damned to eternal April. The poet has never seen it, but he could have been writing about this corridor. On its dull green walls, a mockery of the grass and green leaves of life, the sun never shines. All day and all night the big windows at the ends of the corridor, one at the east wing of the house and one at the west, are wide open, and from whichever airt the wind does blow it always blows cold. The rooms on the north side of the corridor are, as one might expect, colder and darker than the rooms on the south side, or would be if their light and heat depended totally on the sun.

Before the nuns got here and turned the place into a convalescent home it was lived in by a family famous for generations for a special brand of pipe tobacco. The old soldier who is reluctantly, vociferously fading away in a room on the north side of the corridor, says: This house was built on smoke. Just think of that. Smoke.

The old soldier himself belongs to some branch of the family that emigrated to South Africa and made even more money out of burgundy than the people who stayed at home made out of smoke, and there was always as much soldiering as smoke in the family; and big-game hunting, too, to judge by the fearful snarling mounted heads left behind and surviving, undisturbed by nuns or convalescents, in the entrance hall.

—You'll be nice to the old man, won't you, Mother Polycarp had said to him. He'll bore you to death. But he needs somebody to listen to him. He hasn't much longer to talk, in this world at any rate.

So he talks to the old soldier in the evenings and, in the afternoons, to the old priest and historian, dying as methodically and academically as he has lived, checking references, adding footnotes, in a room on the south side of the corridor. At other times he reads in his own room, or has visitors, or wheels Sister Lua's wheelchair in the ample bosky grounds, or leaves the grounds on his own and goes through quiet suburban roads to walk slowly, tapping his stick, in the public park that overlooks, across two walls and a railway, the flat sand and the bay. It is not an exciting life, but it's not meant to be.

He wheels Sister Lua round and round the dark cloisters of the yew-hedge maze from the corner where Jesus is condemned to death to the central circle where he is laid in the tomb. He tells her that he is not Nanky Poo.

—Well, I heard you had poems in that magazine. And I didn't see your name. And there is this poet called Nanky Poo. And he's very good. About the missions.

—Not me, alas, sister. I was never on the missions.

—Know you weren't. A university student.

Although she is always sitting down and being wheeled she is also always breathless and never quite begins or finishes a sentence, and it is necessary to fill in her words and meanings as she goes along. Bird-like, he knows, isn't much of a description, but she is bird-like, little hands like claws because of the arthritis, of course, a little nose like a beak peeking out from under the nun's pucog. To the left corner of her pale unvarnished little mouth, so often twisted with patience in pain, there's a mole with two hairs. She loves the dark green maze that grew up, like the house, out of smoke and was used by the nuns as a setting for a via dolorosa with life-size

42

figures; and backgrounds of good stone columns and arches robbed from the wreckage of some eighteenth-century mansion. His first faux pas with the old historian had to do with those stations of the cross. One dull evening when the talk wasn't going so well he had, just to make chat, said : Don't they have a big day here once a year? People coming in hundreds to do the stations of the cross. What day does that happen on?

The old man pulls the rug more tightly around his long legs. His feet are always cold. In large bodies, Edmund Burke held, circulation is slower at the extremities, but the coldness of the old man's feet is just the beginning of death. He snuffs black snuff expertly from the hollow between thumb and fore-finger, he sneezes, he says with crushing deliberation : Good Friday, my good young man. Even the younger generation should be aware that the Lord was crucified on Good Friday.

He's a carnaptious old bastard and even for the sake of Mother Polycarp, the kindly reverend mother, who is always thanking God for everything, it's sort of hard to suffer him at times. But he has both made and written history, and poems, too, of a learned sort, and collected folksong, and the best people have written about him and discovered an old-world courtesy and all the rest of that rot behind his rude exterior : the old-world courtesy of a Scandinavian sea-rover putting the full of a monastery of shaven-pated monks to the gory hatchet. By comparison the old soldier who has actually killed his man in far-away wars, is a gentleman. But then the old soldier is simply fading away, all battles fought and won, all comrades gone before him, all trumpets sounding from the other side. The old priest, still trying to work, has his last days aggravated by a mind that remembers everything and by the pain of a stomach cancer.

He leaves Sister Lua in the charge of a big red-headed nurse and walks down the main avenue towards suburbia and the park by the sea. The old white-haired vaudeville enter-tainer who has some sort of shaking paralysis, which he says is an occupational disease, waves to him from his seat by the grotto under the obelisk and gives him three letters to post at the postbox outside the gate. They are, he notices, all addressed to well-known celebrities of screen, stage and television : one in Dublin, one in London, one in New York. Out there is the world of healthy living people.

Life and playing children are, of course, all around him in the park by the sea but it isn't quite the same thing. There isn't enough of life there to help him to stop thinking of old men dying. He is very much on his own either because of his sullenness, or because he thinks that while he may be of interest to himself he couldn't possibly be of interest to anybody else. Nothing humble about that, though. In that park he's really a visitor from a special sort of world, from a cold green corridor damned to eternal December : sort of exclusive, though, a rich old soldier, a famous old historian, the artist who is still in touch with the best people; and only the best die in that corridor.

One old man who sits on a green wooden seat, close to the play-hall where the children run when it rains, talks to him as if he would gladly talk longer. He discourages that old man with abrupt sentences for he has, at the moment, enough of old men. He walks on beyond him and along by the tennis courts. A stout bespectacled girl with strong tanned legs plays awkwardly with a tall blond handsome fellow who wins every set and enjoys his superiority, while she seems to enjoy being beaten. A stranger from a strange land, he enjoys, as he passes or rests for a while on a seat and watches, the leaping of her legs. So everybody is happy and the park is beautiful. The blond boy isn't even good at the game and he, the stranger, knows that if it wasn't for the stiff hip, still slowly recovering, he could challenge him and beat him easily. But then the stout girl, legs excepted, isn't really interesting.

He himself is blond and doesn't take too well to the sun. So his favourite seat is in a shady corner under dark horse-chestnuts whose white candles are fading. He likes the place also because nobody else sits there. Strollers seem to accelerate as they walk past. Once in a while children run shouting, hooting through the dark tunnel, from one shire of sunshine into another. Through a fence of mournful laurels and copper beeches he sees the glitter of the sun on the lake. Out of the corner of his left eye he sees a well-built girl in white shorts flat on her back on the sunny grass. Sometimes she reads. Sometimes she raises her legs and, furiously with flashing thighs, pedals an invisible bicycle, faster and faster until it seems as if she has seven or seventeen legs, until the flash of her thighs takes the shape of a white circle. Her belly muscles must be jingling like springs. The joints in her hips, unlike his own, must be in perfect lubricated condition. She is at the moment one of the five women in his life : Polycarp thanking God for the rain and the sunshine, for the hail and the snow; Lua, twisted in her chair; she who, nameless, cycles on her back on the grass; the strong-legged tennis player whose name, he has heard the blond fellow shout, is Phyllis; and A. N. Other.

To the rear of his shady corner there is a privet hedge and a high wooden fence and a gate with a notice that says no admission except on business. That's exactly the way he feels. Adam in Eden must have had just such a corner where he kept his tools and experimented with slips and seeds. But then before Adam and Eve made a pig's ass out of a good arrangement the garden must have looked after itself and needed none of that sweat-of-the-brow stuff. What would old Thor the thunderer, brooding in his room, biting on his cancer, think of that?

Belloc, says the old priest, was a big man who looked as if all his life he had eaten too much and drunk too much. The best way to learn French is to read cowboy and injun stories. They hold the interest better than Racine.

Aware of his own inanity, he says : translations.

Before that face, oblong, seemingly about twelve feet long, like a head cut out of the side of some crazy American mountain, he is perpetually nonplussed into saying stupidities.

—Cowboys and injuns, my good young man, are not indigenous to the soil of France.

—There's a city called Macon in Georgia, U.S.A.

—There's a city called everything somewhere in the States. Naturally they mispronounce the names.

So it goes on. You can't win with the old bastard.

—Darlington, he says, used to call on Hopkins to take him out for walks. Hopkins was for ever and always complaining of headaches. What else can you expect, Darlington would say to him, immured up there in your room writing rubbish. I'm not so sure that Darlington wasn't right.

He is at that time just entering his Hopkins phase and if he wasn't afraid of that granite face, eyes sunken and black and burning, jawbones out rigid like a forked bush struck by lightning, he would defend the poet, quoting his sonnet about the windhover which, with some difficulty, he has just memorised. Yet it still is something to hear those names tossed about by a man who knew the men, and was a name himself. He feels grateful to Mother Polycarp who, as a friend of his family, has invited him to this place for a while, after his year in orthopaedic, so that he can read his books and learn to walk at his ease. In all that green cold corridor, which is really a place for old men, he is the only person who is going to live. He searches for something neutral to say: Wasn't Hopkins always very scrupulous about marking students' papers?

—He was a neurotic Englishman, my good fellow. They never could make up their minds between imperialism and humanitarianism. That's what has them the way they are. Darlington was English, too, of course, the other sort, the complacent Englishman, thinking that only what is good can happen to him, and that all his works are good. Then a young upstart called Joyce put him in a book. That should have been a lesson to Darlington, if they have books in heaven or wherever he went to.

He should, as Mother Polycarp says, be taking notes, thank God, except he feels that if he did so, secretly even in his room, the old lion might read his mind and take offence. The old man laughs seldom, but he's laughing now, perhaps at some memory of two English Jesuits marooned in Ireland, or at some other memory surfacing for a second in the dark crowded

46

pool behind his square forehead. He has kept his hair, a dirty grey, standing up and out as if it had never encountered a comb. The long bony hands tighten the rug about his knees. The cold is creeping upwards.

In the green corridor he kneels for a while at the prie-dieu before the shrine, not praying, just thinking about age and death, and looking up at the bearded face of St. Joseph, pure and gentle, guardian of the saviour child. With a lily in his hand. Another old man and, by all accounts, very patient about it. What in hell is St. Joseph, like Oscar Wilde or somebody, always doing with a lily in his hand? An awkward class of a thing for a carpenter to be carrying.

Before his hip betrayed him he has had a half-notion of being a priest, but a year in orthopaedic, bright nurses hopping all around him, has cured him by showing him that there are things that priests, in the ordinary course of duty, are not supposed to have.

—You're too young, the old soldier says, to be in this boneyard.

He's a small man with a red boozy face, a red dressing-gown, a whiskey bottle and a glass always to his right hand. The whiskey keeps him alive, thank God, Mother Polycarp says. He is, like St. Joseph, gentle but not so pure, rambling on about dirty doings in far-away places, Mombasa and Delhi are much mentioned, about Kaffir women, and about blokes who got knocked off in the most comical fashion. He laughs a lot. He doesn't need a considered answer or a balanced conversation, just a word now and then to show he's not alone. He shares the whiskey generously. He has bags of money and, when he dies, he'll leave the perishing lot to the nuns.

—They do good, you know. Keep perky about it, too. Who else would look after the likes of me? Ruddy boneyard, though. Elephants' graveyard. Get out of here and get a woman. Make sons. Before it's too late. Would get out myself only nobody would have me any more, and I couldn't have them. Only whiskey left. But I had my day. When I was your age I laid

47

them as quick as my batman could pull them out from under me. Three women shot under me at the battle of Balaclava and all that. Fit only for the boneyard now and the nuns. They don't want it and I can't give it. But there's always whiskey, thank God, as the mother says. A field behind the barracks where old wind-broken cavalry mounts went on grass with the shoes off until they died. At least we didn't eat them like the bloody Belgians. Smell of slow death around this place.

He sniffs the whiskey and laughs and then coughs. By night the coughing is constant. Lying awake and listening, the young man has a nightmarish feeling that they are all in prison cells, all dying, which is true, all the living are dying, and after one night the sun will never rise again on the park, and every time the cycling girl spins her legs she's another circle nearer to the grave. His own healthy youth has already collapsed in illness. Life is one collapse after another. The coughing goes on and on. To be a brave soldier and to end up coughing in a lonely room. Let me outa here. No, Sister Lua, I am not Nanky Poo.

—But every day that passes, Mother Polycarp tells him, brings you a day nearer to getting back to your studies, thank God. You made a great recovery in orthopaedic.

She is a tall woman with a long flat-footed step and more rattlings of keys and rosary beads than seem natural even in a nun. When he tells her that, she laughs and says, of course, that she has the keys of the kingdom, thank God. She has a good-humoured wrinkled mannish face, and she is famous everywhere for her kindness and her ability to gather money and build hospitals.

Does she say to the old men: Every day that passes brings you a day nearer heaven, thank God?

She naturally wouldn't mention death as the gate of heaven.

He has a feeling that none of them want to go any farther forward, they look backward to see heaven: on the day a new book was published or a new woman mounted or a new show went well. Heaven, like most things, doesn't last, or could only be an endless repetition of remembered happiness, and would in the end be, like dying, a bloody bore.

In her chair as he wheels her, Sister Lua, chirping like the little robin that she is, prays a bit and chats a bit and, because of her breathlessness and the way she beheads her sentences and docks the tails off them, he has to listen carefully to know whether she is chatting or praying. The life-size figures in the maze of dark yews—fourteen Christs in various postures, with attendant characters from jesting Pilate to the soldiers by the tomb—have acquired a sombre existence of their own. Do they relax at night, yawn, stretch stiff limbs, mutter a curse, light a cigarette, say to hell with show business? He must try that one out on the vaudeville man, shaking his way to the grave, on the seat by the grotto under the obelisk.

—Weep not for me, Sister Lua prays, but for yourselves and for your children.

The lord is talking to the weeping women of Jerusalem and not doing a lot to cheer them up. Some anti-semitical Irish parish priest must have written the prayers that Lua reels off. He didn't think much either of the kind of recruitment that got into the Roman army: These barbarians fastened him with nails and then, securing the cross, allowed him to die in anguish on this ignominious gibbet.

From the prayer book she has learned, by heart, not only the prayers but the instructions that go with them. She says, as the book instructs: Pause a while.

He pauses. The yew-hedges are a dark wall to either hand. Twenty paces ahead, the lord, in an arbour, is being lowered from the cross. The dying has been done.

—Nanky Poo. Nanky Poo.

—Sister, I am not Nanky Poo.

—But I call you Nanky Poo. Such a lovely name.

—So is Pooh Ba.

—Pooh Ba is horrible. Somebody making mean faces. Nanky Poo, you must write a poem for Mother Polycarp's feast-day. So easy for you. Just a parody. Round Linden when the sun was low, Mother Polycarp the Good did go.

—There's a future in that style.

—You'll do it, Nanky Poo?

—At my ease, sister. Whatever Nanky Poo can do, I can do better.

By the laying of the lord in the tomb they encounter A. N. Other. She tries to escape by hiding behind the eighteenth-century cut-stone robbed from the old house, but Sister Lua's birds-eye is too quick and too sharp for her.

—Nurse Donovan, Nurse Donovan, the French texts have arrived.

—Yes, Sister Lua.

—When can you begin, Nanky Poo?

—Any time, sister.

—So useful to you, Nurse Donovan, French, when you're a secretary.

She is a small well-rounded brunette who has nursed in the orthopaedic hospital until something happened to her health. He is in love with her, has been for some time. Nothing is to come of it. He is never to see her again after he leaves the convalescent home. The trouble is that Sister Lua has decided that the girl must be a secretary and that Nanky Poo must teach her French, and it is quite clear from the subdued light in the girl's downcast dark eyes that she doesn't give a fiddler's fart about learning anything, even French, out of a book. Worse still : on the few occasions on which he has been able to corner the girl on her own he hasn't been able to think of a damn thing to talk about except books. How can he ever get through to her that pedagogy is the last thing in his mind?

She wheels Sister Lua away from him to the part of the house where the nuns live. Between the girl and himself Sister Lua has thrown a barbed-wire entanglement of irregular verbs. No great love has ever been so ludicrously frustrated.

A white blossom that he cannot identify grows copiously in this suburb. Thanks be to God for the thunder and lightning, thanks be to God for all things that grow.

No, Sister Lua, I am not Nanky Poo, am a disembodied

spirit, homeless in suburbia, watching with envy a young couple coming, white and dancing, out of a house and driving away to play tennis, am a lost soul blown on the blast between a green cold corridor of age and death, and the children running and squealing by the lake in the park.

Beyond the two walls and the railway line the sea is flat and purple all the way to Liverpool. He envies the young footballers in the playing fields close to where the cycling girl lies flat on her back and rides to the moon on her imaginary bicycle. He envies particularly a red-headed boy with a superb left foot, who centres the ball, repeating the movement again and again, a conscious artist, as careless as God of what happens to the ball next, just so that he drops it in the goalmouth where he feels it should go. The footballer is on talking terms with the cycling girl. He jokes and laughs with her when the ball bounces that way. She stops her cycling to answer him. From his shadowy corner under the chestnuts Nanky Poo watches and thinks about his latest talk with the vaudeville man on his seat by the grotto under the obelisk.

The obelisk has also been built on smoke to celebrate the twenty-first birthday of a son of the house who would have been the great-grand-uncle of the old soldier.

—Vanished somewhere in India, the poor fellow. There was a rumour to the effect that he was eaten by wild beasts. A damn hard thing to prove unless you see it happen. Anyway he did for a good few of them before they got him. Half of the heads in the hallway below are his.

The obelisk stands up on a base of a flowering rockery, and into the cave or grotto underneath the rockery the nuns have, naturally, inserted a miniature Lourdes: the virgin with arms extended and enhaloed by burning candles, Bernadette kneeling by a fountain of holy water that is blessed by the chaplain at its source in a copper tank.

—The candles, says the vaudeville man, keep my back warm.

He wears a faded brown overcoat with a velvet collar. His white hair is high and bushy and possibly not as well trimmed as it used to be. The skin of his shrunken face and bony

51

Roman nose has little purple blotches and, to conceal the shake in his hands, he grips the knob of his bamboo walking-cane very tightly. When he walks his feet rise jerkily from the ground as if they did so of their own accord and might easily decide never to settle down again. The handwriting on the envelopes is thin and wavery as if the pen now and again took off on its own.

—You know all the best people.

—I used to.

He is never gloomy, yet never hilarious. Somewhere in between he has settled for an irony that is never quite bitter.

—You still write to them.

—Begging letters, you know. Reminders of the good old days. They almost always work with show people. I never quite made it, you know, not even when I had the health. But I was popular with my own kind. This one now.

He points to a notable name on one envelope.

—We met one night in a boozer in London when I wasn't working. He stood me a large Jameson straight away, then another, then another. He asked me to dine with him. We talked about this and that. When we parted I found a tenner in the inside breast pocket of my overcoat. While we were dining he had slipped into the cloakroom. No note, no message, just a simple tenner to speak for itself. He wasn't rich then, mark you, although as the world knows he did well afterwards. But he remembers me. He promises to come to see me. Do you know, now that I think of it, this was the very overcoat.

The cycling girl has stopped cycling and is talking to the red-headed footballer. He stands above her, casually bouncing the ball on that accurate left foot. Whatever he's saying the girl laughs so loudly that Nanky Poo can hear her where he sits in gloom and broods on beggary. She has a good human throaty sort of a laugh.

The night there is no coughing, but only one loud single cry, from the next room, he knows that the old soldier has awakened for a moment to die. He rises, puts on slippers and dressing-gown, and heads down the corridor to find the night nurse. But Mother Polycarp is there already, coming stoop-shouldered, beads and keys rattling, out of the old man's room.

—Thank God, she says, he died peacefully and he had the blessed sacrament yesterday morning. He wandered a lot in his time but he came home in the end.

He walks down the stairway to the shadowy main hall. Do the animals in the half darkness grin with satisfaction at the death of a man whose relative was eaten by one or more of their relatives? The front door is open for the coming of the doctor and the priest. Above the dark maze of yew-hedge the obelisk is silhouetted against the lights of the suburb. The place is so quiet that he can hear even the slight noise of the sea over the flat sand. This is the first time he has been out of doors at night since he went to orthopaedic. Enjoying the freedom, the quiet, the coolness, he walks round and round in the maze until his eyes grow used to the blackness and he is able to pick out the men and women who stand along the via dolorosa. They are just as motionless as they are during the day. When he comes back Mother Polycarp is waiting for him in the hallway.

—Now you're bold, she says. You could catch a chill. But every day that passes brings you nearer to freedom, thank God, and you can walk very well now.

She crosses herself as she passes the shrine in the corridor. She says: One thing that you could do now that you are up, is talk to himself. Or listen to him. He's awake and out of bed and lonely for somebody to talk to.

He is out of bed but not fully dressed; and, in a red dressing-gown that must have been presented to him by Mother Polycarp, he doesn't seem half as formidable as in his black religious habit. There is an open book on the rug that, as usual, covers and beats down the creeping cold from his thighs and knees. He is not reading. His spectacles are in their case on the table to his right hand. Above the light from the shaded reading-lamp his head and shoulders are in shadow. For once, since he is red and not black and half invisible, Nanky Poo feels almost at ease with him.

From the shadows his voice says: Credit where credit is due, young man. The first Chichester to come to Ireland was certainly one of the most capable and successful robbers who ever lived. He stole most of the north of Ireland not only from its owners but even from the robbers who stole it from its owners. Twice he robbed his royal master, James Stuart, the fourth of Scotland and the first of England. The man who did that had to rise early in the morning. For although King James was a fool about most things he was no fool about robbery: it was he who got the Scots the name for parsimony. Chichester stole the entire fisheries of Lough Neagh, the largest lake in the British Isles, and nobody found out about it until after he died. *Age quod agis*, as the maxim says. Do what you do. At his own craft he was a master. I dealt with him in a book.

—I read it.

—Did you indeed? A mark in your favour, young man.

—As a matter of fact, sir, the copy of it I read had your name on the flyleaf. Father Charles from your monastery loaned it to me when I was in orthopaedic.

As soon as the words are out he knows he has dropped the biggest brick of his career, and prays to Jesus that he may live long and die happy and never drop a bigger one. He has never known silence to last so long and be so deafening. Even the bulb in the reading-lamp makes a sound like a big wind far away. Blood in the ears?

—They're not expecting me back, so.

—What do you mean, sir?

—You know damned well what I mean. In a monastery when they know you're dead and not coming back they empty your room. There's another man in it now. They were kind and never told me. That room was all I had, and my books. They have sent me to the death-house as they so elegantly say in the United Sates. This here is the death-house. What do you do here, young man?

He is asking himself that question. So far no easy answer has offered itself.

—Books you build around you, more than a house and wife and family for a layman, part of yourself, flesh of your flesh, more than furniture for a monk's cell, a shell for his soul, the only thing in spite of the rule of poverty I couldn't strip myself of, and my talents allowed me a way around the rule, but man goeth forth naked as he came, stripped of everything, death bursts among them like a shell and strews them over half the town, and yet there are men who can leave their books as memorials to great libraries . . .

Sacred Heart of Jesus, he thinks, up there in the shadows there may be tears on that granite face.

—I'm sorry, sir.

—You didn't know, young man. How could you know?

—You will be remembered, sir.

—Thank you. The old must be grateful. Go to bed now. You have reason to rest. You have a life to live.

In his room he reads for what's left of the night. He has a life to live.

Through a drowsy weary morning he feels he wants to leave the place right away. Never again will he see the old soldier. Never again can he face the old scholar.

—Nanky Poo, Nanky Poo, you won't see your old friend again.

—No, sister. He died last night.

—Not him. Your old friend on the seat by the grotto.

Flying from French, A. N. Other cuts across their path through the maze. But she's moving so fast that not even Lua can hail her. Somewhere in the maze and as quietly as a cat she is stealing away from him for ever. Dulled with lack of sleep his brain is less than usually able to keep up with the chirpings of Lua.

—Is he dead too?

Let them all die. Let me outa here. I am not Nanky Poo.

—A stroke, not fatal yet, but, alas, the final one.

—I'll go to see him.

But Mother Polycarp tells him there's no point in that: all connection between brain and tongue and eyes is gone.

—He wouldn't know whether you were there or not.

—Couldn't he see me?

—We don't know. The doctor says, God bless us, that he's a vegetable.

—I wondered had he any letters to send out. I used to post them for him.

—He can't write any more.

A silence. So he can't even beg.

—It's a blow to you, she says. You were his friend. He used to enjoy his talks with you. But it'll soon be over, thank God. Pray for him that he may pray for us. For some of us death isn't the worst thing and, as far as we can tell, he's content.

A vegetable has little choice. Refusing to lie down and rest in that green place of death he walks dumbly through the suburb. The white blossoms blind him. When he leaves this place he will do so with the sense of escape he might have if he was running on a smooth hillside on a sunny windy day. But later he knows that the place will be with him for ever: the cry in the night, the begging letters sent to the stars, the pitiful anger of an old man finding another man living in his room. Crucified god, there's life for you, and there's a lot more of it that he hasn't yet encountered. He expects little, but he will sit no longer expecting it alone in any dark corner.

He would like to be able to tell the cycling girl a really good lie about how he injured his hip. The scrum fell on me on the line in a rather dirty game, just as I was sneaking away and over: that's how it happens, you know.

Or: An accident on a rockface in Snowdonia, a bit of bad judgment, my own fault actually.

Or: You've heard of the parachute club that ex-air force chap has started out near Celbridge.

He would prefer if he had crutches, or even one crutch, instead of a stick which he doesn't even need. A crutch could win a girl's confidence for no harm could come to her from a

56

fellow hopping on a crutch unless he could move as fast as, and throw the crutch with the accuracy of, Long John Silver.

There he goes, thinking about books again. He'd better watch that.

The red-headed footballer is far-away and absorbed in the virtues of his own left foot. For the first time Nanky Poo notices the colour of her hair, mousy, and the colour of her sweater, which today is mauve, because when she lay flat on the grass and he watched from a distance, she was mostly white shorts and bare circling thighs.

He sits down, stiffly, on the grass beside her. She seems not in the least surprised. She has a freckled face and spectacles. That surprises him.

He says : I envy the way your hips work.

If he doesn't say something wild like that he'll begin talking about books and his cause is lost.

—Why so?

—I was laid up for a year with a tubercular hip. I'm in the convalescent over there.

—Oh I know who you are. Sister Lua told me. You're Nanky Poo. You write poetry.

He is cold all over.

You know Sister Lua?

—She's my aunt. I write poetry too. Nobody has ever printed it though. Yet. Sister Lua said that some day she'd ask you to read some of it.

—I'd be delighted to.

—I watched you sitting over there for a long time. But I didn't like to approach you. Sister Lua said you were stand-offish and intellectual.

She walks back with him as far as the obelisk and the grotto. They will meet again on the following day and take a bus into a teashop in the city. They may even go to a show if Mother Polycarp allows him—as she will—to stay out late.

He suspects that all this will come to nothing except to the reading of her poetry which as likely as not will be dia-bolical. He wonders if some day she will, like her aunt, be arthritic, for arthritis, they say, like a stick leg, runs in the blood. But with one of his three friends dead, one estranged and one a vegetable, it is something to have somebody to talk to as you stumble through suburbia. He has a life to live. Every day that passes brings him a day nearer to somewhere else.

So thanks be to God for the rain and the sunshine, thanks be to God for the hail and the snow, thanks be to God for the thunder and lightning, thanks be to God that all things are so.

MAIDEN'S LEAP

T HE CIVIC GUARD, or policeman, on the doorstep was big, middle-aged, awkward, affable. Behind him was green sunlit lawn sloping down to a white horse-fence and a line of low shrubs. Beyond that the highway, not much travelled. Beyond the highway, the jetty, the moored boats, the restless lake-water reflecting the sunshine.

The civic guard was so affable that he took off his cap. He was bald, completely bald. Robert St. Blaise Macmahon thought that by taking off his cap the civic guard had made himself a walking, or standing, comic comment on the comic rural constable, in the Thomas Hardy story, who wouldn't leave his house without his truncheon : because without his truncheon his going forth would not be official.

Robert St. Blaise Macmahon felt like telling all that to the civic guard and imploring him, for the sake of the dignity of his office, to restore his cap to its legal place and so to protect his bald head from the sunshine which, for Ireland, was quite bright and direct. Almost like the sun of that autumn he had spent in the Grand Atlas, far from the tourists. Or the sun of that spring when he had submitted to the natural curiosity of a novelist, who was also a wealthy man and could afford such silly journeys, and gone all the way to the United States, not to see those sprawling vulgar cities, Good God sir no, nor all those chromium-plated barbarians who had made an industry out of writing boring books about those colossal bores, Yeats and Joyce, but to go to Georgia to see the Okefenokee Swamp which interested him because of those sacred drooping melancholy birds, the white ibises, and because of the alligators. Any day in the year give him, in preference to Americans, alligators. It could be that he made the journey so as to be able at intervals to say that.

But if he talked like this to the bald guard on the ancestral doorstep the poor devil would simply gawk or smirk or both and say : Yes, Mr Macmahon. Of course, Mr. Macmahon.

Very respectful, he would seem to be. For the Macmahons counted for something in the town. His father's father had as good as owned it.

The fellow's bald head was nastily ridiculously perspiring. Robert St. Blaise Macmahon marked down that detail for his notebook. Henry James had so wisely said : Try to be one of those on whom nothing is lost.

Henry James had known it all. What a pity that he had to be born in the United States. But then, like the gentleman he was, he had had the good wit to run away from it all.

The bald perspiring cap-in-hand guard said : Excuse me, Mr. Macmahon. Sorry to disturb you on such a heavenly morning and all. But I've come about the body, sir.

Robert St. Blaise Macmahon was fond of saying in certain circles in Dublin that he liked civic guards if they were young, fresh from the country, and pink-cheeked; and that he liked Christian Brothers in a comparable state of development. In fact, he would argue, you came to a time of life when civic guards and Christian Brothers were, apart from the uniforms, indistinguishable. This he said merely to hear himself say it. He was much too fastidious for any fleshly contact with anybody, male or female. So, lightly, briefly, flittingly, trippingly, he now amused himself with looking ahead to what he would say on his next visit to town : Well if they had to send a guard they could have sent a young handsome one to enquire about the . . .

What the guard had just said now registered and with a considerable shock. The guard repeated : About the body, sir. I'm sorry, Mr Macmahon, to disturb you.

—What body? Whose body? What in heaven's name can you mean?

—I know it's a fright, sir. Not what you would expect at all. The body in the bed, sir. Dead in the bed.

—There is no body in my bed. Dead or alive. At least not while I'm up and about. I live here alone, with my housekeeper, Miss Hynes.

—Yes, Mr Macmahon, sir. We know Miss Hynes well. Very highly respected lady, sir. She's below in the barracks at the moment in a terrible state of nervous prostration. The doctor's giving her a pill or an injection or something to soothe her. Then he'll be here directly.

—Below in the barracks? But she went out to do the shopping.

—Indeed yes, sir. But she slipped in to tell us, in passing, like, sir. Oh it's not serious or anything. Foul play is not suspected.

—Foul what? Tell you what?

—Well, sir.

—Tell me, my good man.

—She says, sir, there's a man dead in her bed.

—A dead man?

—The very thing, Mr. Macmahon.

—In the bed of Miss Hynes, my housekeeper.

—So she says, sir. Her very words.

—What in the name of God is he doing there?

—Hard to say, Mr. Macmahon, what a dead man would be doing in a bed, I mean like in somebody else's bed.

With a huge white linen handkerchief that he dragged, elongated, out of a pants pocket, and then spread before him like an enveloping cloud, the guard patiently mopped his perspiration : Damned hot today, sir. The hottest summer, the paper says, in forty years.

The high Georgian-Floridian sun shone straight down on wine-coloured swamp-water laving (it was archaic but yet the only word) the grotesque knobbly knees of giant cypress trees. The white sacred crook-billed birds perched gravely, high on grey curved branches above trailing Spanish moss, oh far away, so far away from this mean sniggering town and its rattling tongues. It was obvious, it was regrettably obvious, that the guard was close to laughter.

—A dead man, guard, in the bed of Miss Hynes, my housekeeper, and housekeeper to my father and mother before me, and a distant relative of my own.

—So she tells us, sir.

—Scarcely a laughing matter, guard.

—No, sir. Everything but, sir. It's just the heat, sir. Overcome by the heat. Hottest summer, the forecast says, in forty years.

That hottest summer in forty years followed them, panting, across the black and red flagstones of the wide hallway. A fine mahogany staircase went up in easy spirals. Robert St. Blaise Macmahon led the way around it, keeping to the ground floor. The guard placed his cap, open end up, on the hall stand, as reverently as if he were laying cruets on an altar, excusing himself, as he did so, as if the ample mahogany hall stand, mirrored and antlered, were also a Macmahon watching, or reflecting, him with disapproval. It was the first time he or his like ever had had opportunity or occasion to enter this house.

In the big kitchen, old-fashioned as to size, modern as to fittings, the hottest summer was a little assuaged. The flagstones were replaced by light tiles, green and white, cool to the sight and the touch. She had always held on to that bedroom on the ground floor, beyond the kitchen, although upstairs the large house was more than half empty. She said she loved it because it had french windows that opened out to the garden. They did, too. They would also give easy access for visitors to the bedroom : a thought that had never occurred to him, not once over all these years.

Earlier that morning she had called to him from the kitchen to say that she was going shopping, and had made her discreet escape by way of those windows. They still lay wide open to the garden. She was a good gardener as she was a good housekeeper. She had, of course, help with the heavy

62

work in both cases: girls from the town for the kitchen, a healthy young man for the garden. All three, or any, of them were due to arrive, embarrassingly, within the next hour. Could it be the young man for the garden, there, dead in the bed? No, at least, thank God, it wasn't her assistant gardener, a scape-grace of a fellow that might readily tempt a middle-aged woman. She hadn't stooped to the servants. She had that much Macmahon blood in her veins. This man was, or had been, a stranger, an older man by far than the young gardener. He was now as old as he would ever be. The hottest summer was heavy and odorous in the garden, and flower odours and insect sounds came to them in the room. The birds were silent. There was also the other odour: stale sweat, or dead passion, or just death? The guard sniffed. He said: He died sweating. He's well tucked in.

Only the head was visible: sparse grey hair, a few sad pimples on the scalp, a long purple nose, a comic Cyrano nose. Mouth and eyes were open. He had good teeth and brown eyes. He looked, simply, surprised, not yet accustomed to wherever he happened to find himself.

—Feel his heart, guard.

—Oh dead as mutton, Mr. Macmahon. Miss Hynes told no lie. Still, he couldn't die in a better place. In a bed, I mean.

—Unhouselled, unappointed, unannealed.

—Yes, sir, the guard said, every bit of it.

—I mean he died without the priest.

With something amounting almost to wit—you encountered it in the most unexpected places—the guard said that taking into account the circumstances in which the deceased, God be merciful to him, had passed over, he could hardly have counted on the company of a resident chaplain. That remark could be adopted as one's own, improved upon, and employed on suitable occasions and in the right places, far from this town and its petty people.

—Death, said the guard, is an odd fellow. There's no being up to him, Mr Macmahon. He can catch you unawares in the oddest places.

This fellow, by heaven, was a philosopher. He was, for sure, one for the notebook.

—Quite true, guard. There was a very embarrassing case involving a president of the great French Republic. Found dead in his office. He had his hands in the young lady's hair. They had to cut the hair to set her free.

—Do you tell me so, sir? A French president? 'Twouldn't be the present fellow, De Gaulle, with the long nose would be caught at capers like that.

—There was a Hemingway story on a somewhat similar theme.

—Of course, sir. You'd know about that, Mr. Macmahon. I don't read much myself. But my eldest daughter that works for the public libraries tells me about your books.

—And Dutch Schultz, the renowned American gangster, you know that he was shot dead while he was sitting, well in fact while he was sitting on the toilet.

—A painful experience, Mr. Macmahon. He must have been surprised beyond measure.

Far away, from the highway, came the sound of an automobile.

—That, said the guard, could be the doctor or the ambulance.

They waited in silence in the warm odorous room. The sound passed on and away: neither the doctor nor the ambulance.

—But that fellow in the bed, Mr. Macmahon, I could tell you things about him, God rest him.

—Do you mean to say you know him.

—Of course, sir. It's my business to know people.

—Try to be one of those on whom nothing is lost.

—Quite so, sir, and odd that you should mention it. For that fellow in the bed, sir, do you know that once upon a time he lost two hundred hens?

—Two hundred hens?

—Chickens.

—Well, even chickens. That was a lot of birds. Even sparrows. Or skylarks. He must have been the only man in Europe who ever did that.

—In the world, I'd say, sir. And it happened so simple.

—It's stuffy in here, Robert said.

He led the way out to the garden. The sound of another automobile on the highway was not yet the doctor nor the ambulance. They walked along a red-sanded walk. She had had that mulch red sand brought all the way from Mullachdearg Strand in County Donegal. She loved the varied strands of Donegal : red, golden or snow-white. To right and left her roses flourished. She had a good way with roses, and with sweetpea, and even with sunflowers, those lusty brazen-faced giants.

—He was up in Dublin one day in a pub, and beside him at the counter the mournfullest man you ever saw. So the man that's gone, he was always a cheery type, said to the mournful fellow : Brighten up, the sun's shining, life's not all that bad. The mournful one says : If you were a poultry farmer with two hundred hens that wouldn't lay an egg, you'd hardly be singing songs.

—The plot, said Robert St. Blaise Macmahon, thickens.

—So, says your man that's inside there, and at peace we may charitably hope, how much would you take for those hens? A shilling a hen. Done, says he, and out with two hundred shillings and buys the hens. Then he hires a van and a boy to drive it, and off with him to transport the hens. You see, he knows a man here in this very town that will give him half-a-crown a hen, a profit of fifteen pounds sterling less the hire of the van. But the journey is long and the stops plentiful at the wayside pubs, he always had a notorious drouth, and whatever happened nobody ever found out, but when he got to this town at two in the morning, the back doors of the van were swinging open.

—The birds had flown.

—Only an odd feather to be seen. And he had to pay the boy fifteen shillings to clean out the back of the van. They were never heard of again, the hens I mean. He will long be remembered for that.

—If not for anything else.

—His poor brother, too, sir. That was a sad case. Some families are, you might say, addicted to sudden death.

—Did he die in a bed?

—Worse, far worse, sir. He died on a lawnmower.

—Guard, said Robert, would you have a cup of tea? You should be writing books, instead of me.

—I was never much given to tea, sir.

—But in all the best detective stories the man from Scotland Yard always drinks a cup o' tea.

—As I told you, sir, I don't read much. But if you had the tiniest drop of whiskey to spare, I'd be grateful. It's a hot day and this uniform is a crucifixion.

They left the garden by a wicket-gate that opened through a beech-hedge on to the front lawn. The sun's reflections shot up like lightning from the lake-water around the dancing boats. Three automobiles passed, but no doctor, no ambulance, appeared. Avoiding the silent odorous room they re-entered the house by the front door. In the dining-room Robert St. Blaise Macmahon poured the whiskey for the guard, and for himself : he needed it.

—Ice, guard?

—No thank you sir. Although they say the Americans are hell for it. In everything, in tea, whiskey, and so on.

Two more automobiles passed. They listened and waited.

—You'd feel, sir, he was listening to us, like for a laugh, long nose and all. His brother was the champion gardener of all time. Better even than Miss Hynes herself, although her garden's a sight to see and a scent to smell.

—He died on a lawnmower?

—On his own lawn, sir. On one of those motor mowers. It blew up under him. He was burned to death. And you could easily say, sir, he couldn't have been at a more harmless occupation, or in a safer place.

—You could indeed, guard. Why haven't I met you before this?

—That's life, sir. Our paths never crossed. Only now for that poor fellow inside I wouldn't be here today at all.

This time it had to be the doctor and the ambulance. The wheels came, scattering gravel, up the driveway.

—He was luckier than his brother, sir. He died in more comfort, in a bed. And in action, it seems. That's more than will be said for most of us.

The doorbell chimed : three slow cathedral tones. That chime had been bought in Bruges where they knew about bells. The guard threw back what was left of his whiskey. He said : You'll excuse me, Mr. Macmahon. I'll go and put on my cap. We have work to do.

When the guard, the doctor, the ambulance, the ambulance attendants, and the corpse had, all together, taken their departure, he sprayed the bedroom with Flit, sworn foe to the housefly. It was all he could think of. It certainly changed the odour. It drifted out even into the garden, and lingered there among the roses. The assistant gardener and the kitchen girls had not yet arrived. That meant that the news was out, and that they were delaying in the town to talk about it. What sort of insufferable idiot was that woman to put him in this way into the position of being talked about, even, in the local papers, written about, and then laughed at, by clods he had always regarded with a detached and humorous, yet godlike, eye?

He sat, for the sake of the experience, on the edge of the rumpled bed from which the long-nosed corpse had just been removed. But he felt nothing of any importance. He remembered that another of those American dons had written a book, which he had slashingly reviewed, about love and death in the American novel. To his right, beyond the open windows, was her bureau desk and bookcase : old black oak, as if in stubborn isolated contradiction to the prevalent mahogany. She had never lost the stiff pride that a poor relation wears as a mask

67

when he or she can ride high above the more common servility. She was a high-rider. It was simply incomprehensible that she, who had always so rigidly kept herself to herself, should have had a weakness for a long-nosed man who seemed to have been little better than a figure of fun. Two hundred hens, indeed!

The drawers of the bureau-bookcase were sagging open, and in disorder, as if in panic she had been rooting through them for something that nobody could find. He had seldom seen the inside of her room but, from the little he had seen and from everything he knew of her, she was no woman for untidiness or unlocked drawers. Yet in spite of her panic she had not called for aid to him, her cousin-once-removed, her employer, her benefactor. She had always stiffly, and for twenty-five years, kept him at a distance. Twenty-five years ago, in this room. She would have been eighteen, not six months escaped from the mountain valley she had been reared in, from which his parents had rescued her. He closes his eyes and, as best he can, his nose. He remembers. It is a Sunday afternoon and the house is empty except for the two of them.

He is alone in his room reading. He is reading about how Lucius Apuleius watches the servant-maid, Fotis, bending over the fire : Mincing of meats and making pottage for her master and mistresse, the Cupboard was all set with wines and I thought I smelled the savour of some dainty meats. Shee had about her middle a white and clean apron, and shee was girdled about her body under the paps with a swathell of red silk, and shee stirred the pot and turned the meat with her faire and white hands, in such sort that with stirring and turning the same, her loynes and hips did likewise move and shake, which was in my mind a comely sight to see.

Robert St. Blaise Macmahon who, at sixteen, had never tasted wine except to nibble secretively at the altar-wine when he was an acolyte in the parish church, repeats over and over again the lovely luscious Elizabethan words of Adlington's translation from the silver Latin : We did renew our venery by drinking of wine.

For at sixteen he is wax, and crazy with curiosity.

Then he looks down into the garden and there she is bending down over a bed of flowers. She is tall, rather sallow-faced, a Spanish face in an oval of close, crisp, curling dark hair. He has already noticed the determination of her long lithe stride, the sway of her hips, the pendulum swish and swing of her bright tartan pleated skirt. For a girl from the back of the mountains she has a sense of style.

She has come to this house from the Gothic grandeur of a remote valley called Glenade. Flat-topped mountains, so steep that the highest few hundred feet are sheer rock-cliffs corrugated by torrents, surround it. One such cliff, fissured in some primeval cataclysm, falls away into a curved chasm, rises again into one cold pinnacle of rock. The place is known as the Maiden's Leap, and the story is that some woman out of myth—Goddess, female devil, what's the difference?—pursued by a savage and unwanted lover, ran along the ridge of the mountain, and when faced by the chasm leaped madly to save her virtue, and did. But she didn't leap far enough to save her beautiful frail body which was shattered on the rocks below. From which her pursuer may have derived a certain perverse satisfaction.

All through her girlhood her bedroom window has made a frame for that extraordinary view. Now, her parents dead, herself adopted into the house of rich relatives as a sort of servant-maid, assistant to the aged housekeeper and in due course to succeed her, she bends over a flower-bed as Fotis had bent over the fire: O Fotis how trimely you can stir the pot, and how finely, with shaking your buttocks, you can make pottage.

Now she is standing tall and straight snipping blossoms from a fence of sweetpea. Her body is clearly outlined against the multi-coloured fence. He watches. He thinks of Fotis. He says again: We did renew our venery with drinking of wine.

When he confronts her in this very room, and makes an awkward grab at her, her arms are laden with sweetpea. So he is able to plant one kiss on cold unresponding lips. The

69

coldness, the lack of response in a bondswoman, surprises him. She bears not the slightest resemblance to Fotis. It was the done thing, wasn't it : the young master and the servant-maid? In the decent old days in Czarist Russia the great ladies in the landed houses used to give the maids to their sons to practise on.

The sweetpea blossoms, purple, red, pink, blue, flow rather than fall to the floor. Then she hits him with her open hand, one calm, deliberate, country clout that staggers him and leaves his ear red, swollen and singing for hours. She clearly does not understand the special duties of a young female servant. In wild Glenade they didn't read Turgenev or Saltykov-Schedrin. He is humiliatingly reminded that he is an unathletic young man, a pampered only child, and that she is a strong girl from a wild mountain valley. She says : Mind your manners, wee boy. Pick up those sweetpea or I'll tell your father and mother how they came to be on the floor.

He picks up the flowers. She is older than he is. She is also taller, and she has a hand like rock. He knows that she has already noticed that he is afraid of his father.

This room was not then a bedroom. It was a pantry with one whole wall of it shelved for storing apples. He could still smell those apples, and the sweetpea. The conjoined smell of flower and fruit was stronger even than the smell of the insect-killing spray with which he had tried to banish the odour of death.

That stinging clout was her great leap, her defiance, her declaration of independence but, as in the case of the Maiden of Glenade, it had only carried her halfways. To a cousin once-removed, who never anyway had cared enough to make a second attempt, she had demonstrated that she was no chattel. But she remained a dependant, a poor relation, a housekeeper doing the bidding of his parents until they died and, after their death, continuing to mind the house, grow the roses, the sweetpea and the sunflowers. The sense of style, the long lithe swinging stride, went for nothing, just because she hadn't jumped far enough to o'erleap the meandering withering enduring ways of a small provincial town. No man in the place could publicly be her equal. She was part Macmahon. So she had no man of her own, no place of her own. She had become part of the furniture of this house. She had no life of her own. Or so he had lightly thought.

He came and went and wrote his books, and heard her and spoke to her, but seldom really saw her except to notice that wrinkles, very faint and fine, had appeared on that Spanish face, on the strong-boned, glossy forehead, around the corners of the eyes. The crisp dark hair had touches of grey that she had simply not bothered to do anything about. She was a cypher, and a symbol in a frustrating land that had more than its share of ageing hopeless virgins. He closed his eyes and saw her as such when, in his writing, he touched satirically on that aspect of life in his pathetic country. Not that he did so any more often than he could help. For a London illustrated magazine he had once written about the country's low and late marriage rate, an article that had astounded all by its hard practicality. But as a general rule he preferred to think and to write about Stockholm or Paris or Naples or Athens, or African mountains, remote from everything. His travel books were more than travel books, and his novels really did show that travel broadened the mind. Or to think and write about the brightest gem in an America that man was doing so much to lay waste : the swamp that was no swamp but a wonderland out of a fantasy by George MacDonald, a Scottish writer whom nobody read any more, a fantasy about awaking some morning in your own bedroom, which is no longer a bedroom but the heart of the forest where every tree has its living spirit, genial or evil, evil or genial.

At that moment in his reverie the telephone rang. To the devil with it, he thought, let it ring. The enchanted swamp was all around him, the wine-coloured water just perceptibly moving, the rugged knees of the cypress trees, the white priestly birds curved brooding on high bare branches, the silence. Let it ring. It did, too. It rang and rang and refused to stop. So he

71

walked ill-tempered to the table in the hallway where the telephone was, picked it up, silenced the ringing, heard the voice of the civic guard, and then noticed for the first conscious time the black book that he carried in his right hand.

The guard said : She's resting now. The sergeant's wife is looking after her.

—Good. That's very good.

It was a ledger-type book, eight inches by four, the pages ruled in blue, the margins in red. He must, unthinkingly, have picked it up out of the disorder in which her morning panic had left the bureau-bookcase. For the first time that panic seemed to him as comic : it wasn't every morning a maiden lady found a long-nosed lover, or something, cold between the covers. It was matter for a short story, or an episode in a novel : if it just hadn't damned well happened in his own house. What would Henry James have made of it? The art of fiction is in telling not what happened, but what should have happened. Or what should have happened somewhere else.

The guard was still talking into his left ear, telling him that the doctor said it was a clear case of heart failure. Oh, indeed it was : for the heart was a rare and undependable instrument. With his right hand he flicked at random through the black book, then, his eye caught by some words that seemed to mean something, he held the book flat, focused on those words until they were steady, and read. The hand-writing was thick-nibbed, black as coal, dogged, almost printing, deliberate as if the nib had bitten into the paper. He read : Here he comes down the stairs in the morning, his double jowl red and purple from the razor, his selfish mouth pursed as tight as Mick Clinton, the miser of Glenade, used to keep the woollen sock he stored his money in when he went to the market and the horsefair of Manorhamilton. Here he comes, the heavy tread of him in his good, brown hand-made shoes, would shake the house if it wasn't as solid on its foundations as the Rock of Cashel. Old John Macmahon used to boast that his people built for eternity. Thud, thud, thud, the weight of his big flat feet. Here he comes, Gorgeous Gussie, with his white linen shirt, he should have frills on his underpants, and his blue eyeshade to show to the world, as if there was anybody to bother looking at him except myself and the domestic help, that he's a writer. A writer, God help us. About what? Who reads him? It's just as well he has old John's plunder to live on.

The black letters stood out like basalt from the white, blue-and-red lined paper. Just one paragraph she wrote to just one page and, if the paragraph didn't fully fill the page, she made, above and below the paragraph, whorls and doodles and curlicues in inks of various colours, blue, red, green, violet. She was a lonely self-delighting artist. She was, she had been, for how long, oh merciful heavens, an observer, a writer.

The guard was saying : She said to the sergeant's wife that she's too shy to face you for the present.

—Shy, he said.

He looked at the black words. They were as distinct as that long-ago clout on the side of the head : the calloused hard hand of the mountainy girl reducing the pretensions of a shy, sensitive, effeminate youth.

He said : She has good reason to be shy. It is, perhaps, a good thing that she should, at least, be shy before her employer and distant relation.

—It might be that, sir, she might mean not shy, but ashamed.

—She has also good reason for being ashamed.

—She says, Mr. Macmahon, sir, that she might go away somewhere for a while.

—Shouldn't she wait for the inquest and the funeral? At any rate, she has her duties here in this house. She is, she must realise, paid in advance.

So she would run, would she, and leave him to be the single object of the laughter of the mean people of this town? In a sweating panic he gripped the telephone as if he would crush it. There was an empty hungry feeling, by turns hot, by turns cold, just above his navel. He was betraying himself to that garrulous guard who would report to the town every word he said. It was almost as if the guard could read, if he could read, those damnable black words. He gripped the phone, slippy and sweaty as it was, gulped and steadied himself, breathed carefully, in out, in out, and was once again Robert St. Blaise Macmahon, a cultivated man whose education had commenced at the famous Benedictine school at Glenstal. After all, the Jesuits no longer were what once they had been, and James Joyce had passed that way to the discredit both of himself and the Jesuits.

—Let her rest then, he said. I'll think over what she should do. I'll be busy all day, guard, so don't call me unless it's absolutely essential.

He put down the telephone, wiped his sweating hand with a white linen handkerchief, monogrammed and ornamented with the form of a feather embroidered in red silk. It was meant to represent a quill pen and also to be a symbol of the soaring creative mind. That fancy handkerchief was, he considered, his one flamboyance. He wore, working, a blue eyeshade because there were times when lamplight, and even overbright daylight, strained his eyes. Any gentleman worthy of the name did, didn't he, wear hand-made shoes?

On the first page of the book she had pasted a square of bright yellow paper and on it printed in red ink : Paragraphs.

In smaller letters, in Indian black ink, and in an elegant italic script, she had written : Reflections on Robert the Riter.

Then finally, in green ink, she had printed : By his Kaptivated Kuntry Kusin ! ! !

He was aghast at her frivolity. Nor did she need those three exclamation marks to underline her bitchiness, a withdrawn and secretive bitchiness, malevolent among the roses and the pots and pans, overflowing like bile, in black venomous ink. She couldn't have been long at this secret writing. The book was by no means full. She had skipped, and left empty pages here and there, at random as if she dipped her pen and viciously wrote wherever the book happened to open. There was no time sequence that he could discern. He read : He

74

says he went all the way to the States to see a swamp. Just like him. Would he go all the way to Paris to see the sewers?

—But the base perfidy of that.

He spoke aloud, not to himself but to her.

—You always pretended to be interested when I talked about the swamp. The shy wild deer that would come to the table to take the bit out of your fingers when you breakfasted in the open air, the racoon with the rings round its eyes, the alligators, the wine-coloured waters, the white birds, the white sand on the bed of the Suwannee River. You would sit, woman, wouldn't you, brown Spanish face inscrutable, listening, agreeing, with me, oh yes, agreeing with me in words, but, meanly, all the time, thinking like this.

Those brief words about that small portion of his dream-world had wounded him. But bravely he read more. The malice of this woman of the long-nosed chicken-losing lover must be fully explored. She was also, by heaven, a literary critic. She wrote : Does any novelist, nowadays, top-dress his chapters with quotations from other authors? There is one, but he writes thrillers and that's different. Flat-footed Robert the Riter, with his good tweeds and his brass-buttoned yellow waistcoat, has a hopelessly old-fashioned mind. His novels, with all those sophisticated nonentities going nowhere, read as if he was twisting life to suit his reading. But then what does Robert know about life? Mamma's boy, Little Lord Fauntleroy, always dressed in the best. He doesn't know one rose from another. But a novelist should know everything. He doesn't know the town he lives in. Nor the people in it. Quotations. Balderdash.

He found to his extreme humiliation that he was flushed with fury. The simplest thing to do would be to let her go away and stay away, and then find himself a housekeeper who wasn't a literary critic, a secret carping critic, a secret lover too, a Psyche, by Hercules, welcoming by night an invisible lover to her bed. Then death stops him, and daylight reveals him, makes him visible as a comic character with a long nose, and with a comic reputation, only, for mislaying two hundred hens, and with a brother, a great gardener, who had the absurd misfortune to be burned alive on his own lawn. Could comic people belong to a family addicted to sudden death? Somewhere in all this, there might be some time the germ of a story.

But couldn't she realise what those skilfully-chosen quotations meant?

—Look now, he said, what they did for George MacDonald. A procession of ideas, names, great presences, marching around the room you write in : Fletcher and Shelley, Novalis and Beddoes, Goethe and Coleridge, Sir John Suckling and Shakespeare, Lyly and Schiller, Heine and Schleiermacher and Cowley and Spenser and the Book of Judges and Jean Paul Richter and Cyril Tourneur and Sir Philip Sidney and Dekker and Chaucer and the Kabala.

But, oh Mother Lilith, what was the use of debating thus with the shadow of a secretive woman who was now resting in the tender care of the sergeant's wife who was, twenty to one, relaying the uproarious news to every other wife in the town : Glory be, did you hear the fantasticality that happened up in Mr. Robert St. Blaise Macmahon's big house? Declare to God they'll never again be able to show their faces in public.

Even if she were with him, walking in this garden as he now was, and if he was foolish enough thus to argue with her, she would smile her sallow wrinkled smile, look sideways out of those dark-brown eyes and then go off alone to write in her black book : He forgot to mention the Twelve Apostles, the Clancy Brothers, and the Royal Inniskilling Fusiliers.

All her life she had resisted his efforts to make something out of her. Nor had she ever had the determination to rise and leap again, to leave him and the house and go away and make something out of herself.

He read : He's like the stuck-up high-falutin' women in that funny story by Somerville and Ross, he never leaves the house except to go to Paris. He doesn't see the life that's going on under his nose. He says there are no brothels in Dublin.

But if Dublin had the best brothels in the long history of sin . . .

Do you know, now, that was not badly put. She has a certain felicity of phrase. But then she has some Macmahon blood in her, and the educational advantages that over the years this house has afforded her.

. . . long history of sin, he'd be afraid of his breeches to enter any of them. He says there are no chic women in Dublin. What would he do with a chic woman if I gave him one, wrapped in cellophane, for Valentine's Day? He says he doesn't know if the people he sees are ugly because they don't make love, or that they don't make love because they're ugly. He's the world's greatest living authority, isn't he, either on love or good looks?

On another page : To think, dear God, of that flat-footed bachelor who doesn't know one end of a woman from the other, daring to write an article attacking the mountainy farmers on their twenty pitiful acres of rocks, rushes, bogpools and dunghills, for not marrying young and raising large families. Not only does he not see the people around him, he doesn't even see himself. Himself and a crazy priest in America lamenting about late marriages and the vanishing Irish. A fine pair to run in harness. The safe, sworn celibate and the fraidy-cat bachelor.

And on yet another page : That time long ago, I clouted him when he made the pass, the only time, to my knowledge, he ever tried to prove himself a man. And he never came back for more. I couldn't very well tell him that the clout was not for what he was trying to do but for the stupid way he was trying to do it. A born bungler.

The doodles, whorls and curlicues wriggled like a snake-pit, black, blue, green, red, violet, before his angry eyes. That was enough. He would bring that black book down to the barracks, and throw it at her, and tell her never to darken his door again. His ears boomed with blood. He went into the dining-room, poured himself a double whiskey, drank it slowly, breathing heavily, thinking. But no, there was a better way.

Go down to the barracks, bring her back, lavish kindness on her, in silence suffer her to write in her book, then copy what she writes, reshape it, reproduce it, so that some day she would see it in print and be confounded for the jade and jezebel that she is.

With deliberate speed, majestic instancy, he walked from the dining-room to her bedroom, tossed the book on to her bed where she would see it on her return and know he had read it, and that her nastiness was uncovered. He had read enough of it, too much of it: because the diabolical effect of his reading was that he paused, with tingling irritation, to examine his tendency to think in quotations. Never again, thanks to her malice, would he do so, easily, automatically, and, so to speak, unthinkingly.

Coming back across the kitchen he found himself looking at his own feet, in fine hand-made shoes, his feet rising, moving forwards, settling again on the floor, fine flat feet. It was little benefit to see ourselves as others see us. That was, merciful God, another quotation. That mean woman would drive him mad. He needed a change: Dublin, Paris, Boppard on the Rhine—a little town that he loved in the off-season when it wasn't ravished by boat-loads of American women doing the Grand Tour. First, though, to get the Spanish maiden of wild Glenade back to her proper place among the roses and the pots and pans.

The guard answered the telephone. He said: She's still resting, Mr. Macmahon, sir.

—It's imperative that I speak to her. She can't just take this lying down.

That, he immediately knew, was a stupid thing to say. On the wall before him, strong black letters formed, commenting on his stupidity.

There was a long silence. Then she spoke, almost whispered: Yes, Robert.

—Hadn't you better get back to your place here?

—Yes, Robert. But what is my place there?

—You know what I mean. We must face this together. After all, you are half a Macmahon.

—Half a Macmahon, she said, is better than no bread.

He was shocked to fury: This is nothing to be flippant about.

—No, Robert.

—Who was this man?

—A friend of mine.

—Do you tell me so? Do you invite all your friends to my house?

—He was the only one.

—Why didn't you marry him?

—He had a wife and five children in Sudbury in England. Separated.

—That does, I believe, constitute an impediment. But who or what was he?

—It would be just like you, Robert, not even to know who he was. He lived in this town. It's a little town.

—Should I have known him?

—Shouldn't a novelist know everybody and everything?

—I'm not an authority on roses.

—You've been reading my book.

She was too sharp for him. He tried another tack: Why didn't you tell me you were having a love affair? After all, I am civilised.

—Of course you're civilised. The world knows that. But there didn't seem any necessity for telling you.

—There must be so many things that you don't feel it is necessary to tell me.

—You were never an easy person to talk to.

—All your secret thoughts. Who could understand a devious woman? Far and from the farthest coasts . . .

—There you go again. Quotations. The two-footed gramophone. What good would it do you if you did understand?

—Two-footed, he said. Flat-footed.

He was very angry: You could have written it all out for me if you couldn't say it. All the thoughts hidden behind your

79

brooding face. All the things you thought when you said nothing, or said something else.

—You really have been reading my book. Prying.

The silence could have lasted all of three minutes. He searched around for something that would hurt.

—Isn't it odd that a comic figure should belong to a family addicted to sudden death?

—What on earth do you mean?

Her voice was higher. Anger? Indignation?

—That nose, he said. Cyrano. Toto the Clown. And I heard about the flight of the two hundred hens.

Silence.

—And about the brother who was burned.

—They were kindly men, she said. And good to talk to. They had green fingers.

It would have gratified him if he could have heard a sob.

—I'll drive down to collect you in an hour's time.

—He loved me, she said. I suppose I loved him. He was something, in a place like this.

Silence.

—You're a cruel little boy, she said. But just to amuse you, I'll give you another comic story. Once he worked in a dog kennels in Kent in England. The people who owned the kennels had an advertisement in the local paper. One sentence read like this : Bitches in heat will be personally conducted from the railway station by Mr. Dominic Byrne.

—Dominic Byrne, she said. That was his name. He treasured that clipping. He loved to laugh at himself. He died for love. That's more than most will ever do. There you are. Make what you can out of that story, you flat-footed bore.

She replaced the telephone so quietly that for a few moments he listened, waiting for more, thinking of something suitable to say.

On good days, light, reflected from the lake, seemed to brighten every nook and corner of the little town. At the end of some old narrow winding cobbled laneway there would be a vision of lake-water bright as a polished mirror. It was a graceful greystone town, elegantly laid-out by some Frenchman hired by an eighteenth-century earl. The crystal river that fed the lake flowed through the town and gave space and scope for a tree-lined mall. But grace and dancing light could do little to mollify his irritation. This time, by the heavenly father, he would have it out with her, he would put her in her place, revenge himself for a long-ago affront and humiliation. Body in the bed, indeed. Two hundred hens, indeed. Swamps and sewers, indeed. Bitches in heat, indeed. She did not have a leg to stand on. Rutting, and on his time, with a long-nosed yahoo.

The Byzantine church, with which the parish priest had recently done his damnedest to disfigure the town, struck his eyes with concentrated insult. Ignorant bloody peasants. The slick architects could sell them anything : Gothic, Byzantine, Romanesque, Igloo, Kraal, Modern Cubist. The faithful paid, and the pastor made the choice.

Who would ever have thought that a lawnmower could be a Viking funeral pyre?

The barracks, a square, grey house, made ugly by barred windows and notice-boards, was beside the church. The guard, capless, the neck of his uniform jacket open, his hands in his trouser pockets, stood in the doorway. He was still perspiring. The man would melt. There was a drop to his nose : snot or sweat or a subtle blend of both. Robert St. Blaise Macmahon would never again make jokes about civic guards. He said : I've come for Miss Hynes.

—Too late, Mr. Macmahon, sir. The bird has flown.

—She has what?

—Gone, sir. Eloped. Stampeded. On the Dublin train. Ten minutes ago. I heard her whistle.

—Whistle?

—The train, sir.

—But the funeral? The inquest?

—Oh, his wife and children will bury him. We phoned them.

—But the inquest?

—Her affidavit will do the job. We'll just say he dropped while visiting your house to look at the roses.

—That's almost the truth.

—The whole truth and nothing but the truth is often a bitter dose, sir.

—As I said, guard, you are a philosopher.

He remembered too late that he hadn't said that, he had just thought it.

—Thank you kindly, sir. Would you chance a cup of tea, sir? Nothing better to cool one on a hot day. Not that I like tea myself. But in this weather, you know. The hottest day, the forecast says.

Well, why not? He needed cooling. The bird had flown, sailing away from him, over the chasm, laughing triumphant eldritch laughter.

In the austere dayroom they sat on hard chairs and sipped tea.

—Nothing decent or drinkable here, sir, except a half-bottle of Sandeman's port.

—No thank you, guard. No port. The tea will suffice.

—Those are gallant shoes, sir, if you'll excuse me being so pass-remarkable. Hand-made jobs.

—Yes, hand-made.

—Costly, I'd say. But then they'd last for ever.

—Quite true, guard.

—He's coffined by now. The heat, you know.

—Don't remind me.

—Sorry, sir. But the facts of life are the facts of life. Making love one minute. In a coffin the next.

—The facts of death, guard. Alone withouten any company.

—True as you say, sir. He was a droll divil, poor Byrne, and he died droll.

—Among the roses, guard.

—It could happen to anyone, God help us. Neither the day nor the hour do we know. The oddest thing, now, happened once to the sergeant's brother that's a journalist in Dublin.

This particular day he's due to travel to Limerick City to report on a flower show. But he misses the train. So he sends a telegram to ask a reporter from another newspaper to keep him a carbon. Then he adjourns to pass the day in the upstairs lounge bar of the Ulster House. Along comes the Holy Hour as they call it for jokes, when the pubs of Dublin close for a while in the early afternoon. To break up the morning boozing parties, you understand. There's nobody in the lounge except the sergeant's brother and a strange man. So the manager locks them in there to drink in peace and goes off to his lunch. And exactly halfways through the Holy Hour the stranger drops down dead. Angina. And there's me man that should be at a flower show in Limerick locked in on a licensed premises, the Ulster House, during an off or illegal hour, with a dead man that he doesn't know from Adam.

—An interesting legal situation, guard.

—Oh it was squared, of course. The full truth about that couldn't be allowed out. It would be a black mark on the licence. The manager might lose his job.

—People might even criticise the quality of the drink.

—They might, sir. Some people can't be satisfied. Not that there was ever a bad drop sold in the Ulster House. Another cup, Mr. Macmahon, sir.

—Thank you, guard.

—She'll come back, Mr. Macmahon. Blood they say is thicker than water.

—They do say that, do they? Yet somehow, in spite of what they say, I don't think she'll be back.

On she went, leaping, flying, describing jaunty parabolas. He would, of course, have to send her money. She was entitled to something legally and he could well afford to be generous beyond what the law demanded.

—So the long-nosed lover died, guard, looking at the roses.

—In a manner of speaking, sir.

—Possibly the only man, guard, who ever had the privilege. Look thy last on all things lovely.

But the guard was not aware of De La Mare.

83

—That's what we'll say, sir. It would be best for all. His wife and all. And no scandal.

—Days of wine and roses, guard.

—Yes, sir. Alas, that we have nothing here but that half-bottle of Sandeman's port. She was a great lady to grow roses, sir. That's how they met in the beginning, she told me. Over roses.

WILD ROVER NO MORE

T H E D A Y M Y sister turned Hannah the Saint from the door because she couldn't find a copper in the house to give her there was, as my mother herself would have said, a row that ten could fight in. It was a Saturday, and Saturdays my mother helped out in the dining-room of the White Hart, the town's best hotel, and also helped out with the family budget; and Friday was normally Hannah's begging day so that my sister and myself, housekeeping and eating fried potatoes off the same pan, were caught copperless and unawares. Fried potatoes never tasted so good eaten off smooth soulless plates as they did taken hot and succulent from the metal, and eating from the pan was more than eating. It was a tiptoe, breathless conflict over property, and territory : your pile, my pile, and keep your potatoes in your own part of the pan.

The door closed and Hannah was gone. The sister sat down opposite me, peeked sharply through wisps of dark hair that were for ever blinding her and coming between her and her food. She said : You robbed when my back was turned.

There was no use in lying to her. So I confessed : Four. Only four tiny ones.

She compensated herself, and with interest, by an expert flick of the fork. She said : Nothing smaller in the house than a florin and it's the only coin in the Catskill jug. I couldn't give Hannah the only florin we have. There'd be murder.

An American aunt home on holiday had left us the jug cut from the wood of a tree that had grown in Rip Van Winkle's mountains, and faithfully on the kitchen mantelpiece it housed the petty cash.

—Hannah's mad anyway, I said and thought that a florin

would be sadly wasted on a poor woman, the wrinkles of her face lined with dirt, who hadn't the right use of her wits.

—She shouts out her prayers at the altar rails. She thinks she's the Blessed Virgin.

—Funny thing, my sister said, when I told her I had nothing to give her. She wrapped the dirty old brown shawl around her, as haughty and high and mighty as if she was queen of England. And do you know what she said?

—How would I know?

—How indeed and you busy robbing my fried potatoes? She said : Sara Alice, I see some people forget old times. Sara Alice, she said. She called me by mother's name. Isn't that odd? But I couldn't give her the only florin in the house. There'd sure as God be murder.

The sister was fourteen and old enough to take in at the pores a feeling of guilt from the encircling air even if she had no formed idea as to what she was feeling guilty about. We finished the fried potatoes in a gloomy foreboding silence and lived to learn there was reason for foreboding because, florin saved or florin given in charity, there was murder anyway.

Buttoned boots with shiny patent toes you could see your face in were then still the fashion for women over forty and my mother, casting an armful of parcels on the kitchen table, collapsed in her old rocking chair while the sister knelt and unbuttoned her boots and pushed her a wooden footstool on which she rested her heels and waggled her toes. On a market day the White Hart dining-room was no paradise for weakly insteps. She said : Gulders of rich farmers from as far away as Strabane shouting for steak and porter as if they were never fed at home.

Her spectacles had misted over with her breathlessness and the effort of carting all those parcels up the Courthouse Hill; and with her hair escaped from hat and hairpins and half-veiling her peeping eyes she waited and listened while my sister told her about Hannah, and wiped the lenses. She was so short-sighted that if she put the spectacles down on the table she couldn't find them again except by groping and the sense of touch. Rocking, she listened, and seemed to continue listening long after my sister's narrative ended, and in a silence that had grown ominously chill. Then suddenly she groped for the glasses as if by seeing she could hear and understand better. The rocking ceased. She rested her tired feet flat on the floor. She said with a calmness that was worse than a shout or the blow of a stick : God in his heaven, don't tell me you turned Hannah from the door without a copper ha'penny.

My sister was frightened and already almost on the edge of tears. She said pathetically : Only one florin in the Catskill jug.

—You should have given it to her. You should have given her the jug. You should have given her the house. Given her something. Eggs. Bread. A pot of marmalade. A cup of tea. But not to turn her from the door with one hand as empty as the other. Pray heaven, the roof doesn't fall on us this blessed night.

The sister was sobbing. My startled imagination saw Hannah like a mad witch of a Meg Merrilees kneeling down to pray prayers of doom on us and our ill-fated house collapsing like so much sand.

—Repeat after me the two of you, she said, God's poor must never be turned away empty.

We repeated the words, my sister in gulps and sobs, my voice shaking.

—Hannah's not only God's poor, my mother said. She's my poor.

We had no notion what she meant. Then my mother cried and cried and that was the most frightening thing of all.

We couldn't understand why she made such a fuss about Hannah except it was that Hannah was religious, and daft enough to think she was the mother of God. The brown wooden angels on the rafters high above the nave of the Sacred Heart Church always, I thought, looked down on the altar rail antics of Hannah with a special sort of disapproving interest. How anyone could so disrupt the holy silence and get away with it, none of us, the young, could ever comprehend. Yet neither angel nor parish priest nor pious parishioner ever protested. Hannah and Joe the Musician, who wasn't quite as outspoken, had the freedom of God's house.

Joe the Musician was stout, short, bald, wore winter and summer an abrased leather motoring coat, played the fiddle for relaxation, owned a small confectionery shop in River Lane, and when the Church was empty and often even during service and ceremony had a sort of roving commission on the epistle side of the nave. He was to be found anywhere between the marble rails and the dark alcove by the door where the baptismal font was. Usually he prayed in a sibilant but unintelligible whisper but in moments of special fervour his voice took sound and shape and the angels above could hear him demanding prosperity and customers in plenty for his wee shop.

—Isn't God good enough to him, we used to say, that he has a wee shop to pray for.

The Lord may have heard him or perhaps he was merely a subtle advertiser. The shop certainly prospered.

But Hannah in a corner of the altar rails half hidden on the gospel side, a close neighbour to the two pews full of black-robed brothers of the Christian Schools, was a fixed star. She had her own place and no one who knew would have knelt there, even when she was wandering the town or absent with her simple daughter in a cottage a mile away where she was less at home, I'd say, that when she was before the altar. She had picked that place possibly because the sunlight when it was good brought the gaudy Munich blues down to it with the intensity of a spotlight from the Lady's mantle spread wide on the window above the tabernacle. Hannah, unlike Joe, had no mundane interests, no appeals to make for prosperity. Her rosary beads two feet long and each bead as big as a horse-chestnut, rattled like stones against the altar rails. She waved her arms then, with the composure of a pompadour, resettled her shawl on her shoulders. Her prayers, breathless and loud, came out in fragments that meant nothing to nobody except herself and the person to whom they were addressed. But we could make out that she spoke of herself as Mary and talked again and again of a heart wounded and pierced. She prayed as she walked too, on the Courthouse Hill, on the High Street or on the mile of road to her cottage, and my sister, who was inclined to fancy, said the blue light from the window followed her.

Once she splattered a handful of holy water from the font at the church door over one of the town's richest and most respected citizens and told him he needed a blessing more than any soldier from the barracks to Calcutta. But apart from that one incident she walked unmolesting and unmolested. No running children mocked her or called her names. We feared her as we did not fear the dirty old giant of a tramp, Mickey Alone, whose true name might have been Malone. One day he gave me twopence to light his stub of a clay pipe but his head was shaking so much with bad drink that I singed the wiry hairs off the tip of his nose and he chased me with his stick and, with pride, I have been telling the story ever since. Or as we did not fear Andy Orr who lived with his mother Tilda in one of the white cottages in the Back Alley and who was the image of Charlie Chaplin enduring a dog's life, and whom I once saw, roaring with Finest Old Red Wine at a shilling a bottle, being frogmarched to the lockup by two sombre embarrassed constables. Or as we did not fear the street-singer, Hit-Him-in-the-Kisser-with-a-Navvy's-Boot-in-our-Back-yard-last-night, who had earned the name because he sang for coppers a song with that curious refrain. He sang also a song about the gallant Forty-Twa and every loyal regiment under the King's command and the South Down militia who were the terror of the land. When he sang that song he paced up and down like a sentry and to simulate a rifle carried a broom-stick at the present, and danced, too, at the end of each verse.

To call names to that trinity and be chased in return was fair game, spice for their lives as for ours. But Hannah in her blue light walked alone under the Lady's mantle, and my

89

sister was so worried after the unfortunate affair of the florin that, for Hannah's intentions, she made the thirty days prayer to the Blessed Virgin, and met Hannah on the street one day and gave her two shillings she had saved. Hannah thanked her, using my mother's name again. That was still a mystery to us because my mother never talked about Hannah and on Fridays sent my sister or myself to the door with the weekly contribution.

In the house we lived in, a twisted stairway went up from the kitchen, and underneath the stairway was the dark cave, called in Scotland and Northern Ireland the logey-hole, a storehouse for brushes and polishing cloths and a den for children. Our next-door neighbour, a tailor and a fat one, obeying some impulse a few hundred thousand years older than himself or tailoring, sought refuge always in his logey hole in thunderstorms.

A year or so after the day of the florin, that secluded corner became of a sad morbid importance to my sister and myself. Our father had died suddenly. The funeral over, our three brothers and three sisters, all older than us, had gone back to their jobs in Belfast, Dublin, Liverpool, London, one brother, our hero, to the Inniskillings at Aldershot. After their going, the house on Saturdays was a painful place where every object from the Catskill jug to my father's wooden shaving bowl had a voice to remind us of the pain of loss. The darkness under the stairs had mercy in it. It seemed easier there to face up to the bewilderment of death, to accept that a hole in the ground in the graveyard on a green hill above the Drumragh River could be the brown gateway to a heaven in the clouds, and that when somebody you knew even so well as your father had gone to heaven you would see or hear him no more until you too had passed through that gateway.

Then one Saturday my sister went rope-skipping, apple, jelly, jam-tart, tell me the name of your sweetheart, with her girl friends, leaving me alone to mind the house, and in the cosy darkness I fell asleep and in my dream saw Hannah's cottage. It was a mile away on the western road from the town at a place we called the Flush. It stood on a low rocky hill fifty yards back from the road. It had one storey, one door, two tiny peeping windows, a roof of corrugated iron once painted red but long rains had streaked and stripped the paint. The place was called the Flush because a small stream came there out of meadowland, crossed the road boldly, not hiding under any bridge and curved off somewhere round Hannah's hill. In my dream the stream was in flood swelling into a torrent until it seemed as if it would swamp Hannah's house, and I could hear her voice complaining. Then I awoke and thought I was still dreaming because to my amazement she was out there in the kitchen talking to my mother.

—On Drumard Wood they crowned me Queen, she was saying. Do you recall those days, Sara Alice?

She sounded sane, yet talk of her being crowned as a queen fitted in as part of her altar-rail ravings, especially when she went on to sing in a cracked quavering voice : Oh Mary, we crown thee with blossoms today, queen of the angels and queen of the May.

—Three spoons, Hannah?

—Three spoons, Sara Alice. How well you remember I always had the sweet tooth.

—I'll never forget those days, my mother said.

Sipping tea, spoons tinkling, they were silent for a while.

—I came to sit with you, Sara Alice, in your sorrow.

—That was thoughtful of you, Hannah. Old friendship is old friendship.

Then Hannah spoke poetry as clearly and sensibly as the schoolmaster. She said : Make new friends but keep the old, those are silver, these are gold.

—But it wasn't May and it wasn't blossoms made the crown, my mother said. It was the last Sunday in July, or the first in August. The beginning of harvest and the first new potatoes. It was Garland Sunday. The young ones now never heard of it, Hannah. That pair of canaries of mine, supposed to be housekeeping. Absent without leave. Vanished without trace.

Like the birds of the air. More tea, Hannah? Is it sweet enough?

—Sweet and strong the way you know I always liked it. Boys and girls together from three parishes and one small town up Drumard Hill to the hazel-wood and the open moor, all together dancing and singing.

She must have put her cup down and gone, holding out her shawl, in a twirl around the kitchen because my mother was laughing and saying Hannah should be on the stage and that she was as light on her feet as a lassie of sixteen.

—All together up the hill hand in hand, Sara Alice. Picking the bilberries from the little bushes hiding in the heather. Then every boy with thread to make a necklace of bilberries for his girl and the leading girl to be crowned queen with the heather, purple and white.

—White for true hearts, Hannah. Purple for passion.

We were all mad jealous the day Tommy came there a stranger and crowned you before all others. He was the finest man we ever saw. We all envied you. I was with him the first day you met him, Sara Alice. Very fine he looked in his good brown suit.

—You have the memory. You're not rambling now, Hannah.

Hannah was singing again. She sang: Ramble away, ramble away, are you the young man they call Ramble Away.

She said: That was a song the girls made about a sailor.

—It was a Holy Thursday, Hannah, and your mother, no better woman ever to those that worked for her, was off to her devotions and I was behind the hotel bar when in he stepped, dying on his feet with the drink and looking for a cure of brandy and burgundy mixed. It was the fashion then.

—He travelled with a crowd of wild men, Sara Alice.

—He was a wild man himself, said my mother.

—At that time he was, she added. A wild rover.

—It's all as clear as if it was yesterday, Hannah said. Tommy's death when they told me and I saw the funeral going down the High Street brought everything back to me, good and bad, grave and gay.

She was crying.

—Drink your tea, Hannah. There's sweet cake here I always get on Saturday for the two canaries and since they're not here we'll demolish it ourselves.

She spoke as a conspirator. Hannah, I felt, was wiping her eyes and smiling. There went our sweet cake while I was hiding and my sister skipping tell me the name of her sweetheart.

—Whiles, Sara Alice, sitting out there listening to the Flush and the wind in the bushes and looking at my poor child I keep thinking long, the afflicted pierced heart, remembering everything. Running out to the hotel yard, all white-washed walls, and the tarred doors of the stables, to see the sun on Easter Sunday dancing as he came over the trees beyond the Fairywater.

—Master Reid, Hannah, that gave me the book of Robert Burns with the poems marked in it I wasn't to look at used to say : Those who do not care to face the bright orb with the naked eye may be content to look at its image in a tub of clean water.

—Your eyes were always weak, Sara Alice.

—I gave him the brandy and burgundy, my mother said, and watched the shake in his hand and the glass rattling off his teeth. A fine young man, I said, are you not ashamed? Have you no religion on a holy Thursday? No home, no parents?

—You were sharp, Sara Alice.

—Somebody had to be sharp. He cried there at the bar like a child.

—Drink and loneliness, Hannah said.

The sunny village street outside like a picture. Not saint or sinner to be seen. They were all at the devotions.

—Drink and loneliness, Hannah repeated. But my, when he steadied up we heard the stories. The tales of a wild rover. The black girls of the Barbadoes. Nova Scotia and Newfoundland, and how he and Pat O'Leary from Cork had planned to break out of the army and head for the Klondyke, and how

93

a patrol of the Dublin Fusiliers on the plains of Africa had fired all night at a waving bush.

My mother was laughing : The Dublins weren't used to country places and bushes, he said. There was never anybody like him to tell stories, true or false. You know, Hannah, he was thirty-five the day he wept over the brandy and burgundy and he hadn't seen home or father or mother since he was eighteen. I brought him back to them for a visit when we were married, not that his mother, the old battleaxe, ever gave me much thanks. The father wasn't too bad but he was as stiff as a ramrod and could never forgive the eighteen-year-old who had betrayed his trust as he called it, as if he owned the Bank of England and his son had mislaid the safe. Sending a boy from the Donegal Mountains to Dublin for the first time with a wallet of money to do a man's business. He saw Capetown before he ever saw Dublin and woke up drunk in the Royal Oak at Parkgate on the outskirts of the city with the money gone and the King's shilling in his fist and the uniform as good as on his shoulders. That was the way they joined the army in those days.

—Wild boys, wild men, said Hannah. Wild rovers. Fine men, but all unsettled by war and foreign places. Even the tinker men from Mayo fell short of them the night of the Lammas hiring fair. Ash plants against belt buckles and the buckles won.

—Discipline he used to say, Hannah, and overall stategy.

—Wandering Ireland, a bunch of old comrades, measuring it with chains to make a map for the King of England as if a map of his own country shouldn't satisfy him. The survey they called themselves, but we called them the sappers. They'd hunt you a mile for calling them sappers. There was great life at the dances when they came and the song they all sang together about the boy that listed in the army at the Curragh Camp because of a broken heart.

My mother spoke slowly then, touching each word as if it were a separate lovely thought : Straight will I repair to the Curragh of Kildare since my true love is absent from me.

—The great dances that we had, Sara Alice, in Langfield Hall. The big farmers' daughters who'd rub a tiny smear of cow dung on a new print frock so that the world would know their father grazed cattle. The dances in Brown's house.

—I preferred the dances in Brown's house, my mother said. They were more friendly and no strangers from the town. I remember one night the procession of ponies and traps in the moonlight along Brown's boreen, the two Clara lakes down in the flat bog, shining like the eyes of a giant. All along the boreen above Conn's Brae we went, and the hazel-woods where John Hart, the tea traveller, lost a wheel of his cart and had to chase it down a mile of woods and across the street before Big Mick Gormley's farmhouse to catch up with it in Big Mick's midden. John said the devil or the fairies were in that wheel. That night in the moonlight the whole convoy sang the song of the wild rover until the woods and hills rang.

Once again she spoke with that low wounded lingering on each word : I went into an alehouse, my money was done, and I asked the landlady to credit me some. She came trippingly to me and sweetly did say she could have as good customers as me any day. But now I've money plenty, money plenty in store, and I'll be the good boy and I'll play the wild rover no more.

—He stopped roving then, Sara Alice. He was a good man and dying about you.

—He'll rove no more ever, Hannah. Death ends all roving.

Then to my fear and horror my mother cried out in a voice I had never heard before, calling and listening for a while as if she expected an answer, and then calling again.

—Tommy, Tommy, Tommy, she cried three times.

All the long day of the funeral she had kept talking, and serving food and drink to all, and the bishop's bottle to the parish priest. She hadn't cried a tear.

—Hush, Sara Alice, hush, don't worry the dead. You were happy with him and he's happy now with God and his blessed mother. How lucky you were and all the parts of the world he might have wandered, to find him, even if he needed

95

brandy and burgundy and a talking to about his holy religion.
I was the spoilt child that my mother thought would wed the
Prince of Wales and my lot was a rascal of a fancy man with
talk for a dozen, and promising me the world, to leave me in
beggary on the streets of Glasgow carrying a child that was
never right with the fit of temperament I had when she was
born.

—True, Hannah, you had it sad, said my mother.

Then as if her first wild cries had been answered she repeated softly : Tommy, Tommy.

After that they may have talked for an hour. In fear and
agony I sat feeling guiltily that, with no right in the world, I
had seen something naked and bleeding. In the darkness I
cried silently for a sunny Thursday and a singing moonlit night
I had never seen. My ears I held shut, and flapped my hands
up and down over them, so that I'd hear not voices but the
happy quacking of ducks, and I could see the ducks. When I
quit that fantasy Hannah was gone and my sister was back
breathless from trying to learn by leaping over a rope, apple,
jelly, jam-tart, what would be the initials of her sweetheart.
She said : Don't cry, mother. Are you crying for da?

—I miss him, Kathleen. But I'm not crying for him. He's
happy in heaven. I'm crying for them that were happy once
and are now neither in heaven nor on earth.

Sitting crying, she may have seen but paid no attention to
my creeping forth from the cave.

Or under the earth, I thought, and recalled from the school
catechism a satisfying piece of resonance about how every knee
in heaven, on earth or under the earth, should bend to honour
the Lord's name.

Hannah the Saint is now long with those who are under
the earth and bend no knee. One day she walked home in
the blue spotlight that followed her from far beyond Munich
and found that the simple daughter had cut the heads of all
her hens and chickens and was screaming about the place. So
they took her away beyond the river which was our euphemism

for the mental hospital on the far bank of the Drumragh, across the water from the dead who were happy in heaven on their green hill. Hannah when her time came died also beyond the river. The cottage by the Flush is gone, too, eaten up by a boa constrictor of a new motor-road that swept away bad corners and made straight the way for a faster world. The Flush itself, that once sparkled across the roadway and dared the traffic and was a boon to thirsty horses, rumbles somewhere through the darkness in the entrails of that monster.

A BOTTLE OF BROWN SHERRY

Mr. Edward came home from hospital on the second day of the second summer holidays we spent at Delaps of Monellen.

That was the year old John Considine, the stone mason, laid the black basalt flagged floor in the hallway of the hotel. While the work was going on the guests used a side-door so that old John, the craftsman, we, the four children, the only children allowed to holiday in that sedate house, and the stuffed brown bear, the ornamental organ that wasn't meant to play, and the framed photograph of the big bearded man leaning on a long rifle and with a dead antlered stag on his shoulders, had the hall all to ourselves. The big man in the picture had also, John told us, shot the bear. John, as he worked, told us an awful lot.

—There's nothing, he would say, like having a trade. Even if it's only cutting thistles.

He did not intend to belittle his own craft and, indeed, his old back arched with pride at his ability to lay the stones smoothly, gently as a mother would lay a child in a cot, on their bed of resilient red sand. Sand and stones came from the coast visible across parkland and over high trees from the top windows of Monellen; and so close that the dazzle of surf and sunshine could brighten the shade of the surrounding greenery, and on a morning after a night of gale, salt and sand blurred the window-panes.

John wore an old bowler hat that he doffed for nothing or nobody, not even for the queenly grandeur of Miss Grania Delap herself, and although his work had him bending and straightening, kneeling and rising again, the hat held its place like a confident cormorant riding one familiar wave. The local

98

louts had nicknamed him Apey Appey for he was hairless from birth as a ha'penny apple, and he had turned his back on all organised religion because he felt embarrassed about taking his hat off in church.

But his round purple cheeks showed that he worshipped frequently and publicly in the seaside taverns. As he bent and worked he puffed the cheeks out comically and talked in spurts, not to himself, but to the stuffed bear, to the tall hunter in the picture, to the flagstones and—although they were outside the house and too far away to hear him—to the three aproned servant-maids who, in sunny moments of leisure, took their sport on a swing under an oak tree in the centre of the lawn.

Once when he knelt at work a robin hopped, picking, in from the lawn and perched on his left heel, and he chatted to the robin, apologising in the end for the cramp that compelled him to move and unsettle his guest.

Of my twin brother and myself and our two sisters, also twins, he never seemed much aware, yet he never made us feel unwelcome. So we stayed with him and carried tools for him and tried to make out who and what he was talking to.

—Aren't you smooth now as a bottle of the best, and shiny black like a well-fed crow in a good harvest? Won't the visitors be coming in droves to see you?

That was his praise for one of the flagstones.

—Don't I smell the sea when I touch you, and see the cliffs you were quarried from? If it wasn't for you and your likes the ocean would be flowing over us, and nothing but fish in Monellen, instead of priests and doctors eating lobsters. Master Gerald there, with the stag on his back like a sack of meal, was the man for the cliffs, hail or shine, gale or calm. Up there, he said, he could expand his lungs like the Lord God. There'll be rich feet and fancy shoes stepping now on you that kept the ocean from flowing over us for so long. And the silver woman looking down on the miracle.

The silver woman was a decorative bare-breasted Juno who

stood with her peacock on the top of the highest dead pipe of the mute ornamental organ.

—'Tis you has the youth in you. 'Tis you're soople.

Slowly, caressingly, he rubbed a stone with the palm of his hand, and could have been talking to the stone or to the bouncing blonde maid who led the others in her frolics on the swing.

The hind-legs of the dead stag were under the armpits of the hunter and pointing up. The fore-legs were over his shoulders and pointing down, and laced to the hind-legs. The antlered head leaned sadly backwards. In a strong thick-nibbed hand an inscription was written under the photograph. It read like this: Carrying a deer a few miles on one's back stimulates a glorious dinner appetite. Love from Brother Gerald and the Maple Leaf.

—Any man, John said, who would walk with that burden to work up an appetite would be liable to get married, no matter how much the family was set against it. Master Gerald, my man, you took all the strength with you the day Edward and yourself saw the light. 'Tisn't you they'd have to send like poor Edward to the doctors of Dublin to have things unknown injected into you.

Straightening up, stamping on a flag to test its steadiness, fixing with both hands the bowler more firmly on his head, he looked out at the bright lawn, the windy woods beyond, and said in a singsong to suit the rhythm of his feet: Swing, Nora Crowley, swing, you that never knew a father, with your hair as bright as the silver woman, and your mother before you that could swing like a branch in the wind.

The Misses Delap tolerated my father and mother bringing four children with them into that haven for elderly ladies, golfing clergymen and doctors, because the Misses Delap were also twins, and Mr. Edward and the absent hunter, Mr. Gerald, as well. The coincidence intrigued Miss Grania—as so well it might.

Miss Deirdre painted beautifully, we thought, and did an

ivy spray on the dining-room overmantel so real that you would have thought it was growing there. She gave us large round sweets as big as billiard balls—they were called, and were, gob-stoppers—and allowed us to stand, as round-jawed as John Considine, but mute and sucking, in her attic studio while she copied old masters out of an art book. She was a gamey old dame in the attic and she taught my brother and myself how to wink, but anywhere lower down in the house she was only a silvery silent wraith. For while she might paint and wink it was Miss Grania bought the lobsters and was boss over all and, although they were twins, Grania seemed and behaved like the elder of the two.

Deirdre's hair was a pale natural silver but Grania, to emphasise her empery, had tinted her hair an assertive colour you might call red, anywhere except in the presence of cooked lobsters. Those morose, doomed-to-be-boiled-alive crustaceans weren't red, of course, when Donnelly from the harbour would tumble five or six of them out of a sack on to the floor of the big basement kitchen. They still wore the secretive colours of the sea and the rock clefts that had sheltered them in a former life, and no lost soul precipitated into eternity could have been more bewildered than they looked as they clacked helplessly on the floor and stared from outshot eyes at the advance of Grania. If they saw little else in their hell or their heaven they certainly saw her. For she brought with her the power of life and death, and she was, at any time, and particularly before her morning toilet, a sight to catch the eye—even of a lobster. She was a tall woman, taller than her twin or than Mr. Edward. Her tinted hair was stiff with metal curlers that, as old John once muttered, were like hedgehogs roasted in a burning bush. Her face, black and yellow with wrinkles, was alarmingly different from the creamy mask it presented later in the day.

Touching a lobster smartly with her right foot, she would say : How now brown cow.

The high-heeled, golden-coloured shoes she wore for that ritual were never seen at any other time of the day, and it did seem to us that they were special shoes for touching and choosing lobsters.

—How now brown cow number two and three and four. Put the others back in the tanks, Donnelly, and give them a chance to repent.

To find themselves keeping guests for money was a come-down in the world for the Delaps. Miss Grania, not so much by direct words as by continuous tyranny, never allowed the guests to forget it. She talked often and with solemn authority about low prices for farm produce and the crushing burden of rates on the owners of landed property. The implication was that only for those two reasons no paying guest would ever have crossed the threshold of Monellen.

After high rates and low prices, the next worst thing in the degenerating world seemed to be afternoon tea.

—Quite the thing, she would say, for salesmen and their wives in commercial hotels, I'm told, but it was never the custom at Monellen.

So it was sherry or port and biscuits, or nothing at all, in the dreamy, tree-surrounded afternoons. My mother, though, seemed to be a privileged person, for when the maids were having their afternoon meal it was permitted for one of them to bring her tea in her bedroom. Perhaps that was because she was that year in an ailing and expectant condition, and Miss Grania may have hoped to coax by kindness another set of twins into the world. As it turned out, she didn't.

But old widowed Mrs. Nulty, who was eighty-five if she was a day, and whose brother was a bishop, had no such expecta-tions and no such privileges. When at one ill-guided, dyspeptic lunch-time, she turned up her nose at a bread pudding made, with currants, by Miss Deirdre, the retribution descended on her—soft-spoken but relentless.

—So they tell me, Mrs Nulty, you didn't like Miss Deirdre's bread pudding. Perhaps it would suit us mutually if next year we severed connections. There are, I'm told, many more up-to-date establishments in the village and on the sea-front.

102

The brother, the bishop himself, had to exert his ghostly influence to save Mrs. Nulty from banishment to Sea View or Ocean Lodge. His Christian name was Alexander and, if he ever had occasion to warm his hands at the drawing-room fire, he did so, standing at the side of the fireplace, and reaching out his fingertips, to the point almost of overbalancing, towards the flames. He wouldn't stand on the hearth-rug because he thought it was made of cat-skin and, like Lord Roberts of Pretoria and many a lesser man, he couldn't stand cats.

—But how little he knew, John Considine said, and all his learning. I snared the rabbits myself.

As you may see, Monellen was a place with its own character, and Grania Delap an undoubted unchallenged queen. Deirdre, in her arty attic, dabbled in oils and water-colours, but the image of Grania could only have been cast in bronze, one conquering foot on a lobster large as a turtle. One of my sisters—greatly daring—once put her foot on the pet tortoise in the garden and hoarsened her voice to say : How now brown cow. But the effect wasn't even funny, and the four of us afterwards glanced around nervously in fear of detection and banishment.

For Monellen was a happy enough place for a holiday— with good food, freedom, open parkland, a toy lake, miles of magic wood, and the stream beyond; and one of the most exciting things about it was that other dominant image, not bronze, but muscled, living oak and iron, that the mediumistic mutterings of John Considine brought forth from the picture of the hunter in the hallway. Here was a giant of a man who shot bears and stags and who once from his foreign travels had brought back with him a dangerous stockwhip with which he demonstrated, beheading daisies on the lawn at thirty paces, and making cracks that set the grazing horses on the far side of the lake galloping wild in terror.

When a boy he had, for a dare and by moonlight, gone climbing for rooks' eggs up one of the highest trees in the woods, only to find when he got to the top that the birds, more matured than he had imagined, began to caw, and some of them even flew away.

—He was so vexed, John said, it was a God's wonder he didn't sprout wings and take after them.

For another dare he went when he was fourteen through the night woods to a pub at the harbour where the trawlers tied up, and drank whiskey, John said, until it came out of his ears; and walked home sober. It seemed likely, indeed, that from an early age he had carried, if not stags, horned goats, at least, on his shoulders.

Insignificant in the shadow of that great image, Mr. Edward, back from hospital, shuffled about the house. John Considine told our father about the day in the winter when the two doctors, grey grave men, had stood over Edward and decided he needed hospital treatment.

—There they stood like two curers over a side of bacon. Smoke a bit here. Slice a bit there. Streaky in one place. Fat in another. They say in the Harbour Bar that Miss Grania sent him off to fit him for marrying to continue the line of the Delaps here in Monellen. Not that she was so pleased when the man in the picture there dirtied his bib out and out by marrying a foreign woman, as dark as these flagstones, and rearing the family in the heat of Africa; and he left the place to her and never faced home again. The Delaps when they kept at home were never much the marrying kind.

Our father's comment was : That reminds me of the woman who said that to have no children was hereditary in her family.

—But not all the doses or doctors in Dublin, John said.

He addressed himself again to his auditors, the stones, who never answered back or interpolated.

—Not all the doses or doctors in Dublin could make the poor sprissawn the man his brother was. A hunched little mouse of a man, creeping about in carpet slippers and apologising to the fresh air for taking liberties with it when he breathes. There does be an unholy difference in the natures of twins.

As if he was reading the future, he looked at the two of us morosely. Our sisters were upstairs having tea with our mother.

Then we all looked far away across the lawn where poor Edward, walking on a stick, mufflered and overcoated even in the sunshine, was going timid as a mole across the grass; and Nora Crowley, propelled by the pushes of the other laughing maids relaxing after their midday meal, was swinging, skirts fluttering, in a flying curve between grass and sky, her blonde hair bright against the dark green of the woods.

The day our sisters gave us the dare and we took it, the four of us were sitting concealed on the carpet of brown needles under a big Lebanon cedar on the fringe of the woods just beyond the swing. The tree made a tent around us. It was a windy sunny day. The maids had gone back to work. From our shelter we had peeped out at Edward on a garden seat, watching them at play, an open book fallen unheeded to the ground before him. Even when they had gone running and laughing away, he didn't bother to pick up the book. Then our father joined him and they talked. While our father had a sonorous rumble of a voice that, behind his red whiskers, rolled all words into one pleasant but meaningless sound, Mr. Edward had a cutting whining beep-beep that would carry each word distinctly to the moon. We only half listened to him because in taunting whispers under the cedar, the sisters were giving us the dare that implied that, even if we were in lands where they were to be found, we would never carry stags nor kill brown bears.

Mr. Edward said : Our lamented father often took the two of us, Gerald and myself, with him when he went to thin young plantations. It was an exhausting and exacting task under his leadership and surveillance. He expected us to be as good almost as he was himself. Gerald often was.

—Not even whiskey then, said Nora. Just a weeshy bottle of mangy abominable sherry.

She had tasted sherry once and simultaneously discovered the word abominable.

James had reasonably pointed out that we were too young, in these puny times, to be served with whiskey in the Harbour

105

Bar. Things had been different in Mr. Gerald's days—or nights.

—Pale or brown, I said, just to be difficult.

—Mr. Gerald was different, said Nora just to be nasty.

—Wet or dry, mocked Kathleen. The two of you would be feared to go through the woods by night.

—We never used big axes, Mr. Edward said, only light hand implements made by Douglas McDonnell, the land steward.

—Why don't ye go yourselves?

—We're ladies.

—We know. Young ladies don't go out at night. They might wet their bloomers in the dew.

But when we had to descend to offensiveness we knew they had us beaten.

—Douglas McDonnell's wife did housekeeper and baked yeast bread, getting the yeast from a friend of hers who had a small brewery in Altnamona. When she heard her friend was dead her only comment was that now she would be ill-fixed for barm.

—We'll make it easy for ye, Nora said. You don't have to drink the sherry in the Harbour Bar. Bring the bottle back with ye to show ye were there.

—We'll help to drink it, Kathleen said.

But Nora said not her, because sherry was abominable.

Except in their differing about the desirability of sherry our two red-headed sisters were enzygotics or identical twins. We never tested their fingerprints, as we did our own, to find—insofar as, not being Scotland Yard men, we could read them—that the books could be right in saying that the coincident sequence of papillary ridge characteristics had never been found to agree even in uniovular twins.

They both married. They were certainly identical in their love of hellery. They worked as one woman in taunting us and egging us on.

We pretended to be boys from Ocean View sent down for

the bottle of brown sherry for our father who was sick in bed with a cramp.

—A sufferer, said one man at the counter of the Harbour Bar, from the Ocean View six-day joint, old cow to cottage pie in six painful moves.

My brother was quick tongued. He said : No. It was last Friday's caviar gave him the heartburn.

Thanks to his wit, our exit from the pub, clutching the bottle, was on a flowing tide of appreciative kindly laughter, and not as shamefaced as it might have been. Yet it was not the exit of a young hero who had drunk whiskey until it came out of his ears and was still sailing on a steady keel.

In that windy August of sudden squalls the dinghies moored in the harbour jumped and tossed their heels on the full turbulent tide, like hairy Connemara ponies restless at a fair. The moon leaped to drown into racing clouds, then surfaced again with a bound and a brightness that made us feel the whole world was watching ourselves and our sinful bottle. So, to hide from its silver revelations, and for the general mystery of the thing, we made the first stages of the return journey by what we called the Secret Passage. There was nothing very secret about it. It was merely a narrow sunken roadway that went inland from east to west across Monellen land to the village of Altnamona, following a right of way that the village people had used, since God knew when, as a short-cut to the shore for shellfish or seaweed for manure, or to dig the succulent sand-eels from the wide white strand when the spring tides had ebbed and the moon was full. Three stone bridges carried over it the private roads generations of Delaps had driven on. We walked steadily in silence and shadow, and were, to be honest, more than a little out of breath with fear. I carried the bottle. Like a stick in the fist it was comfort and company.

—I don't mind the nights, said James, if it's windy.

For he felt and I with him, that no evil thing could be abroad on a night when the wind bellowed so heartily and the moon and clouds played chasing games; and the sound of the orchestra of wind and swaying branches blotted out those subtle, unnerving, unidentifiable sounds that woods and the creatures in them make on calm nights. When we climbed up by the winding steps of an old belvedere to the main avenue, and saw the house, white in moonlight and distance, a curious exhilaration had conquered our fear. Afterwards, on long talk and reflection, we realised we had been possessed. Tall pines and cypresses lined the avenue, gracefully holding back two hunch-backed hordes of red oaks. One of the pines, leaning and sailing with the wind, must have been the highest tree in the world. We looked up, and the tip of it touched and pierced the moon, and at the moment of contact James said : To hell with those girls. We'll kill the sherry.

We were thirteen years apiece and not exactly novices. We had sampled on the sly everything we found at home in sideboard or undrained glass. As altar boys in the parish church we had nipped at the altar wine. Once, too, after a hasty gulp of whiskey James claimed that he had had in the bathroom the most comical double vision.

At my second gulp of the grocer's sherry I made a measured statement about the superiority of altar wine.

James was barking like a dog at the still impaled moon.

—Sure as God, he said, that was the tree he went up for the rooks' eggs.

—It tastes bloody, I said, but at least it's warm, and what better could you hope for from the Harbour Bar?

—Show me a bear and I'll shoot it and stuff it, he shouted. Show me a stag and I'll carry it to Miss Grania. How now brown cow?

He stamped his feet like a dancing Indian and howled into the blustery warm wind. We wrestled for the last drop of the brown sherry, and he had it and drank it, and tossed the bottle off spinning to some place where it fell in silence. We ran round and round in circles shouting about bears and lobsters, brown cows and stags. Then, James leading, we climbed the tree.

We went up easily into the light, regularly spaced branches

as convenient as the rungs of a ladder. It was a comfortable tree to climb and for a while the swaying motion had a most comfortable effect on bellies warm with the cheap rough wine. Patterns of light and shadow, of pasture, tilled fields, woods, laid themselves out below us; and the lake was a glittering circle. Heads in the wild clouds, we turned dazzled eyes from the moon, and rested at the top of the tree, looked down at the lake and saw the moon again, and saw the sight, and thought at first that we were mad in the head with drink.

In days before the Delaps had made money in milling and bought the land, some eighteenth-century lord had brought from London a wandering Italian to plan that lake and the gazebo beside it. In classical afternoons, the lord and his ladies and friends would have been at their ease on the flat, tiled, octagonal roof. There now, in their space, on a stone seat was Mr Edward, as many overcoats on him as an onion, his head bent, his mouth to the nipple of a living enlarged Juno who had stepped down, leaving her peacock behind her, from the organ in the hallway : of Nora Crowley, before God, that never knew a father, and her mother before her that could swing like a branch in the wind, and not a coat in the world on her, or a rag at all higher than her belly button.

She was laughing and tossing her blonde hair back, and pretending to push him away. Hunched with the weight of his coats he was trotting after her round and round the octagon. They were back again at the stone seat. He was kneeling before her and cutting all sorts of capers. They were circling the roof again. We could hear nothing except the wind but we could see that she was still laughing. We laughed a little ourselves, but in sadness and mystery, because we felt sorry for Edward who had never frightened horses with a stock-whip. Yet we would have gone on watching, held by the night of wind and moon and by those antics that seemed to be part of it, if our father's voice hadn't bellowed up at us from the avenue : Come down, you misbegotten monkeys. Come down, you niggering night-owls. What games are you playing up there?

Juno, startled by mistake, vanished with a whisk, like a fish frightened from a clear pool into the shelter of reeds and rocks. Poor many-coated slow-moving Edward was left alone on the eighteenth-century octagon. We looked down into gloom and shadow, and the sherry settled, and our stomachs turned over at the prospect of descending, feet feeling for dark branches, to explain to our father where we had been and what we had been doing on the top of the tree.

—Bird-nesting, said James. Remember we were bird-nesting. For owls' eggs.

I repeated queasily : Bird-nesting.

The thought of soft eggs made me feel ill.

—Go carefully, my father bawled. Don't break your necks.

No cautionary words were needed. We were sick and shivering, and most anxious about our necks. The tree below us was the pit of darkness. When we stepped painfully from the lowest branches, and I opened my mouth to talk about bird-nesting for owl's eggs, release of tension struck me like a kick in the ribs and out came the sherry, not, alas, through my ears and a little the worse for wear. It spattered the grass and pine needles at my father's feet.

—Arboreal activities by moonlight, he was beginning to say.

The woods stank of sour wine.

—Lord God what a reek, he said. Come home quick and wash your teeth before you put me off the drink for life.

The idea seemed to amuse him. So James, always an opportunist, snatched the chance of the moment to rattle out a doctored description of the sight we had seen while bird-nesting.

—He was sitting with Nora Crowley on the bench on the gazebo.

—By God and was he? By the bright silvery light of the moon. And what would he be at there?

—He had his arm round her and he was kissing her.

—Oh, sound man. Begod modern medicine can work the wonders.

He laughed a little, just as we had, and then stopped

laughing. He said, half to himself : Get married or something quickly the four of you, and don't end up lost like poor Edward.

Absent-mindedly, and with a friendly thump apiece on the shoulder-blades he left us at the foot of the back-stairs and we knew that he had, in private, to tell our mother all about it, and that there wouldn't be much more said about where the sherry that had bespattered the pine needles had come from.

Our sisters thought it the joke of the world when we told them precisely what Mr. Edward had been kissing.

—Like a baby, they said.

And there were no secrets, not even the moon's secrets, to be kept from bald John Considine. On his knees, smoothing the listening flagstones, he would go off into fits of shrill giggles and mutters which we, most efficient receiving sets, caught and elucidated : A bottle of brown sherry for two bad boys and a doll to play with for the third. They'll have to send him to the Dublin doctors again to have something else done to him to keep him in the house at night. Anyway, 'twas like the casting of a spell, 'twas the magic of having too many twins about the one house. 'Twas enough to bring Mr. Gerald back over the seas to take possession of the place he owned. Wasn't there a man in Altnamona who talked like a Russian although he was never outside the parish?

So the hunter, we heard, had come back from Africa, or wherever he was, or stepped, stag on shoulders, out of the picture in the hallway, to walk in the stormy moonlit woods. We had more fellow feeling than ever for Edward because we knew that he wasn't the only man, on that night of gale and running moon, to be possessed by his brother's spirit. It was more than sherry had sent us climbing, and it was something more than our own efforts that had brought us safely down into darkness from the remote top of that tree.

When, at art in the attic, we asked Miss Deirdre about Mr. Gerald, she wept a little tear and told us she often tried to get in touch with him by clairvoyance or telekinesis. She explained to us about clairvoyance and telekinesis. She said : You may think it impossible with your harsh practical young minds. But I assure you children that I have in my time seen some very remarkable things. When we were at Dover once there was a lady who had a crystal. This colonel asked her about his son who was somewhere at sea, out China way. The lady described him as having or not having a moustache, whichever was wrong, and said he was cleaning a bicycle. They thought this was a poor show. But shortly afterwards the colonel got a letter with a photograph showing his son either with or without a moustache, whichever the lady had said, and saying that as they were near port, and as he had heard the roads were good in China, he hoped to get a run on his bicycle. Then another lady whose husband was in South Africa was told by the lady with the crystal that her husband was on a pile of boxes in a lake. This, of course, sounded most unlikely, but the lady heard by the next post that there had been a cloudburst, and the only dry place he could get to sit on was a pile of empty ammunition cases . . .

She talked on for a long time.

Grania of the Lobsters, though, was a sceptic, and next year, summarily dismissed, swinging Nora Crowley was gone forever from Monellen.

GOD'S OWN COUNTRY

THE PLUMP GIRL from Cork City who was the editor's secretary came into the newsroom where the four of us huddled together, and said, so rapidly that we had to ask her to say it all over again: Goodness gracious, Mr. Slattery, you are, you really are, smouldering.

She was plump and very pretty and enticingly perfumed and every one of the four of us, that is everyone of us except Jeremiah, would have been overjoyed to make advances to her except that, being from Cork City, she talked so rapidly that we never had time to get a word in edgeways. She said: Goodness gracious, Mr. Slattery, you are, you really are, smouldering.

Now that our attention had been drawn to it, he really was smouldering. He sat, crouched as close as he could get to the paltry coal fire: the old ramshackle building, all rooms of no definable geometrical shape, would have collapsed with Merulius Lacrymans, the most noxious form of dry rot, the tertiary syphilis of ageing buildings, if central heating had ever been installed. Jeremiah nursed the fire between his bony knees. He toasted, or tried to toast, his chapped chilblained hands above the pitiful glow. The management of that small weekly newspaper were too mean to spend much money on fuel; and in that bitter spring Jeremiah was the coldest man in the city. He tried, it seemed, to suck what little heat there was into his bloodless body. He certainly allowed none of it to pass him by so as to mollify the three of us who sat, while he crouched, working doggedly with our overcoats and woollen scarves on. The big poet who wrote the cinema reviews, and who hadn't been inside a cinema since he left for a drink at the intermission in *Gone With The Wind* and never went back, was typing, with woollen gloves on, with one finger; and for panache more than for actual necessity he wore a motor-cycling helmet with fleece-lined flaps over his ears. The big poet had already told Jeremiah that Jeremiah was a raven, a scrawny starved raven, quothing and croaking nevermore, crumpled up there in his black greatcoat over a fire that wouldn't boil an egg. Jeremiah only crouched closer to the fire and, since we knew how cold he always was, we left him be and forgot all about him, and he might well have gone on fire, nobody, not even himself, noticing, if the plump pretty secretary, a golden perfumed ball hopping from the parlour into the hall, hadn't bounced, warming the world, being the true honey of delight, into the room.

It was the turned-up fold of the right leg of his shiny black trousers. He extinguished himself wearily, putting on, to protect the fingers of his right hand, a leather motoring-gauntlet. He had lost, or had never possessed, the left-hand gauntlet. He moved a little back from the fire, he even tried to sit up straight. She picked up the telephone on the table before me. Her rounded left haunch, packed tightly in a sort of golden cloth, was within eating distance, if I'd had a knife and fork. She said to the switch that she would take that call now from where she was in the newsroom. She was silent for a while. The golden haunch moved ever so slightly, rose and fell, in fact, as if it breathed. She said : Certainly, your Grace.

—No, your Grace.

—To the island, your Grace.

—A reporter, your Grace.

—Of course, your Grace.

—And photographer, your Grace.

—An American bishop, your Grace.

—How interesting, your Grace.

—Confirmation, your Grace.

—All the way from Georgia, your Grace.

—Goodness gracious, your Grace.

—Lifeboat, your Grace.

—Yes, your Grace.

—No, your Grace.

—Next Thursday, your Grace.

—I'll make a note of it, your Grace.

—And tell the editor when he comes in from the nunciature, your Grace.

The nunciature was the place where the editor, promoting the Pope's wishes by promoting the Catholic press, did most of his drinking. He had a great tongue for the Italian wine.

—Lifeboat, your Grace.

—Absolutely, your Grace.

—Goodbye, your Grace.

The big poet said: That wouldn't have been His Grace you were talking to?

—That man, she said, thinks he's three rungs of the ladder above the Pope of Rome and with right of succession to the Lord himself.

She made for the door. The gold blinded me. She turned at the door, said to us all, or to three of us: Watch him. Don't let him make a holocaust of himself. Clean him up and feed him. He's for the Islands of the West, Hy-Breasil, the Isle of the Blest, next Thursday with the Greatest Grace of all the Graces, and a Yankee bishop who thinks it would do something for him to bestow the holy sacrament of confirmation on the young savages out there. Not that it will do much for them. It would take more than two bishops and the Holy Ghost . . . .

She was still talking as she vanished. The door crashed shut behind her and the room was dark again, and colder than ever. Jeremiah was visibly shuddering, audibly chattering, because to his bloodlessness and to the chill of the room and of the harsh day of east wind, had been added the worst cold of all: terror.

—Take him out, the big poet said, before he freezes us to death. Buy him a hot whiskey. You can buy me one when I finish my column.

As he tapped with one gloved finger and, with a free and open mind and no prejudice, critically evaluated what he had not seen, he also lifted up his voice and sang : When the roses bloom again down by yon river, and the robin redbreast sings his sweet refrain, in the days of auld lang syne, I'll be with you sweetheart mine, I'll be with you when the roses bloom again.

In Mulligan's in Poolbeg Street, established 1782, the year of the great Convention of the heroic patriotic Volunteers at Dungannon when the leaders of the nation, sort of, were inspired by the example of American Independence, I said to Jeremiah : Be a blood. Come alive. Break out. Face them. Show them. Fuck the begrudgers. Die, if die you must, on your feet and fighting.

He said : It's very well for you to talk. You can eat.

—Everybody, for God's sake, can eat.

—I can't eat. I can only nibble.

—You can drink, though. You have no trouble at all with the drink.

His first hot whiskey was gone, but hadn't done him any good that you'd notice.

—Only whiskey, he said, and sometimes on good days, stout. But even milk makes me ill, unless it's hot and with pepper sprinkled on it.

I pretended to laugh at him, to jolly him out of it, yet he really had me worried. For he was a good helpless intelligent chap, and his nerves had gone to hell in the seminary that he had had to leave, and the oddest rumours about his eating or non-eating habits were going around the town. That, for instance, he had been seen in a certain hotel, nibbling at biscuits left behind by another customer, and when the waiter, who was a friend of mine, asked him in all kindness did he need lunch, he had slunk away, the waiter said, like a shadow that had neither substance nor sunshine to account for its being there in the first place. He was no man, I had to agree, to face on an empty stomach a spring gale, or even a half or a hatful of a gale, on the wild western Atlantic coast.

—And the thought of that bishop, he said, puts the heart

across me. He's a boor and a bully of the most violent description. He's a hierarchical Genghis Khan.

—Not half as bad as he's painted.

—Half's bad enough.

So I told some story, once told to me by a Belfast man, about some charitable act performed by the same bishop. It didn't sound at all convincing. Nor was Jeremiah convinced.

—If he ever was charitable, he said, be sure that it wasn't his own money he gave away.

—You won't have to see much of him, Jeremiah. Keep out of his path. Don't encounter him.

—But I'll encounter the uncandid cameraman who'll be my constant companion. With his good tweeds and his cameras that all the gold in the mint wouldn't buy. How do the mean crowd that run that paper ever manage to pay him enough to satisfy him? He invited me to his home to dinner. Once. To patronise me. To show me what he had and I hadn't. He ran out six times during dinner to ring the doorbell, and we had to stop eating and listen to the chimes. A different chime in every room. Like living in the bloody belfry. Searchlights he has on the lawn to illuminate the house on feast-days. Like they do in America, I'm told. Letting his light shine in the uncomprehending darkness. Some men in this town can't pay the electricity bill, but he suffers from a surplus. And this bishop is a friend of his. Stops with him when he comes to town. His wife's uncle is a monsignor in His Grace's diocese. Practically inlaws. They call each other by their Christian names. I was permitted and privileged to see the room the bishop sleeps in, with its own special bathroom, toilet seat reserved for the episcopal arse, a layman would have to have his arse specially anointed to sit on it. Let me tell you that it filled me with awe. When they have clerical visitors, he told me, they couldn't have them shaving in the ordinary bathroom. I hadn't the courage to ask him was there anything forbidding that in Canon Law, Pastoral Theology or the Maynooth Statutes. God look down on me between the two of them, and an American bishop thrown in for good luck. They say

117

that in the United States the bishops are just bigger and more brutal.

—Jeremiah, I said severely, you're lucky to be out with that cameraman. He'll teach you to be a newsman. Just study how he works. He can smell news like, like . . .

The struggle for words went on until he helped me out. He was quick-witted; and even on him the third hot whiskey was bound to have some effect: to send what blood there was in his veins toe-dancing merrily to his brain.

—Like a buzzard smells dead meat, he said.

Then the poet joined us. Having an inherited gift for cobbling he had recently cobbled for himself a pair of shoes but, since measurement was not his might, they turned out to be too big even for him, thus, for any mortal man. But he had not given up hope of encountering in a public bar some Cyclopean for whose benefit he had, in his subconscious, been working, and of finding him able and willing to purchase those shoes. He carried them, unwrapped, under his arm. They always excited comment; and many were the men who tried and failed to fill them. That night we toured the town with them, adding to our company, en route, an Irish professor from Rathfarnham, a French professor from Marseilles, a lady novelist, a uniformed American soldier with an Irish name, who came from Boston and General Patch's army which had passed by Marseilles and wrecked it in the process. Outside Saint Vincent's hospital in Saint Stephen's Green a total stranger, walking past us, collapsed. He was a very big man, with enormous feet. But when the men from Boston and Marseilles, and the poet and myself, carried him into the hospital he was dead.

All that, as you are about to observe, is another story.

We failed, as it so happened, to sell the shoes.

On that corner of the western coast of Ireland the difference between a gale and a half-gale is that in a half-gale you take a chance and go out, in a gale you stay ashore.

The night before the voyage they rested in a hotel in Galway

City. The wind rattled the casements and now and again blew open the door of the bar in which Jeremiah sat alone, until well after midnight, over one miserable whiskey. Nobody bothered to talk to him, not even in Galway where the very lobsters will welcome the stranger. The bar was draughty. He wore his black greatcoat, a relic of his clerical ambitions. It enlarged his body to the point of monstrosity, and minimised his head. Dripping customers came and drank and steamed and went again. When the door blew open he could see the downpours of rain hopping like hailstones on the street. The spluttering radio talked of floods, and trees blown down, and crops destroyed, and an oil-tanker in peril off the Tuskar Rock. The cameraman had eaten a horse of a dinner, washed it down with the best wine, said his prayers and gone to bed, to be, he said, fresh and fit for the morning. Jeremiah was hungry, but less than ever could he eat : with fear of the storm and of the western sea as yet unseen and of the bull of a bishop and, perhaps too, he thought, that visiting American would be no better. At midnight he drained his glass dry and afterwards tilted it several times to his lips, drinking, or inhaling, only wind. He would have ordered another whiskey but the bar was crowded by that time, and the barman was surrounded by his privileged friends who were drinking after hours. The wind no longer blew the door open for the door was double-bolted against the night. But the booming, buffeting and rattling of the storm could still be heard, at times bellowing like a brazen bishop, threatening Jeremiah. The customers kept coming and crowding through a dark passage that joined the bar and the kitchen. They acted as if they had spent all day in the kitchen and had every intention of spending all night in the bar. Each one of them favoured Jeremiah with a startled look where he sat, black, deformed by that greatcoat, hunched-up in his black cold corner. Nobody joined him. He went to bed, to a narrow, hard, excessively-white bed with a ridge up the middle and a downward slope on each side. The rubber hot-water bottle had already gone cold. The rain threatened to smash the window-panes. He spread his greatcoat over his feet, wearing his socks in bed, and, cursing the day he was born, fell asleep from sheer misery.

Early next morning he had his baptism of salt water, not sea-spray but rain blown sideways and so salty that it made a crust around the lips.

—That out there, said the cameraman in the security of his car, is what they call the poteen cross.

The seats in the car were covered with a red plush, in its turn covered by a protective and easily-washable, transparent plastic that Jeremiah knew had been put there to prevent himself or his greatcoat or his greasy, shiny pants from making direct contact with the red plush.

—Did you never hear of the poteen cross?

—No, said Jeremiah.

They had stopped in a pelting village on the westward road. The doors were shut, the windows still blinded. It was no morning for early rising. The sea was audible, but not visible. The rain came bellying inshore on gusts of wind. On a gravelled space down a slope towards the sound of the sea stood a huge bare black cross: well, not completely bare for it carried, criss-crossed, the spear that pierced, that other spear that bore aloft the sponge soaked in vinegar; and it was topped by a gigantic crown of thorns. The cameraman said: When the Redemptorist Fathers preached hellfire against the men who made the poteen, they ordered the moonshiners, under pain of mortal sin, to come here and leave their stills at the foot of the cross. The last sinner to hold out against them came in the end with his still but, there before him, he saw a better model that somebody else had left, so he took it away with him. There's a London magazine wants a picture of that cross.

—It wouldn't, said Jeremiah, make much of a picture.

—With somebody beside it pointing up at it, it wouldn't be so bad. The light's not good. But I think we could manage.

—We, said Jeremiah.

—You wouldn't like me, he said, to get up on the cross? Have you brought the nails?

He posed, nevertheless, and pointed up at the cross. What

else could he do? We saw the picture afterwards in that London magazine. Jeremiah looked like a sable bloated demon trying to prove to benighted sinners that Christ was gone and dead and never would rise again. But it was undeniably an effective picture. Jeremiah posed and pointed. He was salted and sodden while the cameraman, secure in yellow oilskins and sou'wester, darted out, took three shots, darted in again, doffed the oilskins, and was as dry as snuff. They drove on westwards.

—That coat of yours, said the cameraman. You should have fitted yourself out with oilskins. That coat of yours will soak up all the water from here to Long Island.

—Stinks a bit too, he said on reflection. The Beeoh is flying.

That was meant to be some sort of a joke and, for the sake of civility, Jeremiah tried to laugh. They crossed a stone bridge over a brown-and-white, foaming, flooded river, turned left down a byroad, followed the course of the river, sometimes so close to it that the floodwater lapped the edge of the road, sometimes swinging a little away from it through a misted landscape of small fields, thatched cabins dour and withdrawn in the storm, shapeless expanses of rock and heather, until they came to where the brown-and-white water tumbled into the peace of a little land-locked harbour. The lifeboat that, by special arrangement, was to carry the party to the island was there, but no lifeboatmen, no party. A few small craft lay on a sandy slope in the shelter of a breakwater. Jeremiah and the cameraman could have been the only people alive in a swamped world. They waited : the cameraman in the car with the heat on; Jeremiah, to get away from him for a while, prowling around empty cold sheds that were, at least, dry, but that stank of dead fish and were floored with peat-mould terrazzoed, it would seem, by fragments broken from many previous generations of lobsters. Beyond the breakwater and a rocky headland the sea boomed, but the water in the sheltered harbour was smooth and black as ink. He was hungry again but knew that if he had food, any food other than dry biscuits, he wouldn't be able to eat it. All food now would smell of stale fish. He was cold, as always. When he was out of sight of the cameraman he pranced, to warm himself, on peat-mould and lobsters. He was only moderately successful. But his greatcoat, at least, steamed.

The rain eased off, the sky brightened, but the wind seemed to grow in fury, surf and spray went up straight and shining into the air beyond the breakwater, leaped it and came down with a flat slap on the sandy slope and the sleeping small craft. Then, like Apache on an Arizona skyline, the people began to appear : a group of three, suddenly, from behind a standing rock; a group of seven or eight rising sharply into sight on a hilltop on the switchback riverside road, dropping out of sight into a hollow, surfacing again, followed by other groups that appeared and disappeared in the same disconcerting manner. As the sky cleared, the uniform darkness breaking up into bullocks of black wind-goaded clouds, the landscape of rock and heather, patchwork fields divided by grey, high, drystone walls, came out into the light; and from every small farm-house thus revealed, people came, following footpaths, crossing stiles, calling to each other across patches of light green oats and dark-green potatoes. It was a sudden miracle of growth, of human life appearing where there had been nothing but wind and rain and mist. Within three-quarters of an hour there were a hundred or more people around the harbour, lean hard-faced fishermen and small farmers, dark-haired laughing girls, old women in coloured shawls, talking Irish, talking English, posing in groups for the cameraman who in his yellow oilskins moved among them like a gigantic canary. They waved and called to Jeremiah where he stood, withdrawn and on the defensive, in the sheltered doorway of a fish-stinking shed.

A black Volkswagen came down the road followed by a red Volkswagen. From the black car a stout priest stepped forth, surveyed the crowd like a general estimating the strength of his mustered troops, shook hands with the cameraman as if he were meeting an old friend. From the red car a young man stepped out, then held the door for a gaunt middle-aged lady who emerged with an effort, head first : the local schoolteachers, by the cut of them. They picked out from the crowd a group of twelve to twenty, lined them up, backs to the wall, in the shelter of the breakwater. The tall lady waved her arms and the group began to sing.

—Ecce sacerdos magnus, they sang.

A black limousine, with the traction power of two thousand Jerusalem asses on the first Holy Thursday, came, appearing and disappearing, down the switchback road. This was it, Jeremiah knew, and shuddered. On the back of an open truck behind the limousine came the lifeboatmen, all like the cameraman, in bright yellow oilskins.

—This is God's own country, said the American bishop, and ye are God's own people.

Jeremiah was still at a safe distance, yet near enough to hear the booming clerical-American voice. The sea boomed beyond the wall. The spray soared, then slapped down on the sand, sparing the sheltered singers.

—Faith of our fathers, they sang, living still, in spite of dungeon, fire and sword.

Circling the crowd the great canary, camera now at ease, approached Jeremiah.

—Get with it, Dracula, he said.

He didn't much bother to lower his voice.

—Come out of your corner fighting. Get in and get a story. That Yank is news. He was run out of Rumania by the Communists.

—He also comes, said Jeremiah, from Savannah, Georgia.

—So what?

—He doesn't exactly qualify as a Yankee.

—Oh Jesus, geography, said the cameraman. We'll give you full marks for geography. They'll look lovely in the paper where your story should be. If he came from bloody Patagonia, he's here now. Go get him.

Then he was gone, waving his camera. The American bishop, a tall and stately man, was advancing, blessing as he went, to the stone steps that went down the harbour wall to the moored lifeboat. He was in God's own country and God's own people, well-marshalled by the stout parish priest, were all around him. The Irish bishop, a tall and stately man, stood still, thoughtfully watching the approaching cameraman and Jeremiah most reluctantly plodding in the rear, his progress, to his relief, made more difficult by the mush of wet peat-mould underfoot, growing deeper and deeper as he approached the wall where sailing hookers were loaded with fuel for the peatless island. Yet, slowly as he moved, he was still close enough to see clearly what happened and to hear clearly what was said.

The bishop, tall and stately and monarch even over the parish priest, looked with a cold eye at the advancing camera-man. There was no ring kissing. The bishop did not reach out his hand to have his ring saluted. That was odd, to begin with. Then he said loudly : What do you want?

—Your Grace, said the great canary.

He made a sort of a curtsey, clumsily, because he was hobbled in creaking oilskins.

—Your Grace, he said, out on the island there's a nona-genarian, the oldest inhabitant, and when we get there I'd like to get a picture of you giving him your blessing.

His Grace said nothing. His Grace turned very red in the face. In increased terror, Jeremiah remembered that inlaws could have their tiffs and that clerical inlaws were well known to be hell incarnate. His Grace right-about-wheeled, showed to the mainland and all on it a black broad back, right-quick-marched towards the lifeboat, sinking to the ankles as he thundered on in the soft wet mould, but by no means abating his speed which could have been a fair five miles an hour. His long coat-tails flapped in the wind. The wet mould fountained up like snow from a snow-plough. The sea boomed. The spray splattered. The great canary had shrunk as if plucked. Jeremiah's coat steamed worse than ever in the frenzy of his fear. If he treats his own like that, he thought, what in God's holy name will he do to me? Yet he couldn't resist saying :

That man could pose like Nelson on his pillar watching his world collapse.

The canary cameraman hadn't a word to say.

Once aboard the lugger the bishops had swathed themselves in oilskins provided by the lifeboat's captain, and the cameraman mustered enough of his ancient gall to mutter to Jeremiah that that was the first time that he or anybody else had seen canary-coloured bishops.

—Snap them, said Jeremiah. You could sell it to the magazines in Bucharest. Episcopal American agent turns yellow.

But the cameraman was still too crestfallen, and made no move, and clearly looked relieved when the Irish bishop, tall and stately even if a little grotesque in oilskins, descended carefully into the for'ard foxhole, sat close into the corner, took out his rosary beads and began to pray silently : he knew the tricks of his western sea. Lulled by the security of the land-locked sheltered harbour, the American bishop, tall and stately even if a little grotesque in oilskins, stood like Nelson on the foredeck. He surveyed the shore of rock, small fields, drystone walls, small thatched farmhouses, oats, potatoes, grazing black cattle, all misting over for more rain. Then he turned his back on the mainland and looked at the people, now marshalled all together by the parish priest and the two teachers in the lee of the harbour wall. The choir sang : Holy God, we praise thy name. Lord of all, we bow before thee.

An outrider of the squall of rain that the wind was driving inshore cornered cunningly around harbour wall and headland, and disrespectfully spattered the American bishop. Secure in oilskins and the Grace of state he ignored it. The cameraman dived into the stern foxhole. Jeremiah by now was so sodden that the squall had no effect on him. An uncle of his, a farmer in the County Longford, had worn the same heavy woollen underwear winter and summer and argued eloquently that what kept the heat in kept it out. That soaking salty steaming greatcoat could, likewise, stand upright on its own against the fury of the Bay of Biscay. It was a fortress for

Jeremiah; and with his right hand, reaching out through the loophole of the sleeve, he touched the tough stubby oaken mast, a talismanic touch, a prayer to the rooted essence of the earth to protect him from the capricious fury of the sea. Then with the bishop, a yellow figurehead, at the prow, and Jeremiah, a sable figurehead, at the stern, they moved smoothly towards the open ocean; and, having withdrawn a little from the land, the bishop raised his hand, as Lord Nelson would not have done, and said: This is God's own country. Ye are God's own people.

The choir sang: Hail Glorious Saint Patrick, dear Saint of our isle.

From the conscripted and marshalled people came a cheer loud enough to drown the hymn; and then the sea, with as little regard for the cloth as had the Rumanian Reds, struck like an angry bull and the boat, Jeremiah says, stood on its nose, and only a miracle of the highest order kept the American bishop out of the drink. Jeremiah could see him, down, far down at the bottom of a dizzy slope, then up, far up, shining like the sun between sea and sky, as the boat reared back on its haunches and Jeremiah felt on the back of his head the blow of a gigantic fist. It was simply salt seawater in a solid block, striking and bursting like a bomb. By the time he had wiped his eyes and the boat was again, for a few brief moments, on an even keel, there were two bishops sheltering in the for'ard foxhole: the two most quiet and prayerful men he had ever seen.

—On the ocean that hollows the rocks where ye dwell, Jeremiah recited out as loudly as he could because no ears could hear even a bull bellowing above the roar and movement and torment of the sea.

—A shadowy land, he went on, has appeared as they tell. Men thought it a region of sunshine and rest, and they called it Hy-Breasil the Isle of the Blest.

To make matters easier, if not tolerable, he composed his mind and said to himself: Lifeboats can't sink.

On this harshly-ocean-bitten coast there was the poetic

126

legend of the visionary who sailed west, ever west, to find the island where the souls of the blest are forever happy.

—Rash dreamer return, Jeremiah shouted, oh ye winds of the main, bear him back to his own native Ara again.

For his defiance the sea repaid him in three thundering salty buffets and a sudden angled attack that sent the boat hissing along on its side and placed Jeremiah with both arms around the mast. In the brief following lull he said more quietly, pacifying the sea, acknowledging its power : Night fell on the deep amid tempest and spray, and he died on the ocean, away far away.

He was far too frightened to be seasick, which was just as well, considering the windy vacuum he had for a stomach. The boat pranced and rolled. He held on to the mast, but now almost nonchalantly and only with one arm. The sea buffeted him into dreams of that luckless searcher for Hy-Breasil, or dreams of Brendan the Navigator, long before Columbus, sailing bravely on and on and making landfall on Miami Beach. Secure in those dreams he found to his amazement that he could contemn the snubbed cameraman and the praying bishops hiding in their foxholes. He, Jeremiah, belonged with the nonchalant lifeboatmen studying the sea as a man through the smoke of a good pipe might look at the face of a friend. One of them, indeed, was so nonchalant that he sat on the hatch-roof above the bishops, his feet on the gunwale chain so that, when the boat dipped his way, his feet a few times went well out of sight in the water. Those lifeboatmen were less men than great yellow seabirds and Jeremiah, although a land-lubber and as black as a raven, willed to be with them as far as he could, for the moment, go. He studied on the crazy pattern of tossing waters the ironic glint of sunshine on steel-blue hills racing to collide and crash and burst into blinding silver. He recalled sunshine on quiet, stable, green fields that he was half-reconciled never to see again. He was on the way to the Isle of the Blest.

Yet it was no island that first appeared to remind him, after two hours of trance, that men, other than the lifeboat's crew and cargo, did exist : no island, but the high bird-flight of a dozen black currachs, appearing and disappearing, forming into single file, six to either side of the lifeboat, forming a guard of honour as if they had been cavalry on display in a London park, to escort the sacerdotes magni safely into the island harbour. Afterwards Jeremiah was to learn that lifeboats could sink and had done so, yet he says that even had he known through the wildest heart of that voyage it would have made no difference. Stunned, but salted, by the sea he arose a new man.

The parish church was a plain granite cross high on a windy, shelterless hilltop. It grew up from the rock it was cut from. No gale nor half-gale, nor the gates of hell, could prevail against it.

To west and south-west the land sank, then swept up dizzily again to a high bare horizon and, beyond that there could be nothing but monstrous seacliffs and the ocean. To east and north-east small patchwork fields, bright green, dark green, golden, netted by greystone walls, dotted by white and golden cabins all newly limewashed and thatched for the coming of the great priests, sloped down to a sea in the lee of the island and incredibly calm. The half-gale was still strong. But the island was steady underfoot. Far away the mainland, now a bit here, now a bit there, showed itself, glistening, out of the wandering squalls.

—Rock of ages cleft for me, he hummed with a reckless merriment that would have frightened him if he had stopped to reason about it, let me hide myself in thee. He was safe in the arms of Jesus, he was deep in the heart of Texas. The granite cruciform church was his shelter from the gale, providing him, by the protection of its apse and right arm, with a sunny corner to hide in and smoke in. He was still giddy from the swing of the sea. He was also, being, alas, human and subject to frailty, tempted to rejoice at the downfall and humiliation of another. He hath put down the mighty, he began to chant but stopped to consider that as yet there was little sign of the lowly being exalted.

128

This corner of the cross was quiet. One narrow yellow grained door was securely shut. All the bustle, all the traffic was out around the front porch : white-jacketed white-jerseyed islanders sitting on stone walls, women in coloured shawls crowding and pushing, children hymn-singing in English, Irish and Latin, real Tower of Babel stuff, the cameraman photographing groups of people, and photographing the bishops from a safe distance, and the church from every angle short of the one the angels saw it from. He was no longer a great clumsy canary. He was splendid in his most expensive tweeds. He was, nevertheless, a cowed and broken man.

For back at the harbour, at the moment of disembarkation, it had happened again.

The two bishops, divested of oilskins, tall and black but not stately, are clambering up a ladder on to the high slippy quayside, and they are anything but acrobatic. Jeremiah, a few yards away, is struggling to tear from his body his sodden greatcoat, to hang it to dry under the direction of an island-man, in the lee of a boathouse where nets are laid to dry. The cameraman has jocosely snapped him. Then he directs the camera on the clambering bishops only to be vetoed by a voice, iron and Irish and clanging.

—Put away that camera, the Irish voice says, until the opportune time.

—Why Peter, says the American voice, that would make a fun picture.

—In Ireland we don't want or need fun pictures of the hierarchy. We're not clowns.

It is arguable, Jeremiah thinks. He recalls that archbishops, on their own territory and when in full regimentals, are entitled to wear red boots. But he keeps his back turned on the passing parade in sudden terror that his eyes might reveal his thoughts. He hears the cameraman say : Your Grace, there is on the island the oldest inhabitant, a nonagenarian. I'd like to . . .

But there is no response. The procession has passed on. Fickle, Jeremiah knows, is the favour of princes, particularly

129

when, like the Grand Turk, they are related to you. But whatever or how grievous the cause of offence had been that led to these repeated snubs, Jeremiah feels for the first time, burning through empty belly and meagre body, the corps-spirit of the pressman. Who in hell, anyway, is a bishop that he won't stand and pose like any other mortal man? All men are subject to the camera. Face up to it, grin, watch the little birdie. Only murderers are allowed to creep past, faces covered. If he won't be photographed, then to hell with him. He will be scantily written about, even if he is Twenty Times His Grace. And to hell also with all American bishops and Rumanian Reds, and with all colour stories of confirmations and of simple island people who, more than likely, spend the long winter nights making love to their own domestic animals which, as far as Jeremiah is concerned, they have a perfect right to do.

So here in the corner of the granite cross he had found peace. He didn't need to see the nonsense going on out there. When the time came to type, as no doubt it would, the Holy Ghost would guide his fingertips. The moment on the quayside mingled with the moment in the shelter of the church and he realised, for the first time since anger had possessed him, that he had left his greatcoat still drying with the nets. He had been distracted by a call to coffee and sandwiches intended to keep them from collapsing until the show was over. But to hell, too, he decided with all greatcoats; a man could stand on his own legs. He smoked, and was content, and heard far away the voices of children, angels singing. Then the narrow, yellow, grained door opened, a great venerable head, a portion of surpliced body, appeared, a voice louder than the choirs of angels said : Come here, pressman.

Jeremiah went there.

—On the alert I'm glad to see, His Grace said. Waiting to see me. What can I do for you?

Jeremiah, to begin with, bent one knee and kissed his ring. That little bit of ballet enabled him to avoid saying whether he had or had not been on the alert, waiting for an interview.

—You must be starved, His Grace said. That was a rough journey.

They were in the outer room of the sacristy. The walls were mostly presses all painted the same pale yellow, with graining, as the narrow door. In an inner room the American bishop, head bowed, was talking to two tiny nuns. From one of the presses His Grace took a bottle and a half-pint tumbler and half-filled the tumbler with Jameson neat.

—Throw that back, he ordered. 'Twill keep the wind out of your stomach.

He watched benevolently while Jeremiah gasped and drank. The whiskey struck like a hammer. How was His Grace to know that Jeremiah's stomach had in it nothing at all, but wind? Jeremiah's head spun. This, he now knew, was what people meant when they talked about the bishop's bottle. His Grace restored bottle and glass to the press.

—We mustn't, he said, shock the good sisters.

He handed Jeremiah a sheaf of typescript. He said : It's all there. Names. History. Local lore. All the blah-blah, as you fellows say. Here, have a cigar. It belongs to our American Mightyship. They never travel without them. God bless you now. Is there anything else I can do for you?

Jeremiah's head had ceased to spin. His eyes had misted for a while with the warmth of the malt on an empty stomach, but now the mist cleared and he could see, he felt, to a great distance. The malt, too, had set the island rocking but with a gentle soothing motion.

—There's a man here, he said, the oldest inhabitant, a nonagenarian. The cameraman who's with me would like a picture.

—No sooner said than done, oh gentleman of the press. That should make a most edifying picture. I'll call himself away from the nuns. We'll just have time before the ceremony.

But, for reasons never known to me or Jeremiah, he laughed all the time as he led the way around the right arm of the cross to the front of the church; and brought with him another cigar for the cameraman, and shook hands with him, and offered him his ring to be kissed.

Apart from Jeremiah and the cameraman and the island doctor it was a clerical dinner, the island parish priest as host, a dozen well-conditioned men sitting down to good food, and wines that had crossed from Spain on the trawlers without paying a penny to the revenue.

—One of the best men in the business, said His Grace, although he'd sell us all body and soul to the *News of the World*.

He was talking about the cameraman, and at table, and in his presence. But he was laughing, and inciting the gathering to laughter. Whatever cloud there had been between the relatives had blown away with the storm, or with Jeremiah's diplomacy. So Jeremiah felt like Tallyrand. He was more than a little drunk. He was confirmed and made strong by the sea and the bishop's whiskey. He was hungry as hell.

—And Spanish ale, he muttered, shall give you hope, my dark Rosaleen.

His mutter was overheard, relayed around the table, and accepted as unquestionable wit. He was triumphant. He ate. He fell to, like a savage. He drank, he said afterwards— although we suspected that he had conned the names from a wine merchant's list, red and white Poblet, and red Rioja, and red Valdapenas, and another wine that came from the plain to the west of Tarragona where the Cistercians had a monastery: the lot washed down with Fundadór brandy which the American bishop told him had been the brandy specially set aside for the Conclave of Pope John the Twenty-third.

—Thou art Peter, said Jeremiah, and upon this rock.

Once again the remark was relayed around the table. Awash on the smuggled products of Spain, Jeremiah was in grave danger of becoming the life and soul of the party.

A boy-child had that day been born on the island. The American bishop had asked the parents could he baptise the child and name it after himself.

—Episcopus Americanus O'Flaherty, said Jeremiah.

Pope John's Fundadór circled the board. The merriment knew no bounds. His Grace told how the great traveller, O'Donovan, had dwelt among the Turkomans of ancient Merv, whom he finally grew to detest because they wouldn't let him go home, but who liked him so much they called all their male children after him : O'Donovan Beg, O'Donovan Khan, O'Donovan Bahadur, and so on.

—It was the custom in ancient Merv, said His Grace, to call the newborn babes after any distinguished visitor who happened to be in the oasis at the time.

—It was not the custom in Rumania, said Jeremiah.

Renewed merriment. When the uproar died down, the American bishop, with tears in his eyes, said : But this is God's Own Country. Ye are God's Own People.

Jeremiah got drunk, but nobody minded. Later, outside a bar close by the harbour, he was photographed feeding whiskey out of a basin to a horse. The horse was delighted. The picture appeared in a London magazine, side-by-side with a picture of the nonagenarian flanked by bishops.

—You got him to pose, said the cameraman, when he rusted on me.

He meant, not the horse, but the bishop.

—Jer, he said, you'll make a newsman yet.

So, as Jer, a new man, eater of meat and vegetables, acknow-ledged gentleman of the press, he came back from the Isle of the Blest, sitting on the hatch above the bishops, feet on the gunwale chain. He was not beyond hoping that the swing of the sea and the tilt of the boat might salt his feet. It didn't. The easy evening sway would have lulled a child in the cradle.

—Episcopus Americanus O'Flaherty, he said to the lifeboat-man who sat beside him and who had enough Latin to clerk Mass.

—True for you, said the lifeboatman. Small good that christening will do the poor boy. As long as he lives on that island he'll never be known as anything but An Teasbog Beag

133

—the Little Bishop. If he goes to the States itself, the name could follow him there. His sons and even his daughters will be known as the Little Bishops. Or his eldest son may be called Mac an Easboig, the Son of the Bishop. They'll lose O'Flaherty and be called Macanespie. That's how names were invented since the time of King Brian Boru who bate the Danes.

Behind them the island stepped away into the mist : the wanderer, crazed for Hy-Breasil, would never find it. The rain would slant for ever on rocks and small fields, on ancient forts and cliffs with seabirds crying around them, on currachs riding the waves as the gulls do. Visitors would be enthralled by ancient ways, and basking sharks captured. But as long as winds rage and tides run, that male child, growing up to be a lean tanned young man in white jacket and soft pampooties, leaning into the wind as he walks as his forebears have always done, courteous as a prince but also ready to fight at the drop of a half-glass of whiskey, sailing with the trawlers as far away as the Faroes, will continue, because of this day, to be known as the Little Bishop.

In the foxhole underneath Jeremiah, the American bishop was telling the Irish bishop and the cameraman that in the neighbourhood of the Okeefenokee Swamp, out of which the Suwannee River drags its corpse, and generally in the state of Georgia, there were many Southern Baptists with Irish Catholic names.

The water in the land-locked harbour was deadly still, and deep purple in the dusk. Sleepy gulls foraged on the edge of the tide, or called from inland over the small fields. Jer's greatcoat was still on the island, dry by now, and stiff with salt. He never wanted to see it again.

Shadowy people gathered on the harbour wall. The choir sang : Sweet Sacrament Divine, dear home of every heart.

—Ye are God's own people, said the American bishop. This is God's own country.

—Fuck, said the cameraman and in a painfully audible voice.

He had sunk over the ankles in soggy peat-mould, losing one shoe. But while he stood on one leg and Jer groped for the missing shoe, the bishops and the people and the parish priest and the choir, and the cameraman himself, all joked and laughed. When the shoe was retrieved they went on their way rejoicing.

In Galway City Jer ate a dinner of parsnips and rare roast meat and sauté potatoes that would have stunned an ox; and washed it down with red wine.

Far away the island gulls nested on his discarded greatcoat.

AN OLD FRIEND

Quincey in his long brown overall work-coat leans on the red, corrugated-iron barrier and sings to the river and the tall trees beyond, and to the heron fishing in the shallows, that we're both together dancing cheek to cheek. I'm in heaven, I'm in heaven, and my heart beats so that I can hardly speak.

It is the year of the abdication and Quincey has that morning put his arm around the considerable waist of Miss Annie Mullan.

—Aughaleague, Aughaleague, he says, Aughaleague onward.

He is at that moment standing beside Miss Mullan and facing the local delivery rack in the sorting office. The American letter that he holds in his right hand is not meant for the townland of Aughaleague but for the townland of Lissaneden which is much farther down the alphabet, so that the pigeon-hole for Lissaneden is on the far side of Miss Mullan who is standing to Quincey's right hand and is, at that very moment, slowly, thoughtfully, inserting a letter in the pigeon-hole whose contents will be delivered in the townland of Bomacatall. Quincey is much too much of a gentleman to reach across in front of the lady. To do so would also mean a conflict between the affairs of Lissaneden and Bomacatall. So he reaches around behind her, accurately flicks the letter on its way to Lissaneden, and receives a sharp clean smack on the left ear. That ear clangs and buzzes. His face reddens. Reading out the place names in their alphabetical order he says : Aghee, Altamuskin, Arvalee, Aughaleague, Augher, Ballynahatty, Beragh, Bomacatall, Brackey, Cavanacaw, Clanabogan, Claraghmore, Clogher, Clohogue and Creevan.

As he says afterwards to Bernard : Damn the thing else

could I find to say. To think that that aged faggot who sings hymns on the street every Sunday morning and Saturday night could possibly think that me, or any man aged nineteen and with all the world to pick from, would put his arm around her waist. Lord, catch my flea, catch my flea, catch my fleeting soul. Send down sal, send down sal, send down salvation from the lord.

He chants as Annie Mullan and her faithful few chant outside the Y.M.C.A. on a Saturday night.

It is the year of the abdication. Quincey and Bernard walk from the back of the post office, through the yard where his abdicated majesty's red mail-cars are parked, then down a steep gravelly path and a flight of fourteen concrete steps to a square of matted uncared-for grass on a sort of platform thirty feet or so above the river. On that platform Quincey and Bernard spend as much time as they can steal, leaning on the red corrugated-iron barrier or bulwark, smoking, spitting into the river, talking about girls and telling dirty stories.

It is the year of the abdication and his majesty, while his two servants idle, is in perilous condition.

There is nothing in his majesty's regulations at that time, or before or since, to say that a rural postman shall not shave nor do his morning ablutions in the open air in the townland of Arvalee. The king and the men who make his regulations for him may, at that moment, be too preoccupied to think of that one; and there is a postman who takes advantage of their preoccupation. But only on summer mornings when the air is mild and the bloom on the heather and the lark singing. His eccentricity is celebrated in poetry. A fellow postman who has emigrated to Canada writes all his letters home in verse and one day the head postman reads these lines out of one of the letters :

> *On mornings in summer when there is no fog,*
> *Does Johnny still lather in Arvalee bog?*

Across the river which is wide at that place, fast running and shallow but speckled with still pools, and where, on a lucky day, the two brown-coated loafers can be entertained by one of the town's dryfly experts wading and casting, there is a greystone schoolhouse circled by horse-chestnut trees. At playtime the cries of the racing scuffling children come across sharply to them, a painful reminder to Bernard that childhood and youth are gone forever. They are working men now in a working world, sorting clerks and telegraphists in the employment of his majesty who has just abdicated. Quincey doesn't think that way. His father is a country schoolmaster.

—School. It gave me the creeps. A famous jockey said that all he ever knew about school was that you had to go there.

—It isn't necessary for a famous jockey to be a scholar. He has other ways of earning his living.

—Miss Annie Mullan, Quincey says, will never forgive King Edward. She's sure as God jealous.

—She's loyal to the crown.

—She never lets up about chambering and impurities.

Quincey sings : I'm in heaven, I'm in heaven.

—If it was only Bubbles, he says, that I'd gotten my arm around by accident. When we're both together dancing cheek to cheek.

Bernard says : Bomacatall, Bomacatall, Bomacatall backwards.

Quincey sings : And my heart beats so that I can hardly speak.

As he walks along the sea-front Bernard thinks that in the year of the abdication that must have been the favourite song of millions of people. The gospel-group on the concrete steps above the big swimming-pool are singing : *Everybody ought to love him, everybody everywhere.* He has watched and listened for a while to the four middle-aged ladies with black bonnets and sallow faces, the three middle-aged to elderly men, one with a huge grey moustache, one with bandy legs, none of them as tall as the ladies. *Lord, catch my flea.* The preacher is a pale-faced young man in a dark suit and he has two companions of his own age flanking him : to his right a big red-faced fellow in sandy tweeds whose hands, clasped before him, are huge; to his left a slight pretty brunette in a navy costume but with black stockings and flat spiritless heels. Her face isn't unlike what he thinks the face of Bubbles was thirty-four years ago, turned-up impertinent nose, one eye with the slightest, most attractive, not squint, but a sideways enticing look. But then since he made up his mind to the repentance of this visit he has been seeing the face of Bubbles everywhere, on the street, in restaurants, on trains and buses, in airports, in advertisements on television. The gospel group sings : *Jesus died for every nation, everybody, everywhere.* Below them, in the pool, naked unrepentant limbs flash like silver fish. There are shouts and screams of laughter and then half a dozen voices singing in parody : *On the cross, on the cross where the soldier lost his hoss.* Annie Mullan is long dead and gone to Jesus. *Aughaleague, Aughaleague, Aughaleague onward.*

There is no strand here, just granite rocks below the promenade to his left and the sunny sea churning around them. On one far-out rock five or six black seabirds sit, motionless as buzzards. To the right the shops and boarding houses are brightly painted for the season that's about to open, each man fancying his own colour, and one place glitters with a thousand colours because its owner has imbedded in the pebble-dashing a thousand fragments of coloured glass. High on the headland above him the big hotel dominates the place, nineteenth-century Gothic, the castle of a robber baron raised high above the common people.

—Walk right around under the cliffs this hotel stands on, the hall porter says to him, until you come to the harbour where the fishing-boats are.

The cliff is high above now, black and brown and dripping here and there with rusty water, and he can no longer see the hotel. Nor can he hear the singing from the steps above the pool. The wind is blowing it the other way to disperse the pious words over the distant strand and the bent grass whistling in the dunes. The black birds, cormorants, are still motionless on the rock.

A turn to the left and he is leaning on a low wall looking down on the harbour. The tide is ebbed and five trawlers are settled down, as if never to rise again, on black, salt-stinking mud.

—When we get the government grant, the porter says, we'll deepen the harbour. You can sniff the hogo from here at low tide. But they say it's a healthy smell. Mr. Sloan's house, God pity him, is to your left when you stand at the wall above the harbour. You can't miss it. Only two houses there and the other one's a pub. A long well-kept garden in front of it. Mr. Sloan was a great gardener when he had the health. A fine house in a sheltered corner and everything about it as it should be. To have everything and a fine wife as well, and then to be struck down like that, they say she has to feed him off a spoon. The irony of fate, sir, that's what I call it, I often say we're never half thankful enough.

Quarrelling over something that one of them holds in its beak, a flock of gulls go screaming, fighting, diving, soaring out over the harbour. The sea is lively out there and three homing trawlers wait for high water. The flow may be just beginning, because a long thin tongue of water corners around the head of the mole, darts suddenly up the black mud and is as suddenly withdrawn. A sea-serpent's tongue. An aproned red-headed girl stands at the door of the pub which is down the slope to the right. She shades her eyes with her hands and looks out at the waiting trawlers.

The hand of a gardener quite out of the ordinary has left its mark on this place. He has never known that Quincey gardened. Here are roses and rhododendrons and a long rockery brilliant with blinding white iberis. *You're nearer God's heart in a garden than anywhere else on earth. Oh, laburnum yellow, lilac and the rose, chestnut blossoms mellow in my garden close, and summer coming in. I'm in heaven, I'm in heaven.* But that was thirty-four years ago and the interest in gardening could have begun and developed after he married

140

Bubbles. Here is yellow red-hearted broom, and those fuchsia bushes will soon be in blossom, red flowers with royal purple hearts, deora Dé, the tears of God. *The kiss of the sun for pardon, the song of the bird for mirth, and my heart beats so that I can hardly speak.*

The hunted gull, still struggling to preserve whatever it is that it carries in its beak, has swung back in over the harbour. Three great grey gulls assault simultaneously. The morsel drops dead down to the black mud and the whole screaming family go after it. Dear God, it must be something most delectable. The robbed gull, disconsolate, flies away alone to perch on the rock wall behind the house. The garden would seem to go all the way round to that rock wall. He stands at the front door, under the shade of a candled horse-chestnut, and presses the bell. It is one of those chiming bells. There is a long delay, and he is about to ring again when the door opens so suddenly that he's startled. He has heard no footsteps. For a few seconds it seems as if she doesn't recognise him, or that she does recognise him because he has written to say he's coming, but that she is holding her breath for a moment, trying to add up and subtract what more than thirty years have made of him. She is bare footed and wearing tight red jeans. She has not put on weight. Indeed she is slimmer than he remembers her and her cheeks that were plump with youth and unplanned eating are longer now, somewhat hollowed, but there are no wrinkles showing on the forehead.

—Weight, she says, weight. You put on weight all over.

The awkward preliminary paces before the water-jump have been taken. They laugh and he steps inside and holds her hands and kisses her left cheek, a skin that always tanned well.

—We got your letter, Bernard. It was wonderful of you to remember us after all these years.

—It would have been wonderful if I had forgotten.

Does she blush? It is hard to say with that olive skin. He holds her to him and kisses her cheek again. After all it has been a long time, and beyond a certain age it may be that remembering and returning and repeating are much more satisfying, certainly less bothersome, than beginning anything new. Autumn is no time for ploughing. But her chest, under a white crepe-de-chine blouse, with black spots like a Dalmatian, is flat as a board, as it had not been that evening in the telegraphy room. The land shrivels. The hills are laid low. In the creaking swivelling chair she sat before the tele-printer to show him how the thing worked and he leaned over her and slipped both hands down her loose woollen blouse. No protest, to his honest surprise, a very *toilteanach* girl, a lovely Irish word, and good-humoured about it, a pleasurable ductility about her, as the man said, which spread a calmness over his spirits. The world needed more young women like her, and the devil take the teleprinter. He spun her round and round slowly, still stepping behind her, cupped hands still holding on. Dot, dot, dash, dot.

From the drawing-room to the right a clock chimes. They break, as in boxing. She brushes back a wisp of hair, tinted to keep its original brown, that has come down over her eyes. Her nose is regular, even sharp, and not at all like the nose of the pale flat-heeled girl who sang beside the preacher above the swimming-pool. Her eyes are as he remembers them : brown, short-sighted, in the office she wore spectacles, the left with just the hint of a sideways coy glance, not a cast by no means.

—Have you eaten?

He has, very well, and wined, with merry talkative travelling companions.

—Drink?

—A lovely idea.

He needs more drink because of what he has to say to her.

At a Sheraton sideboard in the dining-room she pours him a rich half tumbler, fine Waterford glass, of black Bushmills and shows him the siphon.

—Drink it all, Bernard. You may be disconcerted at first. He's not what he was.

She sips a pale sherry slowly while he drinks, then refills his glass : I prepared him for your visit. He can hear most of the time, we think. He said he would be glad to see you.

—He said?

—He can write, scribble, make marks, sort of. He's out under the rock now, getting the last of the sun. He loves to see the flowers. But he won't sit in the front where the people can see him. He doesn't mind the local people. He was very popular here. He's one of them. But strangers come down to the harbour. It's very beautiful when the tide's full. You should really see it on a stormy day.

He realises foolishly that he has expected to find Quincey in a long brown working-coat: *I'm in heaven, I'm in heaven, and my heart beats so that I can hardly speak.* The brilliant white iberis climbs up the rock wall behind him, varied with the pink and purple of aubrietia, a stubborn plant that grows in crannies, flower in the crannied wall I pluck you out of the cranny. A border of wallflowers runs along the foot of the wall. Invisible somewhere above, the deprived gull croaks with melancholy at the brutally rapacious ways of his fellows. Blessed mother of God this is nobody he has ever known, this is an oriental image in a gaudy shrine, a withered guru in a Himalayan cave. But the wine in the hotel, the brandy after dinner, the Bushmills on top of that, stand to him like three stout musketeers. He puts out his hand and grasps for a moment the right hand resting on the arm of the wheelchair. It is surprisingly plump and warm. There is a small table, a collapsible leaf, attached to the arm of the chair, and a white pad on it and a blue biro.

—He scribbles on that off and on, Bernard. Not great orthography. But he scribbles.

They sit down on two chairs facing each other, facing the image in the shrine. Should they have knelt? Or said : Master, we have come seeking wisdom.

Like the dead he must know it all by now. Or half of it.

Because Bernard has not yet got to the point where he can look his old friend straight in the face, or the grey distorted mask that he now wears over his face, he finds himself, eyes cast down like a novice monk, contemplating her crimson crotch eloquent in tight jeans, and feeling with his left hand the cold iron of a five-barred gate, and smelling in the darkness the meadow-sweet along a lover's lane in the townland of Arvalee where the postman shaved by the bog pool.

—Orthography, he says.

He finds it impossible to call her Bubbles. Long ago, french-kissing in the long grass of Arvalee, it sounded like a joke : I'm forever blowing bubbles. But it was no name for a woman of fifty with a husband shrunken and helpless in a chair : Bubbles, Blossom, Baby, Trixy, all those names that drooling fathers, melted by tiny hands and dimples and creases in pudgy fat, pass on as sardonic curses to the next generation.

—Orthography, he says. Maxwell, the overseer, you remember him? He used to foam at the mouth if he saw one of us writing backhand. Once upon a time in the post office, he'd say, penmanship was all important.

She remembers Maxwell, a bald, impulsive, long-nosed man who got drunk every Christmas eve when the rush was over, and only then.

—He didn't like younger men to sit down, Bernard says. You could do nothing and get away with it all day long if you did it standing on your feet. One day when I quoted Churchill to him he nearly burst.

—What had Churchill to do with it?

—He said, like the common soldier, never stand when you can sit, never sit when you can lie down.

They have brought their glasses out with them, and a third one, Bushmills, for the guru in the chair. She puts that glass down beside the pad and the pencil. She spoons a little of the liquid into the mouth of the image. She bends down and kisses it lightly on the forehead, dancing cheek to cheek. She says : Poor Quincey has a lot of sitting to do these days.

She sits down again. Sooner or later he knows he will have to look his old friend in the eyes. Those eyes are not dead and can see and may even now be looking at him. Would it not be better if he departed politely and said nothing about what he had intended to say : penance was a macabre, masochistic idea, and whose good was he serving, Quincey's or hers or his own? Thinking desperately, he empties his Bushmills and she goes, laughing, back to the house for the bottle, leaving him alone with the man or the thing or the old friend in the chair, and wine and brandy and Bushmills booming in his ears, and the disconsolate gull croaking on the rock above them, and the air sleepy with the scent of flowers.

That rock wall even in winter would hold off the most inhospitable north-easter. Now it stands as a suntrap for the long evening, a blessed place for a garden and for a paralytic who's a sort of flower. Or shrub, or cabbage, nearer God's heart in a garden? The crimson crotch is no longer there to look at nor the woman to talk to. He can't go on staring at the grass or the chair she sat on, so he looks up and around at his old friend and says : Well, Quincey, it's been a long time.

The face is all sideways. The mask it wears is the silk stocking or the plastic thing that up-to-date bandits pull over their faces to distort without actually concealing. As he watches and smiles the tongue protrudes, tip bent inwards, lips spluttering. The hair incredibly is as blond as it was when they leaned on the red bulwark and Quincey sang across the river. Does she dye it so as to preserve something? The tongue withdraws. The face under the mask twitches. That could be a smile. The right hand creeps around on the little collapsible table and falls on the blue biro. He thinks as he sees, and thanks God, that she is coming back with the Bushmills and the siphon, that she had so often said that she would never marry a blond, that she had said about Quincey that she liked him but that he was a blond.

—Quincey, she says, always wanted a house like this. That is, a house with a garden and a stream at the bottom of it. Now he has the house and the garden and the whole ocean.

It is so plainly something that she says to everybody that no reply is necessary. She refills his glass and leaves the siphon on the grass beside him, and feeds another spoonful to the man in the chair, and rests her hand gently on the blond head. Brendan says : Repetatur haustus.

—I beg your pardon.

—It would be Latin, I suppose, for let the draught be repeated. Or the same again.

—Do you tell me so, professor? Do you still read as much as ever? But I suppose you have to.

He wishes that she would sit down and be still so that he could continue looking at her and, without impoliteness, take his attention away from Quincey, if you can be impolite to the flower in the crannied wall. Yet since Quincey can write or scrawl, or whatever it is, he must be able to hear; and he can certainly see, for his grey eyes flicker at the sudden departure of the despoliated gull. If a man or a flower or a cabbage can hear and see, then he, or it, or they, can feel impoliteness. The gulls, all reunited, are singing a hymn over the harbour. The sunlight is dying. Bernard is afraid that he's getting drunk. When she does sit down she says : Maxwell got drunk only once a year. On a Christmas eve when the worst of the rush was over.

—I remember. The one and only Christmas eve I was there he said to Quincey and myself that you young fellows shouldn't be working so hard. Pulling all the time at his beak of a nose. Go out, he says, and buy yourself a good fish supper in Yanarelli's. He gave us a pound. We were flabbergasted. But when we came back we saw the point. Maxwell and a postman drinking whiskey in the overseer's office, and singing. On His Majesty's premises. And not even a Christmas carol.

They laugh. The man in the chair seems to move but Bernard doesn't dare to look around to check. He stares into a crimson world. She says : And one highly-respected official slept all night in the room where the mailbags were kept because he was too drunk to go home to his wife. And Bernard, do you remember Dick Milligan who used to read all the mail-order catalogues?

—The only books he ever read.

—And buy the oddest things.

146

—And try to resell them in the office.

—Pen-knives and bedside lamps and, once, a baby's bottle.

—And a first-aid kit. You see he came from South Armagh where all the crooked horse-dealers used to come from and he couldn't resist a bargain. Or just the joy of bargaining. It was in his blood.

—And Peter Magee who was chairman of the local British Legion and who always wore a tweed jacket and whipcord breeches and riding-boots in the office.

—And who threw a fit when Mr. Somerville, the cynic, said that when Lady Haig visited the town she walked up the High Street with a ladder in her stocking.

—Magee roared: Lady Haig's the greatest lady in the empire. She couldn't have a ladder in her stocking.

He hasn't noticed it until now but she also is drinking Bushmills. Neat.

He says: They were an odd crowd.

As he stoops for the siphon he notices that the hand has grasped the blue biro, awkwardly, between the second and third fingers, steadying it in the hollow of the thumb, and is moving it slowly over the paper. It is a fascinating sight. But he says nothing about it and retreats guiltily to his crimson memories.

—But we were happy, she says. And do you remember Annie Mullan, the queen of the sorting-office?

—The goddess, you mean. The prophetess. The holy woman, Deborah, who with Barak preserved the people of the lord outside the Y.M.C.A. She was in my mind when I listened to the hymn-singers above the swimming-pool. I was thinking of the day Quincey put his arm around her by accident.

It was on the evening of that day that Bubbles and himself got to know each other over the teleprinter, a most romantic place, but it is unlikely that she'll remember that. She puts her glass down on the ground. She says: What is it, Quincey?

There is a sort of gurgling spluttering noise to his right. He knows that the tongue is protruding again but he refuses to look around and thinks the fool he was, for repentance or any other reason, ever to come near this place. The crimson memories are gone and he is looking at cold grass. The shadow of the house is moving sideways towards them.

—Bernard, Quincey has just said something.

She stands over him and holds the white pad before his eyes, then snatches it away in case Quincey will see that he can't make a damn thing out of the blue squiggles and scrawls. She says : What it says is catch my flea.

She reads very slowly : Catch my flea.

—That's all it says. Quincey, what on earth does it mean? Bernard explains.

Then she is laughing and crying at the same time, and saying : Poor Annie Mullan, poor Annie Mullan, if she only knew.

When the woman comes who helps her to look after her husband they wheel him back slowly into the house. This woman has been a nurse but she married and retired and is a good neighbour and a godsend, and Bubbles says she doesn't know how she could cope without her.

The sunlight has gone. The calls of the seabirds are far away and faintly saying farewell. He holds the warm plump hand once again. She takes from a hallstand a heavy blue cardigan and drapes it around her shoulders. She pats the blond head and kisses the mask or the twisted cheek beneath it.

—I'll drive you back to the hotel, Bernard. Quincey won't mind if I leave him for a while. Will you Quincey? It isn't that often that an old friend calls. Catch my flea, indeed.

As they drive around under the seeping cliff to the sea-front he says to her that they picked a lovely place to live in, and has no sooner come out with that banality than he remembers that only one of them is, in fact, living. She says nothing. But when they come to the place where the avenue goes cork-screwing back towards the hotel she drives straight on instead of turning left, then swings right on a narrow dust-road.

—Kidnapper, he says.

148

Her laugh is a real one : Bubbles laughing long ago in the deep grass of Arvalee. There was one smooth magic place, circled by walls of whins and heather and under a crooked whitethorn.

—I want to show you something. How lovely this place can be.

She is still barefooted. The road twists, goes up more steeply, the last houses drop swiftly back into the shadows. She says : Don't look behind until I tell you. Quincey used to say that from this place you could see five Kingdoms. The Kingdom of Mourne. We're in that. Where the mountains of Mourne sweep down to the sea. Then across the water on a clear day you can see Galloway in the Kingdom of Scotland, and Scawfell in the Kingdom of England, and quite close at hand the Kingdom of Man. Not to mention Snowdon in the principality of Wales.

—That's four kingdoms.

—But look up, he used to say, and you see the kingdom of heaven.

—Fanciful.

He is sick with pain at the thought of the thing in the chair : once a man, playing like a happy child with that fantasy of five Kingdoms, staring across the water to catch in a lucky light a glimpse of Scawfell. He says : There's something I must tell you.

—Bubbles, he adds.

She doesn't seem to hear him, or hears only that mention of her name. She presses his right knee, and swings the car right, and parks. The ascending road has met at right angles another road. Wheels can go no higher. Above and beyond the new road there's nothing but the mountain. She leans against him and kisses his cheek. She says : It's too dark now to see the five Kingdoms. But come out and look. He used to love this place. He used to say that it would impress Bernard if he ever came this way. You see he never forgot you.

Chains clank around him and weigh down his limbs as he steps out of the car. They lean against a drystone wall and he

puts his right arm around her shoulders, protectively, against
the light wind growing colder in the darkness, against the
agony of watching day after day, the twisted shrunken image
in the chair. The land falling away from them is black as tar,
even to the fingers of headlands, but the sea is shining with
the last light and the trawlers that had earlier been prone in
the black mud of the harbour are fanning out to sea. Spots
of light wink from the sea-front. The hotel high on the rock
is like an anchored liner with a party going on for the last
night on board, but they hear no sound other than the
indefinable noises of night on the mountain.

—Now, she says, look up. Slowly, slowly. This is the real
view, the vision.

The mountain is black above them, but rimmed and sharply
outlined by light.

—My god, he cries, it's a giant bird, it's an eagle.

The jagged peak in silhouette is the scrawny featherless
neck and beaked head. The spurs to right and left are spreading wings, covering them, protecting them. The rocky barren
land is alive above them. He might never have said what he
had come to say if it hadn't been that the shadow of the
eagle seemed to cut them off so completely from the rest of
the world. No other kingdoms are visible across the water. He
says: The last time I saw Quincey and yourself, you mightn't
remember it, I had been away from the town for three years.

—You went to higher things, professor.

—And came back on a holiday. The first persons I met on
the High Street were Quincey and yourself.

—You couldn't have met better.

He has rehearsed this speech again and again over the
years. Her levity unsettles him.

—Man and wife.

—Well we had got married. All proper like. In a church.

—I felt about the size of a threepenny bit.

—Whatever for? And why?

It is so dark now that her face is only a blob in the shadow
of the eagle crouching above them. The only light left in the

world is in the hotel and on the sea-front, faint phosphor-escence far out over the water. The trawlers have vanished. His arm is still around her shoulders. But the darkness of Arvalee, perfumed by meadow-sweet, is a long time ago.

—Because of something I'd said to Quincey, three years before that, when I left the town. To the effect that, well the exact words were : I leave you Bubbles, she fornicates.

There is a considerable silence.

—A threepenny bit, Bubbles. And a worn one at that. Believe me I've regretted those words to this day, or night. That day on the High Street I felt so small and lousy that I promised myself to guard my tongue for ever more, amen.

—You've done that, I'm sure.

—I knew I'd never be content until I'd apologised to both of you.

—Did you have to be content? Who in the whole world is content?

—Then when I heard he was ill I knew I had to.

—An apology would hardly set him walking again. But I know he was glad to see you.

Her shoulders are shaking under his arm and he is terrified for the moment that the reason may be anger or grief. Then to his amazement, and mild annoyance, he realises that she is laughing.

—Oh, Bernard, she says, you ageing professorial fool. What does it matter now what was said or done when we were young?

He knows in humiliation that he has been cherishing not repentance but happy daring memories.

—Anyway we did, Bernard, didn't we?

—Did what?

—Fornicate. And great fun it was. But that word. You would use a word like that. Even then. It makes it all so solemn.

She is holding on to him, breathless with laughter.

—You must have learned it from Annie Mullan and the bible and the poor king and the things she used to say about him. Quincey always said that she never forgave King Edward.

—Do you forgive me?

—Bless the boy, what is there to forgive?

She kisses him lightly.

—Why if you hadn't said that to Quincey, he was very shy, he might never, being a blond and knowing how I felt about blonds, might never have had the courage or the curiosity to approach me, or marry me. We have been very happy. We still are. I can protect him. He knows I'm there.

The last light is vanishing from the sea. Somebody is methodically rubbing it out. When they turn again to look up at the eagle it has vanished into the darkness. There will be no moon.

—He never told me, Bernard, he never said a word about that. I suppose he couldn't say it to me. I mean use that word.

—He was always too gentle.

—He used shorter words. Poor Annie Mullan. I hope she found Jesus wherever she went to. That he didn't let her down the way the king did.

They listen for a while but no sound comes up from the sea-front nor the hotel. *Everybody ought to love him, everybody everywhere.*

—I'm not reproaching you, Bernard. I'm so glad you came to see us. I think I can understand why you came. After he had the stroke I nearly took religion, like old Annie or the crowd at the swimming-pool. Only I thought it wouldn't be fair to him to give him nothing to look at but a gloomy face. So we have parties often in the house, and people, and he seems to enjoy them, he seems to be happy. He writes down happy things. I keep everything he writes. I'll show them all to you some day. Tomorrow, before you go. We have good friends.

In a private sitting-room in the hotel his own four good friends are showing no sign of pain. Every man has his own bottle and glass. There is nothing niggardly about the way they take refreshment.

Dominic with the banjo is quietly sipping lager and now and again touching the strings. Peter, back from Boston, has divested himself of a coloured necktie as broad as the fifteen acres and, with shirt-front open for coolness and lung-play and with a glass of Jameson in his hand, is chanting a song about some historic outing from Cork city to the town of Macroom :

"On the journey back home sure we came to some blows,
Tim Buckley thanks God that he still has his nose,
For 'twas struck by an elbow with the devil's own thud. . ."

The stout semanticist with the moustache is drinking vodka and soda, because tonic is fattening, and arguing ecumenism with the grave, wide-browed, senior civil servant who is drinking Paddy Flaherty.

They greet him and the strange woman with loud cries of joy. They say that wherever he goes, even though he's a squat blackavised monster of learning and no matinee idol, he has a handsome woman waiting on him. He notices, as time passes, that she has a particular fancy for the reassuring gravity of Ahearne, the civil servant, and he is momentarily jealous. But what does it matter now? Arvalee is as far away as Eden. She has found a new friend. Under the flowering rock wall Quincey will sit for ever, motionless, wordless, except for the scrawling now and again of happy things on a white pad. Man wants but little here below and my heart bleeds so that I can hardly speak.

When they ask him to do his party piece he is tempted wickedly to sing that song of the year of the abdication. Instead, making in mockery wild gestures in the fashion (he has read) of Burke and Grattan in the golden age of oratory, he begins to recite : Aughaleague, Aughaleague, Aughaleague onwards.

He is already well down into his bottle which is black Bushmills and from which he has helped her. Pouring more of the golden past into her glass, he goes on : Bomacatall, Bomacatall, Bomacatall backwards.

For Dominic and Peter and the stout semanticist some brief explanation is necessary. Ahearne, smiling more or less to himself, seems to understand.

With the nasal whine of an ill-trained and untalented choirmonk Bernard intones : Lord catch my flea, catch my flea, catch my fleeting soul. Send down sal, send down sal, send down salvation from the Lord.

That is the antiphon. Then making the music as he goes along he gives them the hymn :

Lettery, Lissaneden, Tummery and Knocknahorn,
Glengeen, Shanaragh, and Cumber in the summer morn,
Mullaghmore, Tullybleety, Tannagh and old Shanmoy,
Messmore and Mullycarnan where I roamed a happy boy.
Streefe Glebe, Tirooney, Tonegan and old Tremogue,
Drumduff, Gleeneeny, Eskeryboy and Tullahogue.

Dominic has got the idea and is carefully picking out the notes on the banjo. It could be called the song of the sorting-office. There are enough townland names in Ireland to keep a man singing for ever.

THE GREEN LANES

Every evening for several consecutive months, Saturdays and Sundays excepted, he waited for me outside the office of this religious magazine. It was a missionary magazine, quite bright as missionary magazines go, with pictures of Africans in white shirts standing in arranged groups, or of nuns at work in hospitals, or priests on horseback: Father Pat Garrigan from Cavan finds that the way with horses that he learned on his father's farm, near Arva, stands him in good stead on a Nigerian journey.

One elderly priest and myself made up the editorial staff. Myself and one bald hunchbacked man who was well into his sixties made up the despatch and circulation staff. We parcelled up the magazines in that black thick paper used for simulating rock walls in Christmas cribs and posted them to convents here and confraternities there and to private citizens all over the place. We had a thanksgiving column for divine favours received, and articles, edifying, by clerics and lay people, male and female, and short stories and serials, edifying and sentimental, by authors and authoresses, and a bigger circulation by the month than a lot of respectable newspapers had by the day. So that the parcelling was the biggest part of the work, and very dusty thirsty tiring work.

To escape from the dust and the grunting hunchback, from the clerical editor who never talked of anything except the skill and products of ancient Irish metal-workers, was really something. To escape to the company of Marcus and the delights of the Long Hall was to move into another world.

—This, the editor had been saying is a photograph of the De Burgo—O'Malley chalice. I got the postcard for nothing in the national museum.

The hunchback had the biggest brownest eyes I've ever seen in a human being, but they could look wicked looks, something unusual in brown eyes, and they could talk as well as any tongue. What they said to me as they looked at me over the rim of a black parcel was : If he hadn't got it for nothing he wouldn't have it.

—The De Burgos, the Burkes, you understand, the Normans. The O'Malleys, the wild Irish. The chalice is made of silver gilt and weighs thirteen ounces and fifteen pennyweights. It is eight inches in height. The inscription reads: *Thomas de Burgo et Graunia Ni Maile me fieri fecerunt.* As if to say, brought me into existence. The chalice, so to speak, speaks. In the year of the lord, 1696. That's a while ago.

—Grania of the Ships, said the hunchback who was a bit of an historian.

He grovelled and grunted, bald head perspiring, amid piled blocks and pyramids of rock-dark parcels.

—She became a sort of national heroine, said his reverence. But we are told in sober truth that she was a pirate and an immoral woman.

The hunchback staightened up as much as he could : 'Twas the lying Tudors said that. She shamed the lord of Howth into hospitality. She had more style than the King of Spain and the Queen of England.

His warmth surprised me because, like myself he generally listened, or pretended to, and said nothing. The reverend editor ignored him, sniffed so that the tip of his thin nose twitched, took back the photograph which he had just tendered to me, replaced it in its envelope and went his way, his black gown swishing around his square-toed shoes. He had the thickest rubber heels I've ever seen.

From the canyons and corridors between the black parcels my circulation assistant, my brown-eyed Caliban, said : A lot he knows about Grace O'Malley of the Ships, or sanctifying grace, or actual grace. Or hospitality. Two pounds eighteen shillings and sixpence a week and your stamps. No money for a married man.

156

—I never knew you were.

—You thought nobody would take me. Is that it? Anyway nobody did. It's still no wage for a married man.

His red face and high forehead shone like a creased and spotted moon from behind a black mountain of parcelled piety, and news flashes from the mission fields where, like in our dusty office, the labourers, as the lord said, were few.

Outside it was mild and late April, dusk thick in the narrow street between the high houses, the street lamps coming to life one by one. Marcus stood with his back to the high spiked railings that fronted the gaunt Georgian houses, and he himself was as straight as the railings. He had marched with the Dublin Fusiliers, and the British army had a name for being able to straighten a man. He stood, as if hiding, just out of the circle of light from a street lamp. He said : I'm watching that window across the street. Take a dekko.

The window was on the third floor of a five-storey house, counting the basement as the first floor. The house was five windows wide and built of Ballyknockan granite, a grey king amid the princely brick Georgian houses; and I regarded it, every time I passed, with a certain reverence.

—Marcus, do you know who lives there?

—Of course I know.

He mentioned the name of a renowned politician, so renowned and for so long that he had become as venerable as any politician ever could become.

—Of course I know. But it's not him I'm looking at. He's to be seen at any time. Watch that window.

The windows on the first floor were lighted and red-curtained, and light rayed upward from the windows in the basement area. Above that the house was dark.

—The flash of white, he said, watch for the flash of white. The belly of a salmon turning in a pool up the Liffey at Sallins. That's the time to hook them.

We watched the dark window. The evening traffic was lessening in the street. We watched the dark window and were rewarded after a few moments with a definite flash of white.

It flashed, vanished, flashed again, then stayed steady behind the darkened glass.

—What do you think it is? he said.

—Not a notion.

—Use the brains God gave you, if they're not addled up in that place you work in, helping to pollute the free peoples of Africa.

But I couldn't guess what the white blob was. It was still steady at the window.

—God aid your eyesight. It's a maid's white apron. You don't see the rest of her because her dress is black.

—Is her face black too?

—It might be. Though that's not too likely. It's probably just not as white as her apron. Not boiled and starched.

—What's so wonderful about a maid's apron?

—She's looking out. She's looking at us.

—You mean she's looking at you.

—Well, I was here before you. She'd be lonely in that big house.

—They must have twenty servants in the basement.

—Then why isn't she down there? What's she doing alone at a window, looking out? She's homesick. Or yearning.

He took his wide-brimmed grey hat in his hand and waved it at the window. The blob moved, became a flash again, vanished.

—She's shy, he said. I've frightened her.

—You've frightened her apron.

We set off walking towards the warmth and glitter and glisten of the Long Hall, our pub, in George's Street.

—When the long bright evenings come, he said, we'll see more than her apron.

On Sundays, in all seasons and weathers we'd go walking in the hills to the south of the city, up over the Featherbed mountain where the stream overflows, wrestling with oval boulders, from the black tarn—it's the only word—of Lough Bray; higher still and over the ridge to the clear sources of the

Liffey in Calary bog. He was a man for the open air, a fisher-
man and a good man to walk with, for he could, without
saying he was doing it, train you to walk the way the army
trained him : like a machine, with a measured easy tread that,
without strain, covered the ground and could go on for ever.

We talked as we walked, sometimes but not often about the
war. Or, on that topic, he talked and I listened, for he was
a man in his forties and had been there, and I was all of
eighteen and hadn't been anywhere. When he enlisted, he
said, he did the right thing for the wrong motive, to get away
from the mother for a while, just for a change like. There was
something nasty that had happened to Turkish prisoners at
the Dardanelles, and several times he started to tell me that
one but stopped before he got to the details. Once in a while
he would burst into song :

> Long may the colonel with us bide,
> His shadow ne'er grow thinner.
> It would, though, if he ever tried
> Some army stew for dinner.

But mostly, and especially when we walked in the green
lanes on days when we hadn't time to go as far as the hills, he
talked about girls. The green lanes stirred his memory and he
had much to remember, and I was ready to listen and learn,
although now and again I did think that girls and the war
served the same purpose for him : to get him away from the
mother for a while, just for a change like.

The green lanes are no longer green, no longer lanes, no
longer even on the map. The city has eaten them up, and
small semi-detached houses and suburban gardens are all over
that gentle slope above the sea where generations of lovers had
flattened grass under hawthorn hedges and made love in the
open air, not in caves mortgaged to building societies. When,
as we tramped through the maze of narrow paths we came on
a loving couple, they carried on regardless and undisturbed.
By ancient convention they had the freedom of the place and
we were the intruders and should be ashamed to be there.

—But, he'd say, I've my rights here for long and faithful service. I've my citizenship papers.

Here in a hollow under a boortree bush he had had the most thundering experience of his whole career, apart from once in wartime France when the play had surpassed all description. Remembering, he touched gently the bark of the bush : She was a Dublin girl, too. Normally in those days the country girls were the liveliest. They were better fed. You picked them up in the Fun Palace on the quays, the place with the mirrors that show you up in all shapes and sizes. That never ceased to amuse the country girls, they were that simple.

He walked ahead of me, grey hat, brown overcoat, well-polished brown shoes, feet stepping like clockwork. The lanes were narrow. A five-barred iron gate opened a view through high dropping hawthorns, white with blossom, into a field. Down the slope was the sea and the high stacks of dockland. The green slope of that field below the four horse-chestnut trees had been, he told me, more comfortable than a plush circular bed in a rich man's house. There had been wild flowers down there and the white candles of the chestnuts to make posies for a queen.

—There's no harm, you see, in being romantic once in a while. It was unlucky to cut the hawthorn blossoms.

We always entered the green lanes from the road that went by the sea northward from the city. Once in the maze you were steeped in a green silence if you didn't know, that is, that life and whispering were going on all around you. To look down on the maze from a low-flying aeroplane would really be something. But then, he'd say, whip the roofs off all houses and think what God would see.

We always left the green lanes by bending low through a tangled shrubbery and climbing over a pile of stones and rubble where a six-foot stretch of the wall of an old estate had collapsed. The last owner of the estate had sold out to the city for housing development. But since the development had not yet begun, the place was a wilderness bisected by the straight main avenue that went for half a mile between pines and cedars to the burnt-out shell of an eighteenth-century mansion. Children played on the wide grassy margins of the avenue. On one corner of the gravel before the house there was a sort of perpetual card school. The players, interrupted only by nightfall or rough weather stood and swore and shouted and planked their cards with deadly accuracy on the ground. In the most intense moments they squatted like tailors, or Amazon Indians by a jungle fire, and were silent.

Fifty yards behind the house we'd duck through a barbed wire fence, and there was another road and green city buses and a village pub that kept a good pint but had none of the grandeur of the Long Hall.

Half way through May the girl in the darkened room, switched on the light. He took that as a challenge : She wants to see us better. She wants us to know that she sees us : She wants us to see her.

Caught dazzled in brightness that came down like the beam of a lighthouse from the window to the spot where we skulked in the shadows, I tried to work out his meaning. We were later than usual that evening because his reverence had delayed me to tell me all, or all that he knew, about the collar of gold, a hollow necklet, found at Broighter in County Derry and dating from the first century after Christ. The home-going traffic had gone from the street, which was only a narrow side street anyway and the bright noisy flow of life honking like crowded wild geese, and the road to the Long Hall, was fifty yards to our left.

—She probably wants the police or her employer to see us.

—There's no other light in the house.

—They could be hiding behind the dark windows.

—Loitering with intent we are, he said, to see a virgin.

—Hope springs eternal, I said.

—She's from the country by the look of her, Marcus said.

—All maids are from the country.

—There was one that I courted in the conservatory of the

161

6—ABOM * *

burnt-out house at the green lanes. She had thick red hair and a laugh like a horse.

—But soft what light, I said.

We could see her pretty well where she stood spotlighted in the window. She had bronze hair that shone and her face was pale but, at the distance, we could make nothing out of the nature of her eyes. She was plump rather than slender. The black dress, the white apron were plain enough. Her hands were clasped before her breasts and holding some small white object which, with his expert knowledge, he was able to tell me was the hairband that maids would wear in a house of those dimensions.

—A hell of a house to be billeted in, he said. A hibernian harem.

He stood out into the light of the street lamp, took off his hat, bowed with great style and restored the hat quickly to its place. He was sensitive about the bald patch that marred his plentiful crown of dark curly hair. The girl waved back, the white object in her hand fluttered. Then, no mistake about it, she blew him a kiss and vanished.

—That's a beginning, he said as we walked on to the Long Hall. Who can despise the day of small beginnings? I read that once in a book called *Milestones of Progress*.

—Looking out through windows and in through windows is a wonderful thing, he said. Windows are wonderful.

—Like widows.

—I could tell you stories about widows. Beginning with my mother. And windows, too.

Late at night, walking home through narrow streets where the houses abutted on the pavement with no protective patches of garden, he had developed a habit of peeping through curtains or under window-blinds. It wasn't, I really think, that he was a voyeur in the limited, sad or nasty, sense of the word. He was just curious about other people's lives.

—You see the oddest things in other people's houses. Most houses should be on the stage.

Carefree in the glitter of the Long Hall, our pints before

us, we had fun classifying homes we knew into groups to suit the city's theatres. Irish peasant to English light opera, solemn Norwegian to bare-legged burlesque, there was a stage for every home. Always in the Long Hall, a place of many mirrors, there was a shabby, silent little man who drank ale and port wine at the same time but out of separate glasses, an odd ritual; and it amused us, as men of the world, that because of where he sat and we sat, we could see him five times, the man himself and four reflections, five little men, ten little glasses.

Looking at himself, side by side in a mirror with one of the five men, Marcus pulled and pushed at his chin and mouth as if he were shaping plasticine. He was worried at the way the wrinkles were deepening, dry furrows on a dark land, downward from the corners of his mouth.

—Only fatherless girls, you know, go for old men, and they're in the minority. My own mother's house would make a man old before his time. It's so quiet it wouldn't be accepted on any stage. It's so shiny you'd be afraid to sit down.

—But who shines it?

—Oh, I do. But if I didn't the mother would never give me a moment's peace : You'll polish it all right for the woman who comes after me.

The lifelessness of his own home may have set him peeping through curtains and under blinds. As a french-polisher, shining was his business. He affected to dislike it, saying that the man who invented such work or any work, should have kept it to himself. But he was proud of being an exclusive sort of craftsman who could work where and when he pleased. French-polishers were few. The precision, the perfection of the method gratified something of the disciplinarian that the army had found and developed in him. But polishing costly sideboards and tables in big houses, and leaving them behind you at the end of the day for somebody else to study their faces in, was a different thing from polishing in a tiny house at the behest of a nagging widowed mother, always saying her son should get married, always scared to hell that he might.

Once only was I in the house and then only because he

163

couldn't leave me waiting for him outside in the rain. The shine of the tables hurt the eyes. The old mother's thin white face also shone. She was polite and no more. There were no cushions to dim the shine of the chairs, which were hard and slippery under the buttocks. The stage to accommodate such a house had not yet been invented.

The love story of Marcus and the girl at the window was well on the way when I came back from Donegal, where I went once a year for the fluency of my Irish—to the rocks of the Rosses, the stone-wall patchwork of small fields, the white cottages, the turbulent sea, the fuchsia hedges. As in the previous two years the tiny silver-haired sister of Hudie who was seventy, the son of Cormac, who was ninety, McGarvey gave me the parcel of thick home-knitted socks for the reverend editor. She had cherry-blossom cheeks and talked like a bird chirping.

As in the previous two years the hunchback said when he saw the socks, which were grey-white and lumpy and as thick as chain mail : There surely to God must be something wrong with his feet or he wouldn't dare to wear those.

His reverence accepted the socks and went his way, having first told us about the shrine of the Cathach which was made between 1062 and 1098 both years of the lord, to contain a vellum psalter which dated to the year 550. When the O'Donnells of Donegal went into battle they carried the psalter with them as a guarantee of victory, which was why it was called the Cathach or the Battler.

The door closed behind his flat heels and his flapping gown.

—He's a battler himself, said the hunchback, God help us. He hasn't the blood of a louse. The pale thin face of him and the twitchy nose. I should give him some blood.

The parcelling for the month had not yet commenced. My assistant sat on a high stool at the sort of old-fashioned desk that hadn't been much in use since the boyhood of Dickens and made entries in a ledger with a plain pen that scraped and spluttered. On my holiday in Donegal I had decided to look for a better job, something in the world of bright girls and type-writers.

—Give him blood?

—Didn't you know?

He climbed down from the stool.

—But how would you since I never told you? Did you ever see the like of that?

It was a sort of certificate to show that he had been for a vast number of times a blood donor. For a long time I studied it, to show my interest and to hide my surprise. Then he took it back to his wallet and his inner breast-pocket. That day he was wearing an elegant dark-grey suit with a pin stripe, a starched white shirt, and he was so unusually clean-shaven that his strong, tanned, square-chinned handsome face was more than usually noticeable. Although he was an older man than Marcus he hadn't a wrinkle : a bad back, perhaps, but a better stomach.

—Was up there today, he said. That's why the glad rags. A man has to look his best before the nurses. There'd be a lot of people that, if they saw me, wouldn't want my blood. Did you ever know that my mother was an O'Donnell?

We always left by different doors, for he stayed behind me to lock up and to say some prayers for something or somebody in the chapel of the religious house to the rear of the office.

—Everything's going like a house on fire, Marcus said. We'll walk in the green lanes when you've had a bite to eat.

The overcoat had been cast aside. He wore a flannel jacket with a broad check, sharply creased grey pants, a cream shirt and a sporty tie with drawings on it, new suede shoes and, because of the bald patch, a green cloth cap.

—Everything what?

—Everything across the street, man. It's long gone beyond waving at the window.

His face shone with health, and the wrinkles seemed no longer so noticeable. Was it just that the salt air of the Rosses had cleaned and freshened my own eyes, making me see other men

165

as younger and more handsome than they were? That day Marcus smiled more than he usually did. When he smiled he flashed the tips of two shiny teeth, a trick that commonly made him appear cunning but now seemed comic and catching.

—There's nothing better for a man, he said, as he gets older than to start something new and young. There's a chemist in the Coombe has pills would raise the dead.

—What's her name?

—Do you know I've never asked her. So far I've just called her miss.

—Very respectful.

—Or darling. Oh, we're very matey and all. I told her my name was Albert Heaney. But she didn't seem to bother about names. She's sweet and simple.

—You told her a lie.

—Force of habit, I suppose. My poor mother's about the only woman that ever knew my real name.

—Did you walk her in the green lanes yet?

So far, he told me, he hadn't. She didn't have much off-time. Yet that had not impeded the progress of love. By the door in the basement area he slipped in to see her. For the big granite house was by no means as crowded as we had supposed. The venerable politician, no longer active, and his wife spent most of the year either in the sun in the south of France or in a cottage by the Kenmare River. There were so many empty rooms in the place that you could run a disorderly house there without offending anybody. In the absence of the owners the establishment was managed by a few maids and an old house-keeper who was doddering and deaf as a post, and whose sitting-room was on the top-most floor because she liked to look over the roofs of the city towards the blue hills of Wicklow. While she sat at her high window, lifting her heart and her eyes to the hills, the maids in rotation made merry in the base-ment. For the visiting beaux food and drink were laid on at the expense of the absent politician who had never before in his career been of such benefit to the Irish people. It was cheaper by far than walking a girl out and, believe it or not, a broad kitchen table in a dry basement could be as cosy as a green bank or a bed of roses.

—Beds of asphodel, I said.

—Never heard of him. There are so many empty rooms that she thinks the house is haunted. She's more rural than you'd believe possible. From the County Clare.

—From the black stones of the Burren.

—From the stone age if you ask me. You wouldn't credit the extent of her ancient Irish superstition. Salt over the shoulder all the time. She'd sooner walk naked down Grafton Street than put her left shoe on before her right or walk under a ladder. She wears most of her underclothes inside out for good luck, she says, and turns her apron twenty times an hour, when she's wearing it. She's like a chiming chandelier with miraculous medals. But she's gentle and soft as a silk cushion.

His voice, which was normally sharp and clear, softened and shook a little. It startled me. I was listening to love.

—And trusting. She says to me again and again : You won't do me any harm. As if she was expecting nothing out of life but harm. Isn't that an odd one? But down in that basement, man, we could be on our own desert island. The only thing that disturbs or comes between us is the old housekeeper's bell that she rings when she wants somebody to do something for her. She doesn't ring it often though. She's a most undemanding old lady.

With a most aggravating complacence he said : It's the young ones makes the demands. The old ones keep their eyes on heaven or the far-away hills.

But three months later it became obvious that harm had been done and the idyll in the kitchen had ended. The old housekeeper may have been deaf and doddering but she wasn't blind, and the bitter irony was, Marcus told me, that if it hadn't been for her damned bell catching him off his guard on one sleepy Sunday afternoon, the disaster might never have happened.

—You might say, he said, that she's to blame, indirectly.

—Very indirectly. She took her thoughts away from heaven and the hills.

He was not amused and he told me so. A long and carefree life he had had, he said, and never a mishap like this until he made love on a kitchen table in another man's house. Let that be a lesson to all, respect for the domestic hearth and for the homes of our illustrious leaders. That such a thing should come to pass on a patriot's kitchen table. Damn that bell and the hag who rang it for she had also banished the girl in tears and disgrace to wait out the fullness of time with her aunt in a cottage in the green lanes.

—I never knew there was a cottage in the green lanes.

—There are several but nobody ever notices them.

—You could marry her, Marcus.

—And have another woman's face reflected in my mother's polished tables. The way of it is, you see, that I love the girl and I couldn't subject her to tyranny.

The two white tips of teeth did not flash. The lines downward from the corners of his mouth were deeper and darker than ever. It occurred to me to make a joke about the potency of the pills he got from the chemists in the Coombe but I decided against it. He was serious about his love. But it never did enter his mind that he or she could live anywhere else except in the box of a house in Ballybough that he had so brilliantly and grudgingly polished to please his mother.

Summer or winter, our reverend editor was always cold and shivering, perhaps because he really was bloodless, perhaps because he had spent four years in the missions in Africa and had grown to like the heat. Again and again the hunchback would say to me that the editor was a cowled monk, and each time he would laugh happily at his deplorable pun.

—The shrines of the early saints, our editor told us, took interesting, even bizarre, forms. A bronze reliquary shaped like an arm was made in the twelfth century to enshrine the arm of St. Lachtin of Freshford in the County Kilkenny. About 780 the Moylough Belt was made of tinned bronze ornamented with enamel, millefiori and silver panels, to enshrine the belt of a saint. We don't, alas, know which saint or anything about him.

—Except, said the hunchback, that he wore a belt and not braces.

He had been in a strange exalted humour that day and if I hadn't known that he was or said he was, a temperate man, I'd have sworn he was boozed. When his reverence had flat-heeled and flapped it out the door, he said : We'll make a reliquary of asbestos, shaped like two flat feet to enshrine his socks.

He was also wearing his blood-bank clothes with a coloured silk handkerchief, for extra panache in the breast-pocket. But when I asked him had he been donating blood and dazzling the nurses, he looked at me for a long time as if he were testing me for something. His brown eyes could be as still and lightless as deep pools under high banks. He said no, that he had the glad rags on today because the boy was twenty-one. He took his black leather wallet slowly from his inner breast-pocket, unzipped the back compartment in which men normally keep the letters they don't want the wife to find, took out something wrapped in tissue paper, unwrapped it and handed it to me. It was a coloured snapshot of a boy of about seven dressed in a sailor suit and holding, but not playing with, a humming top. He could have been interrupted in his play and made to pose for his picture. He was a very handsome little boy with long golden curls.

—The boy, he said.

—But he's not twenty-one.

—That was taken on his seventh birthday. I took it myself.

—Who is he?

—My son.

—But you told me you weren't married.

—When you're longer in the city you'll find out you can have sons without being married.

—I heard the rumour. Even in the country.

We laughed, and just then the eyes of the boy in the snapshot caught mine. They were the eyes of the father looking up over turrets and battlements of black parcels of piety and letters of thanksgiving and news from darkest Africa. No doubt about it, the eyes stamped them father and son.

169

—He has eyes like yours.

It was an awkward thing to say. Roughly, effectively, he disposed of my awkwardness.

—But as straight as a ramrod, he said. No worry there, God be praised.

As straight as Marcus the soldier and the railings outside the Georgian houses.

—The golden hair was after his mother. Her name was Julia, but I called her Grania for her hair like a queen in history. Grania of the Ships because her husband worked on the Liverpool boat and was away from home six nights out of the seven.

—Does the boy's father know?

—I'm his father. Poor Jimmy, you mean. He'd never guess. He's straight and honest but simple.

—Does the boy know?

—He'll never know. They won't mock at him. It makes me laugh when I give blood.

He rewrapped the snapshot, put it back in his wallet and the wallet back in his pocket. He said : I go to the house often. I'm going there now. Jimmy and myself were always great friends. The boy will have what I have to leave when I die. Mean and all as his reverence is, I managed to hoard a bit.

He followed me to the door, the keys rattling in his hand.

—Wish him a happy birthday from me, I said.

—She's long dead and in Glasnevin, Grania of the Ships. Jimmy never married again. After her, no man would need another woman.

The green lanes, Marcus was able to tell me, looked very different in the early mornings, the times he slipped out to see the girl, because the aunt, who kept a tight eye on her, worked mornings in the city as a cleaner in a block of offices.

Mornings, the green lanes were as quiet as the garden of Eden before the serpent whispered, or after our first parents were driven out. Mornings, the green lanes could actually have been the garden of Eden, for the place must be somewhere, empty for all eternity.

The sound of the city, never at its worst in the mornings, was then very far away. Refreshed by dew the circles of grass, crushed by lovers the previous evening, were springing up again. It was unspoiled virgin earth except where, here and there some couple, more careful of their clothes or more timorous of the damp, had made for themselves mattresses of newspapers. Yesterday evening's headlines, helpless and irrelevant on the ground, showed you how little, anyway, the news of the world outside Eden mattered.

This was rural peace and you could wander for ever through the hedgy maze with only a view, now and again, over a five-barred gate, of Howth Head asleep along the sea or, far to the south, the blue cone of the Sugarloaf Mountain, to remind you that you were in the world at all. The cottages were there and to be seen, yet they sank inoffensively back into the greenery. Until those mornings in the green lanes he had never seen the girl dressed in anything except her house uniform. Out there in Eden she wore a smart green coat so that if it hadn't been for her bronze hair and her healthy country face it would have been hard, at a distance, to pick her out against the background. Green, though, suited her colouring, and love prospered on quiet dewy mornings.

Until the day he looked ahead of him along a green tunnel of a lane and saw her in the company of an older woman. The mother had always told him that green was an unlucky colour. He, as an old soldier, should have been on his guard because at their previous encounter she had asked him to come on parade, next time, two hours later than usual. The children were already playing on the green margins of the avenue. For a change he had entered the place by way of the burnt-out house. The card school was already assembled on its corner of the grass-grown gravel before the house. Because he had time to kill he stood with them for a while, then sat with his back against a fire-scarred Doric pillar and rose a mild winner. He was always lucky at cards.

Advancing as he was then, from the house and not from the seaside, the backs of the girl and the woman were turned to him. The sky was dark with thunder to come. He had worn his overcoat so that he could lay it under them on the grass, and his face was oily with sultry sweat. So he hopped over a five-barred gate into a meadow and found a place where he could peep through the hedge. Who'd ever have thought that a girl so country, so soft and trusting, could have traitorously sold the pass? He saw them clearly enough as they paced back and forward like sentries. The woman's face was dark like the skies and ready for thunder. The hedge he peeped through was of a triple thickness, yet it seemed from what he could see of the girl's face that she was, or had been, weeping. He might have gone out to meet them if it hadn't been that the furious-faced aunt showed the shadow of a dark moustache. The future menaced him, and a polished world in which everything, good and bad, was seen twice. Aunt and niece walked up and down for the best part of an hour. The day by then was as black as night, and the first thunder had rolled, and flickering sheet-lightning brightened the green of meadow and hedges. Once when the pair were long in coming back he judged they had given him up and gone home, and he hopped over the gate and turned towards the sea road, and there they were twenty yards away, coming towards him. In a hoarse voice the woman shouted : Is that the man?

He ran back towards the avenue and the house. She called him sadly by the false name he had given her. He ran from her voice, from the future, from the aunt's shadow of a moustache. The rain came as he ran tangling and twisting through the maze of the green lanes. There wouldn't be a track of him left that even a desert Indian could find. At the meeting of four lanes he ran past the white-washed cottage in which the aunt lived. Rain danced with the sound of kettledrums on the corrugated iron roof. In bedraggled groups the playing children had huddled under the cedars. They cheered after him as he ran sloshing past. The card school had withdrawn into the scorched belly of the building. For a moment he thought he might join them. But on second thoughts he turned his winnings over in his pocket and went on his sodden way. Her good green coat would have been destroyed in the rain.

The shabby, silent little man, who drank ale and port wine, sat and spoke to nobody and didn't seem to know that we could see him drinking ale and port wine in four different mirrors.

—He gets more value for his money than any man in the Long Hall, Marcus said, and laughed at his own joke.

But it was a faltering class of a laugh. He was pale and unshaven, and ashamed before me.

—That very day, do you know, I was going to make a clean breast of it to the old mother. For I loved that girl and would have stood by her if she hadn't betrayed me to the aunt.

—Oh chandeliers and glistening glass, I said, and pints of bass and bottles of port wine. And Johnnie Walker for ever, with his tall hat and red-tailed coat and cream breeches and black knee-boots . . .

—Are you out of your mind?

—That's the song of the Long Hall. I'm writing a prose poem.

—You can trust nobody nowadays. My last and dearest love and she betrayed me.

—Oh silver tankards hanging by the handles and bellying bottles of Bisquit brandy and, on a high rail, ornamental plates with pictures of deep-bosomed ladies and birds in flight and knights in armour. And earthenware kegs of Jamaican rum with pictures of antlered stags. Do you know, Marcus, that the brains of man, like the antlers of a stag, are going to grow too heavy for his head?

—Some people won't have to worry, he said. You're a lot of talk.

We walked in silence through cold wet streets to our usual place of parting. He never waited for me any more in the evenings. He was running from the place where he used to stand up as straight as the railings. She might come to find him there. He never saw her again, nor did she ever find him, if she ever went looking for him. He abandoned the green lanes and, possibly, all the memories that went with them. The green lanes are no longer on the map, and green lanes anywhere into which a man can vanish and be no more are becoming very rare. Bank robbers are photographed, without as much as asking their leave, while they work. A father and mother can sit at home and see their son blown up in the jungle. If a man takes part in serious television discussions he should also remember not to use a false name when booking into hotels with young women who are not his wife.

That was the last summer I ferried socks from the Rosses of Donegal. That better job with girls and typewriters came my way and, anyway, the reverend editor died of cancer and went to where whatever was contrailte with his feet would trouble him no longer.

The hunchback I saw one day, crossing the street, being helped by a handsome young man. They were talking and laughing and he didn't see me.

Marcus fell at the french-polishing and was three months in bed before he died. His face was thin and old the last time I saw him and his sharp voice was failed to a feeble sort of a whisper. He has aged all of a sudden, I thought, but then I remembered that I was, at that moment, the age he was when I first met him. That's the way it is in being friendly for a long time with people older than yourself.

A BALL OF MALT
AND MADAME BUTTERFLY

O n   a   w a r m   but not sunny June afternoon on a crowded
Dublin street, by no means one of the city's most elegant
streets, a small hotel, a sort of bed-and-breakfast place, went
on fire. There was pandemonium at first, more panic than
curiosity in the crowd. It was a street of decayed Georgian
houses, high and narrow, with steep wooden staircases, and
cluttered small shops on the ground floors : all great nourish-
ment for flames. The fire, though, didn't turn out to be serious.
The brigade easily contained and controlled it. The panic
passed, gave way to curiosity, then to indignation and finally,
alas, to laughter about the odd thing that had happened when
the alarm was at its worst.

This was it.

From a window on the top-most floor a woman, scantily-
clad, puts her head out and waves a patchwork bed coverlet,
and screams for help. The stairway, she cries, is thick with
smoke, herself and her husband are afraid to face it. On what
would seem to be prompting from inside the room, she calls
down that they are a honeymoon couple up from the country.
That would account fairly enough for their still being abed on
a warm June afternoon.

The customary ullagone and ullalu goes up from the crowd.
The fire-engine ladder is aimed up to the window. A fireman
begins to run up the ladder. Then suddenly the groom appears
in shirt and trousers, and barefooted. For, to the horror of the
beholders, he makes his bare feet visible by pushing the bride
back into the room, clambering first out of the window, down
the ladder like a monkey although he is a fairly corpulent man;
with monkey-like agility dodging round the ascending fireman,

then disappearing through the crowd. The people, indignant enough to trounce him, are still too concerned with the plight of the bride, and too astounded to seize him. The fireman ascends to the nuptial casement, helps the lady through the window and down the ladder, gallantly offering his jacket which covers some of her. Then when they are halfways down, the fireman, to the amazement of all, is seen to be laughing right merrily, the bride vituperating. But before they reach the ground she also is laughing. She is brunette, tall, but almost Japanese in appearance, and very handsome. A voice says : If she's a bride I can see no confetti in her hair.

She has fine legs which the fireman's jacket does nothing to conceal and which she takes pride, clearly, in displaying. She is a young woman of questionable virginity and well known to the firemen. She is the toast of a certain section of the town to whom she is affectionately known as Madame Butterfly, although unlike her more famous namesake she has never been married, nor cursed by an uncle bonze for violating the laws of the gods of her ancestors. She has another, registered, name : her mother's name. What she is her mother was before her, and proud of it.

The bare-footed fugitive was not, of course, a bridegroom, but a long-established married man with his wife and family and a prosperous business in Longford, the meanest town in Ireland. For the fun of it the firemen made certain that the news of his escapade in the June afternoon got back to Longford. They were fond of, even proud of, Butterfly as were many other men who had nothing at all to do with the quenching of fire.

But one man loved the pilgrim soul in her and his name was Pike Hunter.

Like Borgnefesse, the buccaneer of St. Malo on the Rance, who had a buttock shot or sliced off in action on the Spanish Main, Pike Hunter had a lopsided appearance when sitting down. Standing up he was as straight and well-balanced as a man could be : a higher civil servant approaching the age of forty, a shy bachelor, reared, nourished and guarded all his life by a trinity of upper-middle-class aunts. He was pink-faced, with a little fair hair left to emphasise early baldness, mild in his ways, with a slight stutter, somewhat afraid of women. He wore always dark-brown suits with a faint red stripe, dark-brown hats, rimless spectacles, shiny square-toed brown hand-made shoes with a wide welt. In summer, even on the hottest day, he carried a raincoat folded over his arm, and a rolled umbrella. When it rained he unfolded and wore the raincoat and opened and raised the umbrella. He suffered mildly from hay fever. In winter he belted himself into a heavy brown over-coat and wore galoshes. Nobody ever had such stiff white shirts. He favoured brown neckties distinguished with a pearl-headed pin. Why he sagged to one side, just a little to the left, when he sat down, I never knew. He had never been sliced or shot on the Spanish Main.

But the chance of a sunny still Sunday afternoon in Stephen's Green and Grafton Street, the select heart or soul of the city's south side, made a changed man out of him.

He had walked at his ease through the Green, taking the sun gratefully, blushing when he walked between the rows of young ladies lying back in deck-chairs. He blushed for two reasons: they were reclining, he was walking; they were as gracefully at rest as the swans on the lake, he was awkwardly in motion, conscious that his knees rose too high, that his sparse hair—because of the warmth he had his hat in his hand—danced long and ludicrously in the little wind, that his shoes squeaked. He was fearful that his right toe might kick his left heel, or vice versa, and that he would fall down and be laughed at in laughter like the sound of silver bells. He was also alarm-ingly aware of the bronze knees, and more than knees, that the young ladies exposed as they leaned back and relaxed in their light summer frocks. He would honestly have liked to stop and enumerate those knees, make an inventory—he was in the Department of Statistics; perhaps pat a few here and there. But the fearful regimen of that trinity of aunts forbade him even to glance sideways, and he stumbled on like a winkered

177

horse, demented by the flashing to right and to left of bursting globes of bronze light.

Then on the park pathway before him, walking towards the main gate and the top of Grafton Street, he saw the poet. He had seen him before, but only in the Abbey Theatre and never on the street. Indeed it seemed hardly credible to Pike Hunter that such a man would walk on the common street where all ordinary or lesser men were free to place their feet. In the Abbey Theatre the poet had all the strut and style of a man who could walk with the gods, the Greek gods that is, not the gods in the theatre's cheapest seats. His custom was to enter by a small stairway, at the front of the house and in full view of the audience, a few moments before the lights dimmed and the famous gong sounded and the curtain rose. He walked slowly, hands clasped behind his back, definitely balancing the prone brow oppressive with its mind, the eagle head aloft and crested with foaming white hair. He would stand, his back to the curtain and facing the house. The chatter would cease, the fiddlers in the orchestra would saw with diminished fury. Some of the city wits said that what the poet really did at those times was to count the empty seats in the house and make a rapid reckoning of the night's takings. But their gibe could not diminish the majesty of those entrances, the majesty of the stance of the man. And there he was now, hands behind back, noble head high, pacing slowly, beginning the course of Grafton Street. Pike Hunter walked behind him, suiting his pace to the poet's, to the easy deliberate rhythms of the early love poetry : I would that we were, my beloved, white birds on the foam of the sea. There is a queen in China or, maybe, it's in Spain.

They walked between the opulent windows of elegant glittering shops, doors closed for Sunday. The sunshine had drawn the people from the streets : to the park, to the lush green country, to the seaside. Of the few people they did meet, not all of them seemed to know who the poet was, but those who did know saluted quietly, with a modest and unaffected reverence, and one young man with a pretty girl on his arm stepped

178

off the pavement, looked after the poet and clearly whispered
to the maiden who it was that had just passed by the way.
Stepping behind him at a respectful distance Pike felt like an
acolyte behind a celebrant and regretted that there was no
cope or cloak of cloth of gold of which he could humbly carry
the train.

So they sailed north towards the Liffey, leaving Trinity
College, with Burke standing haughty-headed and Goldsmith
sipping at his honeypot of a book, to the right, and the Bank
and Grattan orating Esto Perpetua, to the left, and Thomas
Moore of the Melodies, brown, stooped and shabby, to the
right; and came into Westmoreland Street where the wonder
happened. For there approaching them came the woman
Homer sung : old and grey and, perhaps, full of sleep, a face
much and deeply lined and haggard, eyes sunken, yet still the
face of the queen she had been when she and the poet were
young and they had stood on the cliffs on Howth Head, high
above the promontory that bears the Bailey Lighthouse as a
warning torch and looks like the end of the world; and they
had watched the soaring of the gulls and he had wished that
he and she were only white birds, my beloved, buoyed out on
the foam of the sea. She was very tall. She was not white, but
all black in widow's weeds for the man she had married when
she wouldn't marry the poet. Her black hat had a wide brim
and, from the brim, an old-fashioned veil hung down before
her face. The pilgrim soul in you, and loved the sorrows of
your changing face.

Pike stood still, fearing that in a dream he had intruded on
some holy place. The poet and the woman moved dreamlike
towards each other, then stood still, not speaking, not saluting,
at opposite street corners where Fleet Street comes narrowly
from the East to join Westmoreland Street. Then still not speaking, not saluting, they turned into Fleet Street. When Pike
tiptoed to the corner and peered around he saw that they
had walked on opposite sides of the street for, perhaps, thirty
paces, then turned at right angles, moved towards each other,
stopped to talk in the middle of the street where a shaft of

sunlight had defied the tall overshadowing buildings. Apart
from themselves and Pike that portion of the town seemed to
be awesomely empty; and there Pike left them and walked in
a daze by the side of the Liffey to a pub called The Dark Cow.
Something odd had happened to him : poetry, a vision of love?

It so happened that on that day Butterfly was in the Dark
Cow, as, indeed, she often was : just Butterfly and Pike, and
Jody with the red carbuncled face who owned the place and
was genuinely kind to the girls of the town, and a few honest
dockers who didn't count because they had money only for their
own porter and were moral men, loyal to wives or sweethearts.
It wasn't the sort of place Pike frequented. He had never seen
Butterfly before : those odd slanting eyes, the glistening high-
piled black hair, the well-defined bud of a mouth, the crossed
legs, the knees that outclassed to the point of mockery all the
bronze globes in Stephen's Green. Coming on top of his vision
of the poet and the woman, all this was too much for him,
driving him to a reckless courage that would have flabbergasted
the three aunts. He leaned on the counter. She sat in an alcove
that was a sort of throne for her, where on busier days she sat
surrounded by her sorority. So he says to Jody whom he did not
yet know as Jody : May I have the favour of buying the lady
in the corner a drink?

—That you may, and more besides.

—Please ask her permission. We must do these things
properly.

—Oh there's a proper way of doing everything, even screwing
a goose.

But Jody, messenger of love, walks to the alcove and for-
mally asks the lady would she drink if the gentleman at the
counter sends it over. She will. She will also allow him to join
her. She whispers : Has he any money?

—Loaded, says Jody.

—Send him over so. Sunday's a dull day.

Pike sits down stiffly, leaning a little away from her, which
seems to her quite right for him as she has already decided that

he's a shy sort of man, upper class, but shy, not like some. He excuses himself from intruding. She says : You're not inthrudin'.

He says he hasn't the privilege of knowing her name.

Talks like a book, she decides, or a play in the Gaiety.

—Buttherfly, she says.

—Butterfly, he says, is a lovely name.

—Me mother's name was Trixie, she volunteers.

—Was she dark like you?

—Oh, a natural blonde and very busty, well developed, you know. She danced in the old Tivoli where the newspaper office is now. I'm neat, not busty.

To his confusion she indicates, with hands moving in small curves, the parts of her that she considers are neat. But he notices that she has shapely long-fingered hands and he remembers that the poet had admitted that the small hands of his beloved were not, in fact, beautiful. He is very perturbed.

—Neat, she says, and well-made. Austin McDonnell, the fire-brigade chief, says that he read in a book that the best sizes and shapes would fit into champagne glasses.

He did wonder a little that a fire-brigade chief should be a quotable authority on female sizes and shapes, and on champagne glasses. But then and there he decided to buy her champagne, the only drink fit for such a queen who seemed as if she came, if not from China, at any rate from Japan.

—Champagne, he said.

—Bubbly, she said. I love bubbly.

Jody dusted the shoulders of the bottle that on his shelves had waited a long time for a customer. He unwired the cork. The cork and the fizz shot up to the ceiling.

—This, she said, is my lucky day.

—The divine Bernhardt, said Pike, had a bath in champagne presented to her by a group of gentlemen who admired her.

—Water, she said, is better for washing.

But she told him that her mother who knew everything about actresses had told her that story, and told her that when, afterwards, the gentlemen bottled the contents of the bath and drank it, they had one bottleful too many. He was too far gone

in fizz and love's frenzy to feel embarrassed. She was his dis-
covery, his oriental queen.

He said : You're very oriental in appearance. You could be
from Japan.

She said : My father was, they say. A sailor. Sailors come
and go.

She giggled. She said : That's a joke. Come and go. Do you
see it?

Pike saw it. He giggled with her. He was a doomed man.

She said : Austin McDonnell says that if I was in Japan I
could be a geisha girl if I wasn't so tall. That's why they call
me Buttherfly. It's the saddest story. Poor Madame Buttherfly
died that her child could be happy across the sea. She married
a sailor, too, an American lieutenant. They come and go. The
priest, her uncle, cursed her for marrying a Yank.

—The priests are good at that, said Pike who, because of
his reading allowed himself, outside office hours, a soupçon of
anticlericalism.

Touched by Puccini they were silent for a while, sipping
champagne. With every sip Pike realised more clearly that he
had found what the poet, another poet, an English one, had
called the long-awaited long-expected spring, he knew his heart
had found a time to sing, the strength to soar was in his spirit's
wing, that life was full of a triumphant sound and death
could only be a little thing. She was good on the nose, too. She
was wise in the ways of perfume. The skin of her neck had a
pearly glow. The three guardian aunts were as far away as
the moon. Then one of the pub's two doors—it was a corner
house—opened with a crash and a big man came in, well
drunk, very jovial. He wore a wide-brimmed grey hat. He
walked to the counter. He said : Jody, old bootlegger, old friend
of mine, old friend of Al Capone, serve me a drink to sober
me up.

—Austin, said Jody, what will it be?

—A ball of malt, the big man said, and Madame Butterfly.

—That's my friend, Austin, she said, he always says that
for a joke.

Pike whose face, with love or champagne or indignation, was taut and hot all over, said that he didn't think it was much of a joke.

—Oh, for Janey's sake, Pike, be your age.

She used his first name for the first time. His eyes were moist.

—For Janey's sake, it's a joke. He's a father to me. He knew my mother.

—He's not Japanese.

—Mind your manners. He's a fireman.

—Austin, she called. Champagne. Pike Hunter's buying champagne.

Pike bought another bottle, while Austin towered above them, swept the wide-brimmed hat from his head in a cavalier half-circle, dropped it on the head of Jody whose red carbuncled face was thus half-extinguished. Butterfly giggled. She said: Austin, you're a scream. He knew Trixie, Pike. He knew Trixie when she was the queen of the boards in the old Tivoli.

Sitting down, the big man sang in a ringing tenor: For I knew Trixie when Trixie was a child.

He sipped at his ball of malt. He sipped at a glass of Pike's champagne. He said: It's a great day for the Irish. It's a great day to break a fiver. Butterfly, dear girl, we fixed the Longford lout. He'll never leave Longford again. The wife has him tethered and spancelled in the haggard. We wrote poison-pen letters to half the town, including the parish priest.

—I never doubted ye, she said. Leave it to the firemen, I said.

—The Dublin Fire Brigade, Austin said, has as long an arm as the Irish Republican Army.

—Austin, she told Pike, died for Ireland.

He sipped champagne. He sipped whiskey. He said: Not once, but several times. When it was neither popular nor profitable. By the living God, we was there when we was wanted. Volunteer McDonnell, at your service.

His bald head shone and showed freckles. His startlingly blue eyes were brightened and dilated by booze. He said: Did I know Trixie, light on her feet as the foam on the fountain?

Come in and see the horses. That's what we used to say to the girls when I was a young fireman. Genuine horsepower the fire-engines ran on then, and the harness hung on hooks ready to drop on the horses as the firemen descended the greasy pole. And where the horses were, the hay and the straw were plentiful enough to make couches for Cleopatra. That was why we asked the girls in to see the horses. The sailors from the ships, homeless men all, had no such comforts and conveniences. They used to envy us. Butterfly, my geisha girl, you should have been alive then. We'd have shown you the jumps.

Pike was affronted. He was almost prepared to say so and take the consequences. But Butterfly stole his thunder. She stood up, kissed the jovial big man smack on the bald head and then, as light on her feet as her mother ever could have been, danced up and down the floor, tight hips bouncing, fingers clicking, singing: I'm the smartest little geisha in Japan, in Japan. And the people call me Rolee Polee Nan, Polee Nan.

Drowning in desire, Pike forgot his indignation and found that he was liking the man who could provoke such an exhibition. Breathless, she sat down again, suddenly kissed Pike on the cheek, said: I love you too. I love champagne. Let's have another bottle.

They had.

—Rolee Polee Nan, she sang as the cork and the fizz ascended.

—A great writer, a Russian, Pike said, wrote that his ideal was to be idle and to make love to a plump girl.

—The cheek of him. I'm not plump. Turkeys are plump. I love being tall, with long legs.

Displaying the agility of a trained high-kicker with hinges in her hips she, still sitting, raised her shapely right leg, up and up as if her toes would touch the ceiling, up and up until stocking-top, suspender, bare thigh and a frill of pink panties, showed. Something happened to Pike that had nothing at all to do with poetry or Jody's champagne. He held Butterfly's hand. She made a cat's cradle with their fingers and swung the locked hands pendulum-wise. She sang: Janey Mac, the child's a black, what will we do on Sunday? Put him to bed and cover his head and don't let him up until Monday.

Austin had momentarily absented himself for gentlemanly reasons. From the basement jakes his voice singing rose above the soft inland murmur of falling water: Oh my boat can lightly float in the heel of wind and weather, and outrace the smartest hooker between Galway and Kinsale.

The dockers methodically drank their pints of black porter and paid no attention. Jody said: Time's money. Why don't the two of you slip upstairs. Your heads would make a lovely pair on a pillow.

Austin was singing: Oh she's neat, oh she's sweet, she's a beauty every line, the Queen of Connemara is that bounding barque of mine.

He was so shy, Butterfly said afterwards, that he might have been a Christian Brother and a young one at that, although where or how she ever got the experience to enable her to make the comparison, or why she should think an old Christian Brother less cuthallacht than a young one, she didn't say. He told her all about the aunts and the odd way he had been reared and she, naturally, told Austin and Jody and all her sorority. But they were a kind people and no mockers, and Pike never knew, Austin told me, that Jody's clientele listened with such absorbed interest to the story of his life, and of his heart and his love-making. He was something new in their experience, and Jody's stable of girls had experienced a lot, and Austin a lot more, and Jody more than the whole shebang, and all the fire-brigade, put together.

For Jody, Austin told me, had made the price of the Dark Cow in a basement in Chicago. During the prohibition, as they called it, although what they prohibited it would be hard to say. He was one of five brothers from the bogs of Manulla in the middle of nowhere in the County of Mayo. The five of them emigrated to Chicago. When Al Capone and his merry men discovered that Jody and his brothers had the real true secret about how to make booze, and to make it good, down they went into the cellar and didn't see daylight nor breathe fresh air, except to surface to go to Mass on Sundays, until they left the U.S.A. They made a fair fortune. At least four of them did. The fifth was murdered.

Jody was a bachelor man and he was good to the girls. He took his pleasures with them as a gentleman might, with the natural result that he was poxed to the eyebrows. But he was worth more to them than the money he quite generously paid after every turn or trick on the rumpled, always unmade bed in the two-storeyed apartment above the pub. He was a kind uncle to them. He gave them a friendly welcome, a place to sit down, free drink and smokes and loans, or advances for services yet to be rendered, when they were down on their luck. He had the ear of the civic guards and could help a girl when she was in trouble. He paid fines when they were unavoidable, and bills when they could no longer be postponed, and had an aunt who was reverend mother in a home for unmarried mothers and who was, like her nephew, a kindly person. Now and again, like the Madame made immortal by Maupassant, he took a bevy or flock of the girls for a day at the seaside or in the country. A friend of mine and myself, travelling into the granite mountains south of the city, to the old stone-cutters' villages of Lackan and Ballyknockan where there were aged people who had never seen Dublin, thirty miles away, and never wanted to, came upon a most delightful scene in the old country pub in Lackan. All around the bench around the walls sat the mountainy men, the stone-cutters, drinking their pints. But the floor was in the possession of a score of wild girls, all dancing together, resting off and on for more drink, laughing, happy, their gaiety inspired and directed by one man in the middle of the floor : red-faced, carbuncled, oily black hair sleeked down and parted up the middle in the style of Dixie Dean, the famous soccer centre-forward, whom Jody so much admired. All the drinks were on generous Jody.

So in Jody's friendly house Pike had, as he came close to forty years, what he never had in the cold abode of the three aunts : a home with a father, Austin, and a brother, Jody, and any God's amount of sisters; and Butterfly who, to judge by the tales she told afterwards, was a motherly sort of lover to him and, for a while, a sympathetic listener. For a while, only : because nothing in her birth, background, rearing or education, had equipped her to listen to so much poetry and talk about poetry.

—Poor Pike, she'd say, he'd puke you with poethry. Poethry's all very well, but.

She had never worked out what came after that qualifying : But.

—Give us a bar of a song, Austin. There's some sense to singing. But poethry. My heart leaps up when I behold a rainbow in the sky. On Linden when the sun was low. The lady of Shalott left the room to go to the pot. Janey preserve us from poethry.

He has eyes, Jody told Austin and myself, for no girl except Butterfly. Reckon, in one way, we can't blame him for that. She sure is the smartest filly showing in this paddock. But there must be moderation in all things. Big Anne, now, isn't bad, nor her sister, both well-built Sligo girls and very co-operative, nor Joany Maher from Waterford, nor Patty Daley from Castleisland in the County Kerry who married the Limey in Brum but left him when she found he was as queer as a three-dollar bill. And what about little Red Annie Byrne from Kilkenny City, very attractive if it just wasn't for the teeth she lost when the cattleman that claimed he caught gonorrhoea from her gave her an unmerciful hammering in Cumberland Street. We got him before he left town. We cured more than his gonorrhoea.

—But, Austin said, when following your advice, Jody, and against my own better judgment, I tried to explain all that to Pike, what does he do but quote to me what the playboy of the Abbey Theatre, John M. Synge, wrote in a love poem about counting queens in Glenmacnass in the Wicklow mountains.

—In the Wicklow mountains, said Jody. Queens? With the smell of the bog and the peat smoke off them.

Austin, a great man, ever, to sing at the top of his tenor voice about Dark Rosaleen and the Queen of Connemara and the County of Mayo, was a literary class of a fireman. That was one reason why Pike and himself got on so well together, in spite of that initial momentary misunderstanding about the ball of malt and Madame Butterfly.

—Seven dog days, Austin said, the playboy said he let pass, he and his girl, counting queens in Glenmacnass. The queens he mentions, Jody, you never saw, even in Chicago.

—Never saw daylight in Chicago.

—The Queen of Sheba, Austin said, and Helen, and Maeve the warrior queen of Connacht, and Deirdre of the Sorrows and Gloriana that was the great Elizabeth of England and Judith out of the Bible that chopped the block of Holofernes.

—All, said Jody, in a wet glen in Wicklow. A likely bloody story.

—There was one queen in the poem that had an amber belly.

—Jaundice, said Jody. Or Butterfly herself that's as sallow as any Jap. Austin, you're a worse lunatic than Pike.

—But in the end, Jody, his own girl was the queen of all queens. They were dead and rotten. She was alive.

—Not much of a compliment to her, Jody said, to prefer her to a cartload of corpses.

—Love's love, Jody. Even the girls admit that. They've no grudge against him for seeing nobody but Butterfly.

—They give him a fool's pardon. But no doll in the hustling game, Austin, can afford to spend all her time listening to poetry. Besides, girls like a variety of pricks. Butterfly's no better or worse than the next. When Pike finds that out he'll go crazy. If he isn't crazy already.

That was the day, as I recall, that Butterfly came in wearing the fancy fur coat—just a little out of season. Jody had, for some reason or other, given her a five-pound note. Pike knew nothing about that. And Jody told her to venture the five pounds on a horse that was running at the Curragh of Kildare, that a man in Kilcullen on the edge of the Curragh had told

188

him that the jockey's wife had already bought her ball dress for the victory celebration. The Kilcullen man knew his onions, and his jockeys, and shared his wisdom only with a select few so as to keep the odds at a good twenty to one.

—She's gone out to the bookie's, said Jody, to pick up her winnings. We'll have a party tonight.

Jody had a tenner on the beast.

—She could invest it, said Austin, if she was wise. The day will come when her looks will go.

—Pike might propose to her, said Jody. He's mad enough for anything.

—The aunts would devour him. And her.

—Here she comes, Jody said. She invested her winnings on her fancy back.

She had too, and well she carried them in the shape of pale or silver musquash, and three of her sorority walked behind her like ladies-in-waiting behind the Queen of England. There was a party in which even the dockers joined, but not Pike, for that evening and night one of his aunts was at death's door in a nursing home, and Pike and the other two aunts were by her side. He wasn't to see the musquash until he took Butterfly on an outing to the romantic hill of Howth where the poet and the woman had seen the white birds. That was the last day Pike ever took Butterfly anywhere. The aunt recovered. They were a thrawn hardy trio.

Pike had become a devotee. Every day except Sunday he lunched in Jody's, on a sandwich of stale bread and leathery ham and a glass of beer, just on the off-chance that Butterfly might be out of the doss and abroad, and in Jody's, at that, to her, unseasonable hour of the day. She seldom was, except when she was deplorably short of money. In the better eating places on Grafton Street and Stephen's Green, his colleagues absorbed the meals that enabled higher civil servants to face up to the afternoon and the responsibilities of State : statistics, land commission, local government, posts and telegraphs, internal revenue. He had never, among his own kind, been much of a mixer: so that few of his peers even noticed the speed with which, when at five in the evening the official day was done, he took himself, and his hat and coat and umbrella, and legged it off to Jody's: in the hope that Butterfly might be there, bathed and perfumed and ready for wine and love. Sometimes she was. Sometimes she wasn't. She liked Pike. She didn't deny it. She was always an honest girl, as her mother, Trixie, had been before her—so Austin said when he remembered Trixie who had died in a hurry, of peritonitis. But, Janey Mac, Butterfly couldn't have Pike Hunter for breakfast, dinner, tea and supper, and nibblers as well, all the livelong day and night. She still, as Jody said, had her first million to make, and Pike's inordinate attachment was coming between her and the real big business, as when, say, the country cattle men were in town for the market. They were the men who knew how to get rid of the money.

—There is this big cattle man, she tells Austin once, big he is in every way, who never knows or cares what he's spending. He's a gift and a godsend to the girls. He gets so drunk that all you have to do to humour him is play with him a little in the taxi going from pub to pub and see that he gets safely to his hotel. The taximen are on to the game and get their divy out of the loot.

One wet and windy night, it seems, Butterfly and this philanthropist are flying high together, he on brandy, she on champagne, for which that first encounter with Pike has given her a ferocious drouth. In the back of the taxi touring from pub to pub, the five pound notes are flowing out of your man like water out of a pressed sponge. Butterfly is picking them up and stuffing them into her handbag, but not all of them. For this is too good and too big for any taximan on a fair percentage basis. So for every one note she puts into her handbag she stuffs two or three down into the calf-length boots she is wearing against the wet weather. She knows, you see, that she is too far gone in bubbly to walk up the stairs to her own room, that the taximan, decent fellow, will help her up and then, fair enough, go through her bag and take his cut. Which, indeed, in due time he does. When she wakes up, fully clothed, in the morning on her own bed, and pulls off her boots, her ankles, what with the rain that had dribbled down into her boots, are poulticed and plastered with notes of the banks of Ireland and of England, and one moreover of the Bank of Bonnie Scotland.

—Rings on my fingers, she says, and bells on my toes.

That was the gallant life that Pike's constant attendance was cutting her off from. She also hated being owned. She hated other people thinking that she was owned. She hated like hell when Pike would enter the Dark Cow and one of the other girls or, worse still, another man, a bit of variety, would move away from her side to let Pike take the throne. They weren't married, for Janey's sake. She could have hated Pike, except that she was as tender-hearted as Trixie had been, and she liked champagne. She certainly felt at liberty to hate the three aunts who made a mollycoddle out of him. She also hated, with a hatred that grew and grew, the way that Pike puked her with poethry. And all this time poor Pike walked in a dream that he never defined for us, perhaps not even for himself, but that certainly must have looked higher than the occasional trick on Jody's rumpled bed. So dreaming, sleep-walking, he persuaded Butterfly to go to Howth Head with him one dull hot day when the town was empty and she had nothing better to do. No place could have been more fatally poetic than Howth. She wore her musquash. Not even the heat could part her from it.

—He never let up, she said, not once from the moment we boarded the bus on the quays. Poethry. I had my bellyful.

—Sure thing, said Jody.

—Any man, she said, that won't pay every time he performs is a man to keep a cautious eye on. Not that he's not generous. But at the wrong times. Money down or no play's my motto.

—Well I know that, Jody said.

—But Pike Hunter says that would make our love mercenary, whatever that is.

—You're a great girl, said Austin, to be able to pronounce it.

—Your middle name, said Jody, is mercenary.

—My middle name, thank you, is Imelda. And the cheek of Pike Hunter suggesting to me to go to a doctor because he noticed something wrong with himself, a kidney disorder, he said. He must wet the bed.

—Butterfly, said Austin, he might have been giving you good advice.

—Nevertheless. It's not for him to say.

When they saw from the bus the Bull Wall holding the northern sand back from clogging up the harbour, and the Bull Island, three miles long, with dunes, bent grass, golfers, bathers and skylarks, Pike told her about some fellow called Joyce—there was a Joyce in the Civic Guards, a Galwayman who played county football, but no relation—who had gone walking on the Island one fine day and laid eyes on a young one, wading in a pool, with her skirts well pulled up; and let a roar out of him. By all accounts this Joyce was no addition to the family for, as Pike told the story, Butterfly worked out that the young one was well under age.

Pike and Butterfly had lunch by the edge of the sea, in the Claremont Hotel, and that was all right. Then they walked in the grounds of Howth Castle, Pike had a special pass and the flowers and shrubs were a sight to see if only Pike had kept his mouth shut about some limey by the name of Spenser who landed there in the year of God, and wrote a poem as long as from here to Killarney about a fairy queen and a gentle knight who was pricking on the plain like the members of the Harp Cycling Club, Junior Branch, up above there in the Phoenix Park. He didn't get time to finish the poem, the poet that is, not Pike, for the Cork people burned him out of house and home and, as far as Butterfly was concerned, that was the only good deed she ever heard attributed to the Cork people.

The Phoenix Park and the Harp Club reminded her that one day Jody had said, meaning no harm, about the way Pike moped around the Dark Cow when Butterfly wasn't there, that Pike was the victim of a semi-horn and should go up to the Fifteen Acres and put it in the grass for a while and run around it. But when, for fun, she told this to Pike he got so huffed he didn't speak for half an hour, and they walked Howth Head until her feet were blistered and the heel of her right shoe broke, and the sweat, with the weight of the musquash and the heat of the day, was running between her shoulder-blades like a cloudburst down the gutter. Then the row and the ructions, as the song says, soon began. He said she should have worn flat-heeled shoes. She said that if she had known that he was conscripting her for a forced march over a mountain she'd have borrowed a pair of boots from the last soldier she gave it to at cut-price, for the soldiers, God help them, didn't have much money but they were more open-handed with what they had than some people who had plenty, and soldiers didn't waste time and breath on poetry : Be you fat or be you lean there is no soap like Preservene.

So she sat on the summit of Howth and looked at the lighthouse and the seagulls, while Pike walked back to the village to have the broken heel mended, and the sweat dried cold on her, and she was perished. Then when he came back, off he was again about how that white-headed old character that you'd see across the river there at the Abbey Theatre, and Madame Gone Mad McBride that was the age of ninety and looked it, and known to all as a roaring rebel, worse than Austin, had stood there on that very spot, and how the poet wrote a poem wishing for himself and herself to be turned into seagulls, the big dirty brutes that you'd see along the docks robbing the pigeons of their food. Butterfly would have laughed at him, except that her teeth by this time were tap-dancing with the cold like the twinkling feet of Fred Astaire. So she pulled her coat around her and said : Pike, I'm no seagull. For Janey's sake take me back to civilisation and Jody's where I know someone.

But, God sees, you never knew nobody, for at that moment the caveman came out in Pike Hunter, he that was always so backward on Jody's bed and, there and then, he tried to flatten her in the heather in full view of all Dublin and the coast of Ireland as far south as Wicklow Head and as far north as where the Mountains of Mourne sweep down to the sea.

—Oh none of that, Pike Hunter, she says, my good musquash will be crucified. There's a time and a place and a price for everything.

You and your musquash, he tells her.

They were wrestling like Man Mountain Dean and Jack Doyle, the Gorgeous Gael.

—You've neither sense nor taste, says he, to be wearing a fur coat on a day like this.

—Bloody well for you to talk, says she, with your rolled umbrella and your woollen combinations and your wobbly ass that won't keep you straight in the chair, and your three witches of maiden aunts never touched, tasted or handled by mortal man, and plenty of money and everything your own way. This is my only coat that's decent, in case you haven't noticed, and I earned it hard and honest with Jody, a generous man but a monster on the bed, I bled after him.

That put a stop to the wrestling. He brought her back to the Dark Cow and left her at the door and went his way.

He never came back to the Dark Cow but once, and Butterfly wasn't on her throne that night. It was the night before the cattle-market. He was so lugubrious and woebegone that Jody and Austin and a few merry newspaper men, including myself, tried to jolly him up, take him out of himself, by making jokes at his expense that would force him to come alive and answer back. Our efforts failed. He looked at us sadly and said : Boys, Beethoven, when he was dying, said : Clap now, good friends, the comedy is done.

He was more than a little drunk and, for the first time, seemed lopsided when standing up; and untidy.

—Clap now indeed, said Jody.

Pike departed and never returned. He took to steady drinking in places like the Shelbourne Hotel or the Buttery in the Hibernian where it was most unlikely, even with Dublin being the democratic sort of town that it is, that he would ever encounter Madame Butterfly. He became a great problem for his colleagues and his superior officers in the civil service, and for his three aunts. After careful consultation they, all together, persuaded him to rest up in Saint Patrick's Hospital where, as you all may remember, Dean Swift died roaring. Which was, I feel sure, why Pike wasn't there to pay the last respects to the dead when Jody dropped from a heart attack and was waked in the bedroom above the Dark Cow. The girls were there in force to say an eternal farewell to a good friend. Since the drink was plentiful and the fun and the mourning intense, somebody, not even Austin knew who, suggested that the part of the corpse that the girls knew best should be tastefully decorated with black crepe ribbon. The honour of tying on the ribbon naturally went to Madame Butterfly but it was Big Anne who burst into tears and cried out : Jody's dead and gone forever.

Austin met her, Butterfly not Big Anne, a few days afterwards at the foot of the Nelson Pillar. Jody's successor had routed the girls from the Dark Cow. Austin told her about Pike and where he was. She brooded a bit. She said it was a pity, but nobody could do nothing for him, that those three aunts had spoiled him for ever and, anyway, didn't Austin think that he was a bit astray in the head.

—Who knows, Butterfly? Who's sound or who's silly? Consider yourself for a moment.

—What about me, Austin?

—A lovely girl like you, a vision from the romantic east, and think of the life you lead. It can have no good ending. Let me tell you a story, Butterfly. There was a girl once in London, a slavey, a poor domestic servant. I knew a redcoat here in the old British days who said he preferred slaveys to anything else because they were clean, free and flattering.

—Austin, I was never a slavey.

—No Butterfly, you have your proper pride. But listen : this slavey is out one morning scrubbing the stone steps in front of the big house she works in, bucket and brush, carbolic soap and all that, in one of the great squares in one of the more classy parts of London Town. There she is on her bended knees when a gentleman walks past, a British army major in the Cold-stream Guards or the Black Watch or something.

—I've heard of them, Austin.

—So this British major looks at her, and he sees the naked backs of her legs, thighs you know, and taps her on the shoulder or somewhere and he says : Oh, rise up, lovely maiden and come along with me, there's a better life in store for you somewhere else. She left the bucket and the brush, and the stone steps half-scrubbed, and walked off with him and became his girl. But there were even greater things in store for her. For, Butterfly, that slavey became Lady Emma Hamilton, the beloved of Lord Nelson, the greatest British sailor that ever sailed, and the victor of the renowned battle of Trafalgar. There he is up on the top of the Pillar.

—You wouldn't think to look at him, Austin, that he had much love in him.

—But, Butterfly, meditate on that story, and rise up and get yourself out of the gutter. You're handsome enough to be the second Lady Hamilton.

After that remark, Austin brought her into Lloyd's, a famous house of worship in North Earl Street under the shadow of Lord Nelson and his pillar. In Lloyd's he bought her a drink and out of the kindness of his great singing heart, gave her some money. She shook his hand and said : Austin, you're the nicest man I ever met.

Austin had, we may suppose, given her an image, an ideal. She may have been wearied by Pike and his sad attachment to poetry, but she rose to the glimmering vision of herself as a great lady beloved by a great and valiant lord. A year later she married a docker, a decent quiet hard-working fellow who had slowly sipped his pints of black porter and watched and waited all the time.

Oddly enough, Austin told me when the dignity of old age had gathered around him like the glow of corn-stubble in the afterwards of harvest.

He could still sing. His voice never grew old.

—Oddly enough, I never had anything to do with her. That

way, I mean. Well you know me. Fine wife, splendid sons, nobody like them in the world. Fine daughters, too. But a cousin of mine, a ship's wireless operator who had been all round the world from Yokohama to the Belgian Congo and back again, and had had a ship burned under him in Bermuda and, for good value, another ship burned under him in Belfast, said she was the meanest whore he ever met. When he had paid her the stated price, there were some coppers left in his hand and she grabbed them and said : give us these for the gas-meter.

But he said, also, that at the high moments she had a curious and diverting way of raising and bending and extending her left leg—not her right leg which she kept as flat as a plumb-level. He had never encountered the like before, in any colour or in any country.

THE WEAVERS AT THE MILL

Baxbakualanuxsiwae, she said to herself as she walked by the sea, was one of the odd gods of the Kwakiutl Indians, and had the privilege of eating human flesh. That pale-faced woman with the strained polite accent would devour me if her teeth were sharp enough. She even calls me, intending it as an insult, Miss Vancouver, although she knows damned well in her heart and mind, if she has a heart, that I don't come from Vancouver.

She loved the vast flat strand, the distant sea, the wraith-like outline of rocky islands that looked as if they were sailing in the sky, the abruptness with which a brook cradled by flat green fields became a wide glassy sheet of water spreading out over the sand.

A thatched cottage, gable end to the inshore gales, was palisaded against the sea by trunks of trees driven deep into the sand. On the sea-front road that curved around the shanty village, wind and water had tossed seaweed over the wall so regularly that it looked like nets spread out to dry. All the young men she met on the road wore beards they had grown for the night's pageant : not the melancholy, wishy-washy, desiccated-coconut pennants of artistic integrity but solid square-cut beards or shaggy beards that birds could nest in. To walk among them was a bit like stepping back into some old picture of the time of Charles Stewart Parnell : stern men marching home to beleagured cabins from a meeting of the Land League.

That woman would say : They are all so handsome.

She was long-faced, pale and languid, the sort of woman who would swoon with craven delight at the rub of a beard. Yet she could never persuade the old man to abandon his daily careful ritual with cut-throat razor, wooden soap bowl, the strop worn to a waist in the middle, the fragments of news-paper splattered with blobs of spent lather and grey stubble.

—Eamonn, she would say to her husband, if you'd only grow a beard you'd look like Garibaldi with his goats on the island of Caprera.

—I have no knowledge of goats. I'm not on my own island any more.

To the girl she would say : If your bags are packed I'll run you at any time to the station.

—My bags are always packed. There's only one of them. A duffle-bag, she'd answer. But if it doesn't inconvenience you too much I'd like to stay another day. There are a few details I want to fill in.

It needed nerve to talk to a woman like that in her own house. But what could the girl do when the old man was plaintively urging her not to go, not to go, pay no heed to her, stay another day.

They had breakfast in bed every day and lunch in their own rooms, and all the time until four in the afternoon free. It was in some ways the most relaxed life the girl had ever known. She had been there for a week since she had come from London across England, Wales, the Irish Sea and a part of Ireland, to write one more article in the magazine series that kept her eating. It was a series about little-known heroes of our time.

The woman had met her at the train. She drove a station-wagon piled high in the back with hanks of coloured wool. They drove round the village, foam glimmering in the dusk to their right hand, then across a humped five-arched stone bridge and up a narrow, sunken, winding roadway to the old Mill House in the middle of gaunt, grey, eyeless ruins where—above the river foaming down a narrow valley—two hundred men had worked in days of a simple local economy. Four grass-grown waterwheels rusted and rested for ever.

—Only my weavers work here now, she said. That's what the wool's for. Aran sweaters and belts—criosanna, they call them here—and scarves and cardigans. We sell them in the States where you come from.

She sounded as friendly as her over-refined, Henley-on-Thames voice could allow her to sound.

—Canada, the girl said. British Columbia. My father worked among the Kwakiutl Indians.

—Can't say I ever heard of them. What do they do?

—They were cannibals once. For religious reasons. But not any longer. They catch salmon. They sing songs. They carve totem poles. They weave good woollens, too. With simplified totem designs.

—How interesting.

The car went under a stone archway topped by a shapeless mass that she was to discover had once represented a re-arising phoenix—until rain and salt gales had disfigured it to a death deeper than ashes. They were in a cobbled courtyard and then in a garage that had once been part of a stables.

—You want to write about my husband's lifeboat exploits when he was an islandman.

—The famous one. I was asked to write about it. Or ordered. I read it up in the newspaper files. It was heroic.

She slung the duffle-bag over her shoulder and they walked towards the seven-windowed face of the old stone house. From the loft above the garage the clacking of looms kept mocking time to their steps. The woman said : Do you always dress so informally?

—I travel a lot and light. Leather jacket and corduroy slacks. You need them in my business. A protection against pinchers and pawsey men.

—You're safe here, said the woman. The men are quiet. All the young ones have just grown lovely beards for a parish masque or a pageant or something. You mustn't tire him too much. Sometimes he can get unbearably excited when he remembers his youth.

His youth, the girl reckoned, was a long time ago.

She spread out her few belongings between the old creaking mahogany wardrobe and the marble-topped dressing-table, and tidied herself for dinner, and remembered that she had left her typewriter, smothered in wool, in the station-wagon. The newspaper that had told her about the rescue had been fifty years old; and Eamonn, the brave coxswain and the leader of the heroic crew, had been then a well-developed man of thirty. The newsprint picture had faded, but not so badly that she couldn't see the big man, a head taller than any of his companions, laughing under his sou'wester with all the easy mirth of a man who had never yet been afraid.

From her bedroom window she could look down into the courtyard and see girls in blue overalls carrying armfuls of wool from the wagon up an outside wooden stairway to the weaving shed. The thatched roofs of the village were, from her height, like a flock of yellow birds nestling by the edge of the sea and, far across the water, the outlines of the islands of Eamonn's origin faded into the darkness, as distant and lost for ever as his daring youth and manhood. Yet she knew so little, or had reflected so little, on the transfiguring power of time that she was ill-prepared for the gaunt, impressive wreck of a man who came slowly into a dining-room that was elaborately made up to look like a Glocamorra farmhouse kitchen. He sat down on a low chair by the open hearth and silently accepted a bowl of lentil soup with fragments of bread softening in it. He didn't even glance at the low unstained oak table where the girl sat most painfully, on a traditional three-legged wooden chair. Dressed in black, her black hair piled on her head, her oblong face, by lamplight, longer and whiter than ever, the woman sat aloof at the head of the table. Two girls, daytime weavers magically transformed by the touch of the creeping dusk into night-time waitresses, blue overalls exchanged for dark dresses, white aprons, white collars, served the table; and a third stood like a nurse behind the old man's chair. He slopped with a spoon, irritably rejecting the handmaiden's effort to aid him. He recited to himself what was to the girl an unintelligible sing-song.

—Merely counting, the woman said. In Gaelic. One, two,

three, and so on. He says it soothes him and helps his memory. I told him what you want. He'll talk when he's ready.

Suddenly he said : She cracked right across the middle, that merchant vessel, and she stuffed as full as a fat pig with the costliest bales of goods and furniture and God knows what. I can tell you there are houses on this coast but not out on the islands where the people are honest and no wreckers, and those houses are furnished well to this day on account of what the waves brought in that night.

The voice came out like a bell, defying and belying time, loud and melodious as when he must have roared over the billows to his comrades the time the ship cracked. Then he handed the empty soup bowl to the nervous weaver-hand-maiden, sat up high in his chair, bade the girl welcome in Gaelic, and said to the woman : She's not one of the French people from the hotel.

—From London, said the woman.

—There's a fear on the people in the village below that there won't be a duck or a hen or any class of a domestic fowl left alive to them with the shooting of these French people. The very sparrows in the hedges and God's red robins have no guarantee of life while they're about. They came over in the beginning for the sea-angling and, when they saw all the birds we have, nothing would satisfy them but to go home to France for their guns. They say they have all the birds in France shot. And the women with them are worse than the men.

—Les femmes de la chasse, said the woman.

—Patsy Glynn the postman tells me there's one six feet high with hair like brass and legs on her like Diana and wading boots up to her crotch. God, Pats said to me, and I agreed, the pity Eamonn, you're not seventy again, or that the Capall himself is dead and in the grave. He'd manipulate her, long legs and boots and all.

—Our visitor, said the woman, is not here to write about the Capall.

—Then, girl from London, 'tis little knowledge you have of writing. For there have been books written about men that weren't a patch on the Capall's breeches. A horse of a man and a stallion outright for the women. That was why we called him the Capall.

With a raised right hand and cracking fingers the woman had dismissed the three girls. This was no talk for servants to hear.

—That John's Eve on the island, the night of the bonfires and midsummer, and every man's blood warm with poteen and porter in Dinny O'Brien's pub. Dinny, the old miser that he was, serving short measure and gloating over the ha'pennies. But, by God, the joke was on him and didn't we know it. For wasn't the Capall in the barn-loft at the back of the house with Dinny's young wife that married him for money, for that was all Dinny had to offer. She had to lie down for two days in bed, drinking nothing but milk, after the capers of the Capall and herself in the loft. He walked in the back door of the bar, his shirt open to the navel, no coat on him and the sweat on him like oil. Two pints he drank and saw for the first time the new barmaid, a niece of Dinny, that had come all the way from Cork City, and the fat dancing on her and her dress thin. So he lifted the third pint and said : Dhia ! Is trua nach bhfuil dara bud ag duine.

Feeling that she did understand, and close to coarse laughter, the girl said that she didn't understand. Coldly and precisely the woman said : To put it politely he regretted that he was merely one man, not two.

—But he saved my life did the Capall. For the gale swept us, and the eight men we took off the broken vessel, eastwards before it to a port in Wales. There was no turning back in the teeth of it. There we were trying to moor the boat by the mole in another country when, with weariness and the tossing of the water, didn't I slip and go down between the wall and the boat, to be crushed, sure as God, if the Capall hadn't hooked his elbow in mine and thrown me back into the boat the way a prize wrestler would. Remember that bit, girl, when you write the story, and thank God you never met the Capall on a lonely road. He came from a place called the Field of the Strangers that was the wildest place on the whole island. From the hill above it you could see the wide ocean all the way to Africa, and the spray came spitting in over the roofs of the little houses, and the salt burned the grass in the fields. There was no strand in it, no breakwater, no harbour or slip for boats. Nothing man ever built could stand against that ocean. You held the currach steady and leaped into it from a flat rock as you shot out to sea. But there were men of strength and valour reared there who could conquer valleys before them and throw sledge-hammers over high houses. Dried sea bream we ate, boiled or roasted over hot sods, the strongest sweetest food in the world. And rock birds taken in nets where they'd nest in the clefts of the cliffs. Bread and tea for a treat, and potatoes boiled or brusselled in the griosach.

The woman explained : Roasted in the hot peat ashes.

—Then a cow might break a leg in a split in the rocks and have to be destroyed. A black disaster in one way. But in another way a feast of fresh meat and liver with the blood running out of it, food for men. All out of tins nowadays, and nobody has his own teeth.

The woman said : You were, Eamonn, talking about the lifeboat.

—Good for its own purpose the lifeboat, he said. But you couldn't feel the heart of the sea beating in it as you could in the canvas currach. We had one fellow with us that night who always had ill luck with currachs. Three of them he lost, and once he nearly lost his life. So we put him in the crew of the lifeboat to break his ill-fortune, and the trick worked. It could be that the sea didn't recognise him in his new yellow oilskins. Three days in that Welsh town we sweated in kneeboots and oilskins, having nothing else to wear, and the gales blowing in against us all the time. But the welcome we got. Didn't a depu-tation of ladies come to us with a white sheet of cloth to draw our names on, so that they could embroider our names for ever on the flag of the town's football team. Didn't the Capall write himself down as Martin McIntyre the Horse. There was the laughing, I can tell you, when the ladies wanted us to tell them why we put the title of the horse on Martin. They made heroes out of us. It was a sea-going town and there wasn't a woman in it hadn't a son or a husband or a lover on the salt water.

The attendant girls had come back silently. His great head, shaggy with uncombed white hair, sank down. With a napkin one of the girls mopped a splatter of soup from the green leather zipper jacket and, startlingly, with the yeeow of a shout a young fellow would give at a country dance, he came awake and slapped her buttocks before she could leap, laughing and blushing, and seemingly well used to the horseplay, out of his reach. The woman looked at the servant and then at her food. She said : Don't tire yourself.

—Never saw the tired day, he said, that the smell of a young girl wouldn't put life into me.

—Tell me more, said the girl, about the sea.

—What would you want to know about the sea and you from the smoky heart of London?

—I'm not from London.

—From Canada, said the woman. Her girlhood companions were cannibalistic Indians.

—On an island, the girl said.

He was wide awake, and interested, and upright. How tall he was when he sat up straight.

—Tell me, he said, about your wild Indians and your island.

Because he had hard blue eyes with a compelling icy light in them, and because for her benefit he had so carefully dredged his memory, she wanted to tell him. She wanted to tell him even more because as soon as he showed interest she had sensed the first stirrings of antagonism in the woman.

—Eamonn, the woman said, our guest may be tired.

—Tell me a little, he said. It's lucky to begin a story by lamplight.

—Nothing much to tell, she said. Don't think of me as sitting in the middle of a pack of noble savages, chewing on a hunk of Tyee salmon while they ate long pig. I didn't grow up with drums and war chants throbbing around me. I was some

205

miles distant, on the other side of the hill. Of course I had plenty of contact with the confused no-man's-land Indian that the white man has made. Studied their history and sociology at college. But when I was a little girl the closest I got to them was to run to the top of the hill and peep down through cedar branches at the noble Indians pulling the guts out of salmon. Sounds bitter I know. But beauty and nobility had left them for a long while. And in our village the groups were so divided that not even the minds of the children could meet. When I was a girl I remember trying to get a little Indian girl to tell me some of her words. She stayed sullen and very silent. Then finally she and her little friend giggled and spat out one word. Matsooie—that was what it sounded like. I found out later that she had simply been saying : what's the matter with you? It was a rebuff.

—It's sad, he said, when people don't understand you, no matter what you do or try to do. We'll talk more tomorrow, girl, when you've rested after your journey.

—I've talked too much, she said. I came to listen to you.

He rose alertly when she passed him and shook her hand in a solemn old-fashioned way. He belonged to a time when men shook hands elaborately at every meeting and parting.

Later—very much later—she thought drowsily that she heard his slow tread on the old creaking stairs, his coughing in the next room as he lay down on his bed; and far away the faint sound of the sea along the shore and around the islands.

She carried two notebooks always in the right-hand pocket of her leather jacket.

All women, said the hopeful man she had met on the Irish Mail, are lascivious.

One of the notebooks was paper-backed, spined with spiral wire, and with tear-out leaves. It was for ephemera and tem-poralities—in other words, her work. The other book was stiff-backed, with stable, ruled leaves for the recording of the experiences she would use when the day would come and she'd sit down really to write. The stiff-backed book had another

206

quality: it kept the weaker member straight in her jacket pocket, for she found nothing more maddening than note-taking on a page that was bent like a crescent.

The people she met she divided into two classes: tear-outs or stiff-backs.

This wonderful old man, an aged hero recalling islands, immured here by a female dragon, was as notable a stiff-back as she had ever encountered.

When the clacking of looms awoke her in the morning, she sat up in bed and reached for ball-point and stiff-back where she had left them in readiness on the bedside table. Or was it the looms had awakened her, or the purring of the motor-car engine in the cobbled yard, or the morning coughing of the old giant in the next room? For an ancient stone house, she thought, the walls were thin. But then she studied the slant of the ceiling, and realised that her room was only half a room and that the sound of coughing came to her, not through old stone, but through a wooden partition. She went to the window and looked out at three of the blue weaving girls walking in single file from the station-wagon to the weaving-shed and carrying hanks of coloured wool: obedient African kraal girls with burdens on their heads and disciplined by some wrinkled Zulu queen. Then the woman drove away under the faceless phoenix. When the girl was settled back in bed again, he spoke to her through the wall: I can hear you're awake. Has she driven off to do the shopping?

—Good morning, she said. She's driven off somewhere.

—Good morning to you, girl. Did you sleep well?

Her answer was lost in a fit of his coughing, and when his throat had cleared again, he said: No more rising with the lark for me. Nor the seagull itself. I'm old and lazy now. But I mind my father, the oldest day he was, walking barefoot in the dawn, the old greasy sailor's cap on his head, to the flagstone at the corner of the house, to look at the sea and the surf on the white strand, to sniff the wind and to tell the weather for the day to come. He had his own teeth to the age of ninety. If he was inland and far from the sea, he could tell by the smell of the wind whether the tide was ebbing or flowing. But it wasn't often he went inland, and he was never happy in an offshore wind.

This was the most wonderful way in the world to conduct an interview. The metallic voice came muted, but clear, through the timber. The looms, the sea, and the river made their noises. The wind muttered around grey stone. She could sit snug in bed, both notebooks open, and make notes at her ease without embarrassing her subject.

—Tell me more, she said.

He said : Tell me about your wild Indians.

So to entice him to talk, she talked about Quathiaski Cove at the mouth of the river, and about the wits among the Scots and Irish settlers who nicknamed it Quart of Whiskey Cove, about the great argonauts of salmon homing up the Campbell River, about people of many nations, Scots, Swedes, Irish, Indians, Chinese, Japanese, living in one way or another on the rich red body of the salmon.

—The very air in that place smells of salmon. When my mother first took me to visit Vancouver I thought there was something wrong with the place, something missing. Finally she told me I felt that way because I could no longer smell the salmon.

—Like myself, he said, when I came here with her. This far inland you can't sniff the salt properly.

—And tell me about their songs, he said. In my days on the island there were sweet singers and old men who could tell stories to last the night.

So, for his sake, she remembered that when she had been a little girl she had sneaked out one night to listen to the singing of the Indians. One song particularly stayed in her memory. Years afterwards, when she and her people had long left the place, she went north by boat with her father to revisit the haunts of her childhood. To one old noble chieftain she spoke of the songs—and of that special song. He answered her about all the forms of songs : morning songs, harvest songs, giving songs to be chanted at the potlatch when a man gave all he had to his neighbours, gambling songs, lullabies. And song after song he sang until she stopped him and said : That's it. That's the song I loved when I was a little girl.

Then, with tears in his eyes, the old chieftain said : That's my gambling song, written for me by my own songwriter.

Her story faded into coughing that rattled the partition between them. Later he said in a hoarse carrying whisper : Don't go away soon, girl. Stay as long as you can whether she wants you to or not.

It wasn't easy to think of any response.

—She doesn't like strangers about the place. She's cold, God help her, and has no failte in her. Even when I was married to my first wife, and herself only a stranger visiting the islands, she was always jealous to find me in the middle of a crowd.

—You were married before?

—To a woman of my own people. And year after year herself came as a tourist until my wife died. Then I went away with her and we were married in London. A watery class of a wedding they give you in cities. It wasn't love, as they call it. She was too grand for that. But she was there always—and willing. The islands do something to visiting women. And with creams and perfumes and the best clothes out of the London shops she was different from any woman I'd ever smelled or seen. You know how it is with a strong imaginative young fellow, and he only a few months married.

—I can guess, she said. Some minor poet said something about white arms beckoning all around him.

—Minor or major he was poet enough to know what he was talking about. We haven't slept heads on one pillow for twenty years now, but in secret corners in those old days we'd play hide and seek in our pelt on the bare rocks—when it was a sin moreover. And look at me now, here, wrapped in coloured wool, and broken in health, and surrounded by stupid women, weaving.

Propped by pillows, and taking notes, she squatted like a tailor, and made up her mind. She would stay a week if she could, just to please the old man and—her blood warming to the conflict—to spite that cold dried fish of a woman. In his youth, to judge by his talk, the old man had eaten better.

When he heard the station-wagon returning he said : I'll doze for a while now. She wouldn't like to hear us talking through the wall. She was hinting last night she'd run you to the station for the late train. But don't go, don't go, stay as long as you can.

They had a week of mornings together talking through the wall. Reading her notes afterwards she found that morning mingled with morning. One morning, though, was distinct because it had been a morning of gale and rain. The coy red-and-purple blossoms were being whipped off the tormented fuchsia bushes, and when she stepped out for her daily walk— the sea was too tossed for a swim—the sand and salt were in her eyebrows and gritting between her teeth. Bloated by a night of rain the brown mad river bellowed around the dead millwheels and, for once, the clack, the mocking one-two-three of the looms couldn't be heard.

Through the wall and the frequent fits of coughing he had said to her : I've grown younger since you came. A gift to me from the god of the sea himself, a beautiful young girl from a far island.

As a clergyman's daughter, the object of as many jokes as an Aberdonian, she was calmly aware of her looks : neither better nor worse than they were. She laughed. She said : I've a nose like a pack saddle, and a square face and freckles, although they tell me I've honest eyes.

—But you're young, he said.

After a silence she heard his dry choking laughter : There's a lump on my own nose still where I had it broken and I no more than a boy. The way it happened is a story will tickle you. There was this free and easy girl, a rare thing on the islands I can tell you—with the close way we lived. She wasn't an island girl, whatever. She came from the mainland in the tourist season and, as the song says, her stockings were white and you'd love to be tickling her garter, even if she was no better than a servant-maid in a lodging-house. This evening weren't we lined up to see her, like penitents going to confession, at the bottom of the orchard behind the house she worked in, and when Pat's Jameseen stepped out of his fair place in the line to go ahead of me, I fought him and, although he cracked my nose, hammered him back.

The dry laughter went on, choking now not with phlegm but with remembered devilment.

—That was the way with me when I was young. A chieftain among my own people, like your fine Indian, and respected by all. Then when my first woman died I never wanted to see the islands again. The English woman had it easy to carry me to the smoke of London where, as God is my judge, I came near to choking. The islands pulled at me again, even though I got only this far and no farther. Old as I am, I think at times I'll take a boat and return. But they don't want me any more since I married a stranger, and grew grand, and left.

—It would be fun, said the girl, if we could go to an island I know in Spain. Life is simple and gentle there, and the food good, cooked over an open fire. Some rough wine, wild and coarse, but with a kind flavour. A little music and reading and story-telling by lamplight, and water all around.

—That would be a holiday to remember, he said.

With the gale that morning they didn't hear the station-wagon returning, and it was the woman opening the door of the old man's room that interrupted them. Afterwards, while the old man slept, she said, over black coffee, to the girl : Any time you're ready I'll run you to the station.

A conflict like this was, in some ways, worse than blows or eye-scratching. As steadily as she could the girl said : If it doesn't upset your arrangements too much I'd love to see the pageant. It would add colour to the story.

—Colour, the woman said. Well, the beards, yes. Please yourself. But don't talk to the girls so much. It holds them up at their work. They lose. I lose. They're paid by piece-work.

Walking out into the gale the girl, for the sake of peace and the old man, avoided the weaving-shed where, she had been glad to think, the sullen faces of the underpaid weavers brightened when she entered. She loved the soft coloured wool, the intricacies of warping mills and heddles, the careful spacing of the threads. When you looked at the process you were as much part of it as the woolwinder and the sound of the looms was comforting, not mocking.

In the hotel bar the French hunters, driven in by the tempest that had also driven the birds to shelter, clustered around Diana who wore tight red pants and sneakers. Through a red beard like a burning bush the barman told her how five years ago the old man had run amok: Terrified the bloody country for a week. Wandering around with a loaded shotgun. Shooting and spearing salmon in the pool below the old mill. Then pleurisy laid him low and he was never the same again. Out on the islands they're savages. Half-crazy with inbreeding.

The raised wind-driven sea was sucking around the tree trunks that palisaded the white cottage. She walked, fighting the gale, along the thin line of sand the water had not devoured.

Baxbakualanuxsiwae, she recalled, shared his house with his wife, Qominoqa, a frightful female who cooked his ghoulish meals. A female slave, Kinqalalala, rounded up victims and collected corpses, well-hung meat in the house of the gods.

The thunder of the waves made her want to run and shout. One Sunday morning the small, deep-toned drums of the potlatch had set the whole village vibrating, until her father was forced to abandon his pulpit and say with a good humour more than Christian: Let us marvel at the force of tradition which is also one of the works of the Lord.

Once, in one of the books in her father's library, she had read that the Dinka people of the southern Sudan had a special sort of priest known as Masters of the Fishing Spear. These men, if they had great names as heroes, could be honourably killed when old and failing, by being buried alive at their own request and before all their assembled kin.

The islands, lost in spume and low-running clouds, were not to be seen.

In the dusk the bearded young men came in twos and threes under the featureless phoenix, across the courtyard, out by another gateway at the back of the weaving-shed, and up the hill to the mounded rath that was to be the open-air, torch-lit stage for their pageant. They wore white shirts and saffron kilts, cowskin pampooties made on the islands and dyed all colours, and thick woollen stockings cross-gartered to the knees. Most of them carried long wooden spears with silvered cardboard heads, and cardboard shields bright with brassy tacks. Some of them carried and some of them even played the bagpipes.

The blue weaving girls gathered on the landing outside the door of the shed, and cat-called, and addressed the bearded heroes by their ordinary everyday names and nicknames. They asked with irony if the men were going to the wars or to stick flounder on the flat sands with the flowing tide. When one bandy-legged, hairy-kneed veteran tottered past carrying a huge harp, and preceded by the curate who was directing the pageant, the blue girls held each other up, embracing in paroxysms and pantomimes of suppressed mirth.

—Never yet, the old man said, did I hear tell of one of these pageants that wasn't a holy laugh in the end. The Orangemen in the North, they say, had a pageant about the landing of King Billy in Carrickfergus harbour. But the sea was choppy that day and the boat tilted and didn't his majesty land on his arse in the water. And in Straide in Mayo they had a pageant about the eviction of the family of Michael Davitt who founded the Land League. But they built the mock cabin so strong that all the guns of Germany, let alone the battering rams of the boys who were pretending to be the bailiff's men, couldn't knock it down. Still and all, for the laugh, we'll go up to the rath and drink porter and eat pork sausages with the rest. It'll be a fine night with a full moon.

—At your age, Eamonn, that's the worst thing you could do.

—At my age?

He tossed aside the blackthorn he leaned on and, on the flat flag at the door of the house, hopped, but stiffly, from one foot to the other.

—These days I'm a two-year-old. The Indian maiden here will lead me up the slope. Minnehaha.

The woman's eyelids came down—it seemed one after the other, and very deliberately—to hide her eyes.

—Please yourself, then. Those girls have wasted enough time. I'll go up later with coffee and sandwiches.

His arm was around the girl's shoulders as they walked up a twisting boreen towards bonfires reddening in the dusk.

—Kings lived on this high hill, he said. All gone now, and dead and buried, generations of ancient kings, but the mounds and the ramparts are as solid as the day they were raised.

For one night, she thought, the kings had returned. She sat beside him on a rug on the mound. They were sheltered by a blossoming whitethorn from the light seawind. She held his hand. A huge round moon was motionless in a cloudless sky. Under its influence, and in the glow of a dozen bonfires, the bearded, cross-gartered country boys, the one decrepit harper, were no longer comic.

It was a masque, not a pageant. In a hut in a forest a dozen old broken men, remnants of a beaten clan, waited sadly and with little hope for the fulfillment of a prophecy that told of the coming of a young hero to lead them back to victory.

—This, said the oldest of them, is the last day of the year of our foretold salvation, and the last hour of the last day, yet the prophecy still stands even if it was made by one of the faery women who make game of men.

Her own old man moved closer to her on the rug.

The blue girls were just ending the long day's weaving. The coffee and sandwiches, and the woman with them, were still a good hour away; and also the thought that her duffle-bag and typewriter had been stored, for simpler departure, in the hotel with the red-bearded barman. She felt a brute, but she had a job to do—such as it was—and an old man's dream couldn't go on for ever, nor could she any longer defy a woman who didn't want her about the place.

When he pressed her hand she returned the pressure. She felt the great bones from which the flesh had melted away. She could have wept.

—The pity, he said, I didn't meet you when I was a young blade.

—I wasn't born then.

—We'd have found our own island and lived on it.

—There was a Japanese poet, she said, who was born in 1911, the year after Halley's Comet. He reckoned with a sad heart that he'd never see the comet since it wouldn't come again until 1986. That it was the same case with human encounters. His true friend would appear after his death. His sweetheart had died before he was born.

—A fine young man there, he said.

For who should arrive at that moment but the red barman himself, striding from darkness into the glare of the fires. Spear on shoulder. With the firelight glinting in his bush of a beard he could only be the hero who was promised. The crowds, seated on the slopes of the rath, cheered him. He was a popular man. For the broken old men he brought venison from the forest, cakes impaled on spears, and rolling barrels of ale from an enemy fortress he had that day captured single-handed. Also a sackful of golden goblets, made out of cardboard, and all the tokens, including a severed head in a sack, to prove he was the man of destiny. The exigencies of the drama did not, mercifully, call for the production of the severed head.

Then the harper harped on his harp and, far away in the shadows, the pipers played, slowly advancing towards the circle of fires to show that they were an army of young men following their unique leader. The watching crowds broke up into groups to eat sausages and pigs' feet and to drink porter. The dancing began on the rough dry grass. Led by two of the pipers, the dancers moved to find a better surface between the weaving-shed and the millhouse. Then the woman was there, and the curate with her helping her to carry cups and sandwiches and the coffee pot.

—Not pigs' feet, Eamonn. Not all that greasy fat.

—'Tisn't often now I have a night out under the moon.

—A midsummer night, she said. Madness.

—I could leap through bonfires, woman. I feel like twenty.

Pour milk on the ground for the good people who lived here before kings were heard tell of. It's not lucky to let them go hungry.

—What silly waste, the woman said.

Slowly the girl tilted her cup and let the coffee drain down to the grass. She said : They might fancy coffee.

His great hand was in the bowl of brown sugar and the fistful he took he tossed into the air, scattering it over the crowd. Faces, some laughing, some curious, turned towards them in the firelight.

—The world knows, he said, that the good people have a sweet tooth. Halley's Comet, Minnehaha, will come again.

They laughed loudly together. She noticed that they were again hand in hand. The curate, pretending to answer a call from one of the bearded men, moved away. The woman poured more coffee. By the farthest fire the girl saw the red man standing and beckoning. He probably had notions above his state in life, but he could give her a lift to the nearest town, and her leather jacket was stout enough to resist even the paws and the pinches of a man mentioned in prophecy. When the barman moved off down the slope towards the millhouse, she excused herself.

—Come back soon Minnehaha, the old man called after her. Don't delay. It's a fine night for seeing comets.

—Eamonn, isn't it time you went in out of the night air?

Like in movies about Italy, the girl thought, everything ends with a carnival. She walked down the slope, taking his second youth with her, towing the sailing islands behind her. She was the sea receding for ever from a stranded master of the sea.

By torchlight in the cobbled courtyard blue weaving girls danced with bearded warriors who had cast aside their spears.

She walked on under the stone phoenix that could never arise again because it had merely decayed, never been purified by fire and burned to ashes.

With car, duffle-bag and typewriter, the red barman was waiting. She sat beside him and was driven off to find her next little-known hero.

216

DOWN THEN BY DERRY

THE FIRST TIME Tom Cunningham ever saw Sadie Law's brother, Francie, that brother was airborne between the saddle of a racing bicycle and a stockade filled with female lunatics. Francie is not the chief part of this story, nor is his sister, but since he has been mentioned, it might be fair to his fame and memory to say who he was and what he was doing in the air in that odd place.

A resident medical officer in the district's mental hospital had, years before, been a believer in athletics as curative therapy for the crazy : running and jumping and the lord knows what. So he set those who were out of cells and strait-jackets, and otherwise capable, at the running and jumping, barring, for good reasons the throwing of the hammer or the discus, or the tossing of the caber—which can be dangerous occupations even for the sane. Then the medical officer, to introduce a sanative, competitive spirit, organised an annual sports meeting, with cups, shields and lesser prizes. The thing grew and grew. That medical officer died and went to Valhalla. The annual meeting continued to grow until it was one of the most notable sporting events in that part of the country. Professionals competed. The crazy men and women, those of them who could be out and about, were now only two small corralled sections among the spectators. They had been pushed back into the shouting or gibbering shadows where everybody, except the man in Valhalla, thought they belonged.

Francie Law was a famous track cyclist. That was how he came to be there in the air. There was one bad corner on the packed cinder track. This day there was a pile-up and Francie was catapulted clean, to land among the lunatic ladies. He survived. It was as a hero-worshipper bearing grapes to

Francie's hospital bedside—Francie, wherever he was, always smelled of embrocation—that Tom Cunningham first met Francie's sister, Sadie, who was almost as famous as her brother, but not for track-cycling.

—She's Number One, according to all the talk, Tom said to his favourite friend who was five years younger than him.

Tom was nineteen.

—And she liked me, Tom said. We have a date. She wore a black leather coat with a belt. There was a good warm smell off it. Like the smell of the plush seats at the back of the cinema where all the feeling goes on. Hot stuff, boy. Also the smell of embrocation. Rub it up good. Frank Mullan told me she was okay and easy to get, if you once got to know her. And the May devotions are on the way. Long evenings. Warm grass. And Frank Mullan should know. He knows them all.

Of course it goes without saying that the devotions on May evenings in the parish church, with the high, limping, Gothic spires, went away back to something far before the worship of holy purity and the blessed virgin, to some pagan festival of the rites of spring. This he found out afterwards by reading, and by much dull talk, in more sophisticated places, heaven help us, than his own native town. But in the spring of that year he neither knew nor worried about such things, as he knelt beside Tom Cunningham in the side aisle to the left hand of the high altar.

Oh, those brown angels cut in wood of a slightly lighter colour than the wood of the beams to which they provided a figurehead finish. They swooped out towards each other over the nave and eyed the praying people. Once he had tried to write a poem about them :

> In church the angels cut in wood,
> In row on row arranged,
> Stand always as before they stood,
> And only I am changed.

But it wouldn't work. The angels weren't standing, for God's sake, they had no legs or feet to stand on, or, if they had, those legs were buried in the wood of the beams from which winged torsos and long-haired oaken heads seemed to have instantaneously, ecstatically, emerged. Times, he still saw those angels in his dreams, soaring, in a sort of a way, over altar, incense, monstrance, praying priest, responding mumbling people, over Tom Cunningham in the side aisle making cute sideways eyes and secret signs at Sadie Law who knelt with her favourite friend directly under the angels in the nave. Whatever about bullshit talk and the rites of spring, the devotions on May evenings was where you met people for good or evil; and all around the church, high on a hill with its hopalong spires, the rolling country was rich in deep grass and the birds were making mocking calls along hidden lovers' lanes. The high grassy embankments along the railways that went out of the town to the Donegal sea at Bundoran, or to Dublin or Belfast, or down then by Derry to the northern sea, were a sort of secret world where only lovers went in the long evenings. No respectable girl would be seen walking along the railway. The art was in not being seen.

His daughter, who was eighteen years of age, said to his mother who admitted to being eighty-five : Dad must have been happy here in this town in his schooldays. He's always singing a song. Well, not singing exactly. It has no particular tune. No beat. Dad's a bit of a square. It goes more like an African chant.

—Wallawalla boom boom, said his son who was fourteen.

—John, said the daughter, mind your manners. Granny doesn't dig Swahili. No granny. The song begins like this. Thrice happy and blessed were the days of my childhood and happy the hours I wandered from school, by green Mountjoy's forest, our dear native wildwood, and the green flowery banks of the serpentine Strule.

—Mountjoy forest, he said, was part of the estate of Lord and Lady Blessington. Back in the days of the great Napoleon. That was an old song.

—He was a good scholar, his mother said. He was very fond

of reading poetry out loud. In the mornings after breakfast. Before he went to school.

As if he wasn't there at all. His daughter giggled.

He was accustomed to his mother rhapsodising in this way, talking about him to other people in his presence. Once she had said to a friend of his : He would be the best man in Ireland if it wasn't for the little weakness.

Afterwards his friend had said with great good humour : with you standing there I couldn't very well ask her which weakness she meant.

Another time and under similar circumstances she had said to the same friend : His father, God rest him, put on some weight when he passed forty, but he never swelled like that.

Pointing to him. As if, by God, the son, had had a dropsical condition.

To her grand-daughter and grandson she said : He read Shelley. If Winter comes can Spring be far behind. I liked that. Shelley was a good poet. Although my own mother could never understand about Tennyson and the brook. She used to say : Poor fellow, could nobody stop him. I think she thought it was about some unfortunate man that had something astray with his bowels. Then there was one poet that droned on and on about Adam and Eve and the fall of Satan.

She spat mildly and politely towards the fireplace where, winter or summer, there was always a fire. She preserved many old country customs. One was to spit when, by inadvertence or necessity, one mentioned a name of the devil—and his names were legion.

Twenty-eight years later he was still a little ashamed that he had inflicted on his mother's patient ears the monotony of Milton, even to the utter extremity of the Latin verses.

—Milton, he said, a bit of a bore.

But nobody paid the least attention to him. So he closed his eyes and his mind to the lot of them : the mother, old, wrinkled, wearing a battered old felt hat that looked like a German helmet, but with an eye as bright and inquisitive as it must have been when she was a lively singing country girl, and the man she was to marry was walking round and round the South African veldt; and he himself wasn't even a fragment of an imagination, or a gleam or a glint in his father's eye; the daughter, pert, small, lively, endlessly talkative; the son, tall, easy-going, slouching when he walked—as his grandfather had done. It was uncanny to observe such resemblances.

Since not one of the three of them paid any attention to him he shut his eyes and his mind to them and went on his own through the town, and back to the past that had made the town and him.

The two tall limping Gothic spires rose high above the hilly narrow streets. Those two spires and the simple plain spire of the Protestant church—that would be Church of Ireland, for the Methodists and Presbyterians did not rise to spires—could be seen for a distance of ten miles. They soared, they were prayers of a sort, over the riverine countryside.

The taller spire was all of two hundred and thirty feet high, thirty of that being for the surmounting cross. To climb up the inside of that spire you went first by a winding stone stairway to the organ loft, then by a steep straight wooden stairway to the shaky creaky platform where the sexton stood when he pulled the bell-rope, then up a series of perpendicular ladders to the place where the two bells were hung, sullen and heavy, but ready at the twitch of a rope to do their duty. From that eminence, one hundred and fifty feet up, you could look down on everything. The town was almost flat, no longer all humps and hills and high ridged roofs and steep narrow streets. Down there was the meeting place of two rivers, the Camowen and the Drumragh : a sparkling trout-water, a sullen pike-water. Who could comprehend the differences there were between rivers, not to speak now of the Amazon and the Seine and the Volga and the Whang-ho and the Ohio, but even between neighbouring rivers destined to marry and to melt into one? United, the waters of Drumragh and Camowen went on under the name of the Strule, sweeping in a great horseshoe around the wide holm below the military barracks, tramping and tossing northwards to meet yet another river, the Fairywater, then to vanish glistening into a green-and-blue infinity.

Except you were the sexton, or some lesser person authorised by him, you were not, by no means, supposed to be up there at all. Dusty boards, with crazy, dizzy gaps between them, swayed and bent under your feet. Vicious jackdaws screeched. The blue-and-green infinity into which the sparkling water vanished was the place where Blessington's Rangers had once walked, speaking Gaelic, great axes on shoulders. They cut down the trees to make timber for war against Bonaparte, and money to keep Lord and Lady Blessington, their daughter, and the ineffable Count D'Orsay gallivanting.

One day coming home from school alone—that was a time of the day when it wasn't easy to be alone but, with cunning, it could be managed—he had found the door at the foot of the stone stairway open and had taken the chance that it was open by accident. It was. He made the climb. He saw the world. He was alone with the jackdaws and the moan of the wind. Then on the way down the perpendicular ladders he had missed a rung, slipped, screamed with the jackdaws, grabbed desperately and held on. Just about where the sexton would stand to pull the bell-rope he had vomited a sort of striped vomit that he had never seen before. Even in boyhood there was the fear of death.

Nobody, thank God, had ever found out who had thus paid tribute, made offertory, in the holy place. For weeks afterwards he had felt dizzy even when climbing the stairs to his bedroom.

When the war was over and Boney beaten, the gallivanting lords and ladies had no more use for the woodsmen of Mount-joy. For the last time they walked down there below in the old Flax Market that hadn't changed much since 1820 : in their rough boots and frieze coats, axes on shoulders, speaking a guttural language that was doomed almost to die, singing, drinking, fighting among each other, but standing shoulder to shoulder or axe to axe against the world. The paltry townsmen and shopkeepers must have breathed easily when the woodsmen went north to Derry to board the American boat.

As a boy he had known of them and walked among their shadows in the Old Market: No more will we see the gay silver trouts playing, or the herd of wild deer through its forest be straying, or the nymph and gay swain on its flowery bank straying, or hear the loud guns of the sportsmen of Strule.

On those May evenings the steeplejacks were swinging on the spires, tiny black dwarfs sitting in wooden chairs at the ends of ropes. They were pointing the stones, which meant that they smeared in fresh cement, netted the soaring prayers in nets of new white. Snug and secure in deep warm grass on a railway embankment from which there was a view both of the tips of the roofs of the town and of one deep curve of the slow pike-infested Drumragh River, Tom and Sadie, Tom's friend and Sadie's friend, lay on their backs and watched the dwarfs on the steeples.

—Why, Angela said, did they not build one steeple as long as the other?

—As high, he said, you mean.

—High or long, she said, what's the difference?

She had a wide humorous mouth that, some evening, with the help of God, he would get around to kissing.

—It all depends, Tom said, on which way you're going. Like up or down or sideways.

—Why, she repeated.

She was a stubborn girl. He held her hand.

—In this life, Tom said, there is nothing perfect.

—No, he said.

Because he knew.

—Two men were killed on the smaller steeple. So they stopped.

—Brian, said Tom, always has a better story. Say us a poem, Brian.

—That's no story. It's gospel truth.

Tom and Sadie were kissing, gurgling. Angela tickled his palm.

—That's a job, he said, I wouldn't have for all the tea in China.

He meant being a steeplejack.

Tom surfaced. He said: I'm not so sure. I wouldn't mind being able to get up as high as that.

Sadie said: You could always try.

With her left hand she gently massaged Tom's grey-flannelled crotch.

He watched Sadie's small moving hand. He wondered how many people within a ten-mile radius, in the town, in villages, from farmhouse doorways, walking along laneways, or fishing, or lying on grass, were watching the steeplejacks on the spires.

For no reason that he could explain he thought it would be exciting to see that face again, the wide humorous mouth, the brown hair that curled like two little brown horns over her temples, the plump fresh cheeks. The hair, though, wouldn't be brown any more. Don't forget that. Look for something older. Three years older than yourself: a reasonable gap of years, once upon a time, for a girl who could teach and a boy who was willing, even afraid, to learn.

—That woman, his daughter said, who writes you those letters from Indiana. What part of this town did she live in? When she was a girl, I mean.

The three of them were walking down the steep High Street. Behind and above them, where two narrower streets met to form the High Street, was the eighteenth-century courthouse, high steps before it and Doric columns, dominating the long undulations of High Street and Campsie Avenue until the houses ended and the point of vision was buried in deep trees.

He told them that there had once been in the town a police-man so lazy that he hated to walk. So he sat all day, when the day was sunny, on the courthouse steps. When his superior officers asked him what he thought he was at, he defended himself by saying that he had the whole town under observation.

This grey day, the last sad day but one of the old year, would have been no day for sitting on the steps.

They laughed at the memory of the lazy policeman, and

descended the steep street. The daughter said : You never met her, all the times you were in the States?

—I never even met her, I only saw her, when we were young together here in this town. She's a shadow, a memory.

—Shadows, she said precisely, don't write letters. Memories might.

—One time last year, he said, I had hoped to meet her. I was, so to speak, passing that way. That is, within a few hundred miles or so of where she lives. That's not far, out there.

—Just next door, his son said.

—It was in March, he said, and I was on the way north to give a lecture in Minnesota. I crossed Indiana.

—See any Injuns dad, said the son.

—No, what I mostly remember about Indiana is big barns and ducks, the big ducks that we call Muscovy ducks. Never saw so many Muscovy ducks, anywhere else in the world.

—But then dad, his daughter said, you never were in Muscovy.

—Or if he was, said the son, he never told us.

In March in Indiana the endless flat brown land still shivered. The harness-racing tracks by the roadside were soggy and empty. The last of the snow lay here and there in sordid mounds. Cattle, with a certain guilty look about them, foraged among the tall battered corn-stalks of last year's harvest. There was ice at the fringes of creeks and rivers that looked far too small to negotiate such interminable expanses of flat land. Great round-roofed barns stood aloof from, yet still dwarfed, the neat houses. Flat and sombre the land went every way to a far horizon . . .

—A small American penny, his daughter said, for your wandering thoughts.

He told her that in one small field near the city of Lafayette he had seen a flock of more than two hundred Muscovy ducks. The field had been between a railway and a line of power pylons.

—Nothing, he explained, more emphasises distance in flat land than a line of pylons striding on and on for ever, giants marching, carrying cables on their shoulders, until they vanish east or west.

—Or north or south, his son said.

—Now, she said sweetly, we know all about electricity. Dad, you're such a dear old bore. We couldn't care less about ducks or pylons. We want to know about the woman who writes you those marvellous letters from Indiana.

—She was an orphan, he said. In an orphanage. In Derry City.

—So far so good, his son said.

—She was taken out of the orphanage by this woman and reared in this town. She suffered a lot from illness. She wore a leg-splint when she was a child. She grew up. She read books. My father used to talk a lot about her. He used to say : You should meet that young woman. She's a wonder.

—But I was in college in Dublin, by that time, coming and going and somehow or other I never did get the opportunity of speaking to her. My memory is of a rather long beautiful face, sort of madonna, and fair hair. Framed like an old picture in glass and wood, against a background of coloured magazines and paperbacked books. Because my last recollection of her is that she was working in the bookstall in the railway station. During the war she went off to London, married an American. Then seven or eight years ago she read something I'd written and wrote to me. That's the whole story.

She had written : You may have a vague recollection of who I am when you read my name. Then again you may not. It's been a long time. About thirty years. But I remember you very well, indeed : on your way to school, to church, walking the roads around our town, always, it seemed to me, alone.

That would be a romantic young girl confusing an average sullen lout of a fellow with her private image of Lord Byron.

—We rarely said more than hello. We lived in the same town all our growing years. We walked the same roads, knew the same people, and didn't meet at all. We might have shared a common interest. I loved books, poetry, music, but had little opportunity to enjoy any of them. I did manage to read quite a lot, and to remember poetry, and get a little music on an old radio. I walked, and thought of the books I'd read, and repeated the poetry to myself, and could hear the music again along the quiet roads. Thus I survived the town I was born in. Though mostly I remember it with love, because of Margaret, the woman who reared me. She was gentle, poor, uneducated, but with a lively mind and kind to all things living—especially to me when she took me from the nightmare of the orphanage in Derry, haunting me even now with its coldness, the crooked hilly streets of Derry, the jail, the Diamond, the wide Foyle which is really our own Strule, and the ships.

—Another penny for your thoughts, his daughter said. Or a measly nickel.

They turned right from the Market Street along the Dublin Road, past a filling station and a Presbyterian church, a toylike gasworks, the old white houses of Irishtown. Beyond Irishtown, he told them, was the Drumragh River and the old humped King's Bridge where James Stuart, falling back from the walls of Derry, had watched the town burn behind him.

Then they were ascending through a pleasant affluent suburb.

—No, he said, this wasn't the part of the town she lived in. We're not going that way just at the moment.

They were, in fact, walking to say a prayer at his father's grave. Everywhere he went he carried with him for luck a white stone from the grave. A white stone from the grave of a kind man would have to be lucky, wouldn't it, if there was the least pick of reason in the universe? But in a drunken moment in Dublin City he had loaned the stone to a man who ran greyhounds, and this particular greyhound had won, and the man had begged to be allowed to keep the stone. Today he would say his prayer and take away with him another white stone.

The Protestants lay to the left of the cemetery's main avenue, the Catholics to the right, and between them, on a slight rise, the stone oratory, cold and draughty, where on harsh days the last prayers were said over the coffins. He never remembered the wind around the corners of that oratory as

being, even in summer, anything but bitterly cold. This last
dead day, but one, of the year it was unbearable. Bravely the
boy and girl knelt on the damp earth and prayed. He knelt
with them, not praying, talking without words to the man
under the clay, or somewhere in the air around him, and
around him wherever in the world he went : the dead hover
for ever over the living.

Low dark clouds travelling, or being forced to travel, fast,
bulged with rain. To the lee of the empty oratory the three of
them stood and looked over the forest of obelisks and Celtic
crosses, Sacred Hearts and sorrowing mothers, at the distant
sweep of the flooded Drumragh, at where the railway line used
to cross it by a red metal bridge. The bridge was gone and the
railway too—sold for scrap. But three hundred yards to the
east of the river, there was still the stone bridge under the
embankment—it looked like a gateway into an old walled
city—and the lovers' lane that led into the fields, and across
the fields to the wooded brambly slope above one of the
deepest, most brooding of the river's pike-pools.

Would it be sin or the beginning of living to touch the
hidden flesh of Angela? His dream of fair women was all about
the creeping hand, the hair, the warmth. That was all that Tom
and the other boys talked about.

She lay on her back in the brambly wood—the pike hovering
in the pool below them—and he fumbled fearfully, and tickled
her, his hand timidly outside her dress. But when she reached
for him he rolled away. She laughed for a longer time than
seemed necessary. From the far side of a clump of bushes he
heard Tom say to Sadie : There must be nothing in Brown's
house that doesn't smell of embrocation.

—The grave was very weedy, the daughter said.

—So I noticed. Your grandmother pays good money to have
it kept clean and covered with white stones. On the way out
I'll call to the caretaker's house and talk to him.

The clay in the centre of the grave had sunk. He was glad
that neither son nor daughter had noticed that. It would be

228

so painful to have to explain to young people, or even to one-self, that clay sank so when the coffin underneath had collapsed.

The hotel they stopped in was a mile outside the town, a domed mid-nineteenth-century house, miscalled a castle, on a hill top with a view of the heathery uplands the Camowen came from, and quite close to a park called the Lovers' Retreat, but known to the soldiers in the barracks as Buggers' Den.

The aged mother was safely at home in bed, in her small house across the narrow street from those gigantic limping spires. She liked to be close to the quietness of the church, the glowing red circle around the sanctuary lamp where she remembered and prayed for and to the dead man.

Leaving her in peace they had walked through the lighted crowded town, along a quiet dim suburban road, over a bridge that crossed the invisible talkative Camowen—there was a good gravelly trout pool just below that bridge. They dined late in a deserted dining-room. Along a corridor there was the noise of merriment from the bar. His son asked him which room had been the haunted room in the days when the hotel had been a castle.

—For the sake of the ghost, the daughter said, let's hope it wasn't where the bar is now.

—Ghosts, he told her, might like company.

—Not mine I pray, she said.

—Fraidy cat, the son said. A ghost couldn't hurt you.

—That ghost, he told them, couldn't hurt anyone. The story was that the people who lived here called in the priest and he blessed the room and put the ghost in a bottle.

—Poor ghost, she said.

—But where, she wondered, did the priest put the bottle.

—On the river, the son said. And it floated over the sea, to England, and somebody found it and opened it, and got a ghost instead of a message.

He saw them to their rooms. No ghost could survive in such up-to-date comfort. No ghost could rest in peace in any of the coloured bottles in the bar. The noisy local drinkers had gone

229

home, taking their din with them. A few commercial men, talking of odds and ends, drinking slowly but with style, sat in an alcove. He joined them.

—Did you like it out there, they asked him.

—You were a friend of Tom Cunningham, they said.

—It's good out there. Fine people. Hospitable. The sort of people I meet.

—Tom went into the Palestine police after the war, they said. Then he went farther east. Never heard of since.

—Chasing the women in China, they said.

—But the crime in America, they said. Did you ever come up against that?

—It's there. But I never came up against it. Except in the newspapers.

—By God, they said, they have picturesque murders out there. We never have anything here except an odd friendly class of a murder. But out there. That fellow in Chicago and the nurses. And the young fellow that made the women in the beauty parlour lie down like the spokes of a wheel and then shot the living daylights out of them.

—The one that sticks most in my mind . . .

They were all attention.

. . . was the girl in the sump. This sump is an overflow pond at the back of a dry-cleaning plant. One morning a man walking by sees a girl's leg standing up out of the water.

—Clothed in white samite, they said. Mystic, wonderful.

—Seems she had been by day a teller in a bank and by night a go-go dancer in a discotheque. One day she walks out of the bank with a bagful of thousands of dollars. She is next encountered in the sump, one leg surfacing, her hands tied behind her back, her throat cut, the bag and the dollars gone. A barman from the discotheque is also missing.

—All for love, they said.

The long cold day, the search for the past, the drink, the warm company, had made him maudlin.

—When I read the newspapers today there are times I think I was reared in the Garden of Eden.

230

—Weren't we all, they said.

But it hadn't been the Garden of Eden for one waif of a girl, now a woman in far-away Indiana. From Atlanta, Georgia, where he had been for two years he had remailed to her the local newspapers that had come to him from this town.

She had written : That photograph of the demolition of the old stone railway bridge at Brook Corner saddened me. I recall that bridge with affection. When I'd spent about fourteen months flat on my back in the County Hospital, and was at last permitted up on crutches, I headed, somewhat shakily, under that bridge to begin the first of many walks. I still remember the bridge framing the road beyond like a picture, and the incredible green of the fields, the flowering hedges, the smell of hawthorn. The bridge became for me a gateway : to happy solitude. When I had trachoma and thought I might go blind my bitterest thought was that I might never again see the world through that bridge. Margaret's brother, Fred, was my companion and consolation in those dark days. He had been hired out at the age of six to work with a farmer and Margaret remembered seeing the golden-curly-haired child going off in the farmer's trap.

—Perhaps that was why Fred never cared to work. He hadn't, for about twenty-five years before he died, not because he couldn't but simply because he didn't want to. Oh, on a number of occasions he worked, briefly, for farmers at harvest time, was rarely paid in cash but in kind; and only on condition that his dog, Major, could accompany him. Major barked all day, every day, as though indignant at his master's labours, and much to the chagrin of the other workers and the farmer. But since, when he wanted to, Fred could work as well as the others, his services were always desired and he was permitted to stay, dog and all.

—He was a strange silent man who sat by the fire all day with a far-off look in his eyes. He had very blue eyes. He rarely spoke to anybody outside the house. He was my sole companion during many long hours when I was confined to bed.

231

I would read to him and ask him to spell and he would deliberately mis-spell and would be delighted when I would sharply correct him. I never knew how much I loved him until he died.

—Margaret housekept for Morris, the lawyer, who lived in the Georgian house beside the church with the high spires, and that left Fred and me a lot alone, and Fred would cook for me. Once, after I had been with Margaret several months, some sadistic neighbour woman told me that I was being sent back to the orphanage. So terrified was I that I hobbled up to the church and stood for hours across the street from the lawyer's house, waiting, the wind moaning away up in the spires in the darkness, until Margaret came and comforted me, led me home by the hand to Fred and Major and numerous cats, and a one-legged hen who had a nest in the corner and who was infuriated if another hen ever came to the back door in search of scraps.

His room was haunted, sure enough. He had sat too late, drunk too much, perhaps released the ghosts from the bottles. Oaken angels sang from the ceiling. A tearful crippled girl waited in the darkness at the foot of spires lost also in the windy darkness, no longer magic towers from which one could see the world. The leg of a girl who had stolen for love stood up like a stump of wood out of stagnant water.

Very cautiously he had asked his mother : Do you remember a family called Law? Are they still in the town? One of them, I think, was a famous racing cyclist.

Cautiously : because in her eyes there were times when he was still fourteen or less and there were people that he wasn't supposed to know.

—Oh, I remember the Laws. They were famous, indeed.

Around the house she had a fancy for dressing as if she were a pirate chief. Or perhaps it was a gipsy queen. Sometimes instead of the helmet-shaped hat she wore a white gipsy head-handkerchief; and a long red dressing-gown and a Galway shawl with the corners tucked back under her oxters and pinned behind.

—One of them called in to see me one morning after Sunday mass. A Law or a half-Law or a quarter-Law or a by-Law. You wouldn't have much time for the like of them. Not condemning anyone for the weakness, but there were more distant cousins in that clan than was natural. Or godly.

That seemed to be that.

—You wouldn't have expected much of the Laws, she said. But it's heartrending to see the fate of some families that had every chance that God and man could give them.

—Like who, for instance?

—Like many I've seen. Like the Glenshrule family, for one.

The red bull of Glenshrule roared through his haunted dreams.

—Glenshrule's sold, she said, and in the hands of strangers.

The bull, he supposed, had been sold to make bovril.

Two private roadways led into the old house at Glenshrule, one from the steep by-road along which the crippled girl had hobbled to find peace, one from the road that led west to the Donegal sea. To either hand on either road it was all Glenshrule land, green, bountiful, a little unkempt, cattle country, little tillage. The three bachelor brothers of Glenshrule were gentlemen farmers : which meant whipcord breeches and booze and hunting horses. But they were frank, reckless, generous, easy in their money and good breeding, and made no objection to the townspeople using their private roads for circular walks on Sunday afternoons. Roving boys used those roads all the time, and the fields around them, and the only prohibiting notice to be seen told you to beware of the red bull.

—Christ, look at the size of him, Tom cried with an artist's enthusiasm. Boy, if you were built like that you'd be welcome anywhere.

They sat on a five-barred iron gate. Between them and the bull's private meadow was the additional fortification of a strong wooden gate. He was an unruly bull. His red coat shone. He had a head near as big as the head of the mouldy bison they had seen in the Old Market in Bostock and Wombell's travelling menagerie. He rooted at the ground with one fore-

233

foot. The great head rose and fell. He didn't roar. He rumbled all the time like a train, far away, going into a tunnel.

—There's a lot to be said, Tom said, for being a bull.

—Everybody puts up with your tantrums.

—There's more to it than that.

Then the lady of Glenshrule, the one single sister of the three bachelor brothers, rode by on a bay mare. To acknowledge that they existed she raised her riding-crop, she smiled and said : Don't tempt him. Don't enter the meadow. Bulls eat boys.

—Boys, Tom muttered.

He was very bitter.

—There's also a lot to be said, he said, for being a bay mare.

She was bareheaded. She was blonde. She was twenty-five. She was blonde, she was blonde, she was blonde and calm-faced, and all the officers in the barracks pursued her. Years afterwards—altering the truth, as memory always does—he thought that he had then thought about queen and huntress, chaste and fair. But he hadn't. He had been too breathless to think of anything except, perhaps, that Sadie and Angela, lively and provoking as they could be, were still only in the servant-maid class.

She rode on towards the Donegal road. The sound of the hooves died away. The red bull, calmed, had lain down on the grass.

—One Sunday evening I sat beside her in the church, Tom said. My right leg against her left. It burned me. I can feel it still.

He rubbed his right thigh slowly, then sniffed his hand.

—I swear to God, he said, she pressed her thigh against mine. It made short work of the holy hour.

That was the year Tom and himself had been barred from the town's one cinema because Tom, ever an eager and enquiring mind, had discovered the anti-social use of hydrogen sulphide. A few sizzling test-tubes planted here and there in the darkness could have tumultuous effects on the audience. Old Mr. Pritchard—he was so old that it was suspected he had fought in the

234

Zulu war—was heard to say in a barracks-square voice that some bloke here needed a purge of broken bottles. But three burly ushers simply purged Tom and his companion from the audience, two of them to hold Tom, the other to herd the companion before him.

Such a splendid deed and its consequences gave the two of them the glory of outlaws among their contemporaries. And to be barred from the delights of Eddy Cantor's Rome, or of Broadway with its gold-diggers, or of Wallace Beery's Big House, meant more nights in the Old Flax Market. That was fair enough, because the Old Flax Market was the place for outlaws. Black-uniformed constables patrolled the streets but, unless there was very audible drunken disorder, they left the Old Flax Market alone. No flax was ever sold there any more.

—The ghosts of the woodsmen are still here, he told Tom. This was their place when they came to town.

—You and those bloody woodsmen. You're a haunted man.

The unpaved three acres of the Old Market were sodden and puddled. A sharply-defined half-moon cut like a cleaver through wispy running clouds. He shouted at the moon : No more will the fair one of each shady bower hail her dear boy of that once happy hour, or present him again with a garland of flowers that they oft times selected and wove by the Strule.

—And poetry, boy, will be your ruination. Poetry will get you nowhere with Angela. Move in man. Angela demands action.

The moon, even if it was only half a moon, was useful to outlaws in a land of outlaws. For there were only three gas-lamps in the whole of the Old Flax Market and gas-lamps were little use on windy nights or when somebody, for fun or hellery, wished to quench them. One lamp was on a wall-bracket at the corner of a rowdy dance hall. It lighted, when it was allowed to, the wooden stairway to the door of the dance hall, and the people ascending or descending or standing in groups making noise. One lamp lighted the covered cobbled entry-way from the High Street. The third lighted the muddy uncovered exit to a dark riverside walk from which an irate lover had, about that time, heaved his fancy into the river.

—Let's have a look, Tom said, at the Jennett's corner. You'd see things there you never saw at the pictures.

—But look, he said, there goes the Bluebottle, her legs like elevenpence marked on a new bucket.

The drum boomed, the horn blared from the dance hall. The half-moon coldly shone on the Strule waters that flowed by one side of the Old Market.

—If your woodsmen ever walked here you can bloody well guess what they were after.

A tall thin girl in a blue coat was being eased into the shadows by a drunken man.

—Would you believe it, Tom said, she fought like a cat here one night with one of the Fighting McDermotts. The one with the dinge in his temple where some decent man brained him with a bottle of port-wine. When she wouldn't go with him he shouted he'd tell her father that sent her out for money, and her uncle that broke her in. She tore the red face off him.

—He rings the bell, her uncle.

—They say he rang the bell for her when she was thirteen.

There then was the terror of the dark walk by the river. The uncle who rang the bell as one of the last town-criers was a figure out of a German fairy-tale, a pied piper, tall hard hat, tailed coat, long grey moustache, a small man with a voice of thunder, swinging his handbell, shouting out fragments of news : that a group of strolling players would perform in the town hall, that the water supply would be turned off—for repairs to pipes in this or that part of the town, that such and such a house property would be auctioned. Was it credible that a comic fairy-tale figure should also be a part of some sniggering story? The Bluebottle vanished ahead of them into some riverside bushes. Where the river made an elbow bend a group of smoking muttering men waited at the Jennet's corner. Her shady bower was a wooden shelter put there by the town council to protect Sunday walkers from sudden showers. The council had not intended to cater for the comfort of the Jennet and her customers. She was a raw-boned red-headed country girl whose husband was in the mental hospital.

236

—Good natured and charges very little, Tom said.

Some of the shadowy courtiers called after them.

—But, boy, a little bit too open to the general public for men of taste like ourselves. Take me back to sweet sinful Sadie. Or the lady of Glenshrule on her bay mare.

She rode on to the Donegal road, the hooves dancing clippety-clop, and the bull lay down in the meadow.

—What went wrong there, he said to his mother. They had everything.

—What would go wrong but debt and drink and the want of wit. The three brothers fled to Canada.

—They followed the woodsmen.

His mother didn't hear him.

—And my, she said, she looked lovely when she rode out astraddle on that bay mare.

—Tom Cunningham would have agreed with you.

—Oh, Tom Cunningham was a rare one. Very freckled when he was a little boy. And curly-haired. I'm amazed you remember him. He went to the war and never came back when it was over. But then you always had a good memory.

—I always had.

—She lived alone after the brothers left, and she never married, and went on drinking. There was a bit of scandal, too. But I never paid much attention to that sort of talk. She died in the ambulance on the way to hospital. But not, thank God, without the priest. For one of the curates was driving past just at that moment.

On the road she had ridden over on the bay mare.

—The Lord, his mother said, has everything mixed with mercy.

—He must have a lot of mercy for orphans, he said.

—Tell granny that story, dad, about the girl in the rain. The woman who writes to you. When she was a child, I mean.

She could still be outside there, the ghost of a frightened child, standing in the darkness at the foot of the spires. But one day in the orphanage playground she had broken out in rebellion.

—A sudden storm came up. The nuns called us in. We were to shelter, cold and miserable, in a sort of arcade or cloister. I started in with the rest, but suddenly I stopped and ran back to the playground. It was pouring. I was alone. The nuns called me. I wouldn't come. I danced around that playground in my bare feet, hair and dress soaking wet. Repeated calls failed to move me. Two nuns came after me. I ran and danced from one side to the other, dodging the hands that tried to clutch me. I laughed and danced in the wind and rain. I'd wait until they got close and then I'd run like the wind. Their long robes were heavy with water. They were exhausted. But I was exhilarated. Until suddenly I collapsed and was dragged inside. Mute and terrified and expecting to be lashed. I don't know why, but my defiance was forgiven.

—It was a ballet, his daughter said. The truant in the rain.

—Nuns on the run, said the son.

The German poet, long ago, went walking in the botanical gardens, saw plants, that elsewhere he had seen only in pots or under glass, growing cheerfully under the open sky. Might he not discover among them, the original plant from which all others are derived? After all, the poet thought, it must exist, the innermost nucleus.

A crazy idea. A wise old woman dressed like a gipsy or a pirate chief. A pert young girl curious about the American woman who had once been an orphan child in this town. Sadie Law with her leather coat and the smell of embrocation. A blonde horse-riding queen and huntress dying of drink in the back of an ambulance. Two sad creatures, nick-named, one for the colour of her only coat and the hard meagre shape of her body, the other because it was said, with sniggers, that she was hopeless of progeny and disreputable in her ancestry. Angela running hand in hand with him on a wet Saturday afternoon through the Old Flax Market.

The place was empty that day. Not even the ghosts of the woodsmen walked in the grey light and the rain. He couldn't remember where Sadie and Tom had been at that time. The

Jennet's corner was also empty. In the wooden shelter, hacked with names and odd obscenities and coy references to local love affairs, they sat on a creaky seat and kissed and fumbled. Then around a corner of the shelter came the Jennet herself, leading a staggering cattle-drover, his ash-plant in his hand.

—Wee fellow, he said with great camaraderie, I suppose you're at the same game as myself.

—He's too bashful, Angela said.

—He'll live to learn, the Jennet said. They all do.

The rain ran down her bony face. Wet yellow hair stuck out from under a red tam o'shanter. Her eyes were of such a bright blue as to make her seem blind.

—The good book, the drover said, says that the wise man falls seven times. And, as sure as my name is Solomon, I'm going to fall now.

So the wee fellow retreated from the shelter, dragging Angela with him for a little way until she dug her heels into the muddy ground. The river was a brown fresh, taking with it broken branches and hay from flooded meadows, sweeping on, down then by Derry our dear boys are sailing. Now he remembered that that day Angela had been wearing a sou'wester and Sadie's black coat, a little big for her but a stronghold against the rain.

—What do we need to run for? You might learn something.

He said nothing.

—Wee boy, she said. I'm going back for a peep.

He stood alone looking at the turbulent river, looking across the river at the limping spires, one proud and complete, one for ever unfinished, a memory of defeat and death. What would a wild woodsman have done? Down along the river valley it was said that there were trees on which the woodsmen, just before they left, had carved their names so strongly that the letters could still be read. But that must be a fable, a memory out of the old song: Their names on the trees of the rising plantation, their memories we'll cherish, and affection ne'er cool. For where are the heroes of high or low station that could be compared with the brave boys of Strule?

—That was as good as a circus, Angela said. You've no idea in the world what you missed.

At breakfast in the hotel in the morning the chatty little waitress shook his belief in himself by saying to him and his children that she had never heard of anybody of his name coming from this town.

—The great unknown, his daughter said.

—Fooling us all the time, the son said. He came from Atlanta, Georgia.

But then it turned out that the waitress came from a smaller town twenty miles away and was only eighteen years of age.

—Off we go now, said the daughter, to see where granny came from.

—Bring no whiskey to Claramore, his mother said. There was always too much whiskey in Claramore. Returned Americans coming and going.

The son and the daughter wished her a happy new year.

—Drive down the town first, she said. I owe a bill I must pay.

—Won't it wait?

She was dressed in high style: widow's black coat, high hat and veil, high buttoned boots for walking in country places.

—Never begin the new year in debt was a good maxim. I'll stick to it while I have breath.

Her grand-daughter, sitting beside her in the back of the hired car, giggled. Sourly he accepted the comments, one unconscious, one conscious, of two other generations on his own finances.

He drove down the High Street. They waited for her outside a hardware shop. The sky was pale blue, cloudless, and last night's unexpected white frost lay on the roofs and spotted the pavements. His daughter said: Granny never heard of a credit card.

More sordidly the son said: Nor hire purchase. Nor a post-dated cheque.

—It was a different world, mes enfants. They paid their way or went without.

But he knew that he had never worked out where—in the world that he had grown into—that terrifying old-fashioned honesty had gone : no debt, no theft, no waste. Beggars were accepted, because Joseph and Mary and the Child Jesus had gone homeless into Egypt. But debt was a sort of sin.

—Eat black bread first, she would say. But let no man say you're in his debt.

He had never taken to black bread. He hadn't told her that in a briefcase in the boot he had two bottles of Jack Daniels as a gift for his cousin—and for himself. A decent man could not with empty hands enter a decent house, and two bottles of American whiskey would be a fit offering to a house that had sent so many sons and daughters to the States.

She was back in the car again, settling herself like a duchess, her small red-headed grand-daughter helping her to tuck a rug around her knees. She refused to believe that a moving vehicle could be heated like a house.

It was a twelve-mile drive, first down the Derry road, over the steep hill that, in spite of all the miracles of macadam, was called, as it had been called in the eighteenth century, Clabber Brae. Then west, over the Drumquin railway crossing. There was no longer any railway to cross. Once upon a time the crossing-keeper's daughter had been as famous as Sadie Law. Then by Gillygooley crossroads where, one June day, Tom and himself, coming tired from fishing perch in the Fairywater, had seen Angela climbing a gate into a ripe meadow just opened for the mower. Her companion was a stocky-shouldered black-avised soldier. That much they could see. A hundred yards ahead, Tom rested from his cycling and was silent for a long time. Then he said : Boy, I'd leave that one alone for the future.

—She's leaving me alone. Who's she with?

—The worst in the barracks. Fusilier Nixon. And he'll never rank higher.

—Why so?

—Four years ago when he came back from India he was all but drummed out for raping a slavey in the soldiers' holm.

—There's a great view of the holm from the tall spire.

—If you had been up there you could have seen the fun. His bacon was saved by a major whose life he saved, or something, in India. And God help the slaveys. The offspring of that bit of love at first sight is now toddling around Fountain Lane. I'll point him out to you some day. You'd have something in common.

They cycled on.

—I'll tell Sadie, Tom said, what we saw. Sadie has some sense. She wouldn't want to be seen in the company of Fusilier Nixon.

Their bicycles bumped over the railway crossing. The keeper's daughter waved, and called : Hello, Tom Cunningham.

—Cheer up, boy. You'll get another girl.

—I suppose I will.

—From here to China the world's full of them.

—I liked Angela.

He found it hard not to sob. Angela peeping around a corner at the animals in the circus. Angela in the clutches of a black-chinned brute. He had, too, really liked her. More than thirty years later he foolishly looked for her face on the streets of the old town and the face he looked for could not, in reason, ever be there. He would see, instead, a Madonna—whom, also, he had never known—against a background of the coloured covers of magazines.

Now as he drove on, he looked at the gate that Angela had climbed into the meadow. But one gate was very like another and, under white frost, all meadows were the same. Although this valley to him would always be summer holiday country. Every mile of it he had walked or cycled. A hay-shed by a prosperous farmhouse meant for him mostly the sultry July hush before the rain came, the smell of sheds and barns, heavy rain on tin roofs, or soda bread and strong tea by peat fires on open hospitable hearths.

There now across the stilled, white fields was the glint of water at the pool where Tom and himself would first strike the Fairywater. The road climbed here, up over the stony place

242

of Clohogue, then switchbacked for miles in and out of hazel glens, over loud rough brooks, then on to a plateau, high, very high; and visible in such clear frosty air, and a good seventy miles away by the edge of the Atlantic, the pigback of Muckish Mountain, the white cone of Mount Errigal, the Cock of the North. Claramore was just below the plateau. It was a place of its own, in a new valley.

From the Barley Hill beyond the old long white farmhouse you could also see those two far-away mountains and, in the other direction and looking down the valley of the Fairywater, the tips and crosses of the two limping Gothic spires, but not the smaller plain spire of the Protestant church.

—On a calm evening, his cousin said, they seem so close that you'd imagine you could hear the bell ringing for the May devotions.

He asked his cousin: Do the young people still climb Drumard in autumn to pluck the blayberries?

—We've heard a lot about those same blayberries, his daughter said. To pluck and eat them, dad says, was a memory of some ancient pagan feast.

—The young people, his cousin said, have their own pagan feasts.

The four of them walked on the boreen that crossed the Barley Hill to the place where the men were building a house for his cousin's son and the bride he would bring home with him in three months' time. Hard frost had slowed up the building work. Among the men, half-loitering, working just enough to keep warm, keeping as close as possible to an open brazier, his cousin passed round one of the bottles of bourbon. They drank from cracked cups and tin mugs, toasted the health of the visitors, of the bride-to-be, wished luck for ever on the house they were building. High above a jet plane, westward-bound out of Prestwick, made its mark on the cold pale blue.

—They'll be in New York before you, his son said.

The drinking men, circling the brazier, saluted the travellers in the sky and raised a cheer. It was only a few hours to New York from the Barley Hill or the pagan blayberries of Drumard.

Breath ascended in puffs as white as the jet's signature. On the far side of the hill from the long farmhouse the Fairywater, glittering black, looped through frosted bottom-land.

—Phil Loughran, that used to work for you, he said. He was about my age. Where did he go?

The Black Stepping Stones were at that bend of the Fairywater, the seventh bend visible from where they stood; and above the Black Stones the pool where the country boys went swimming. Willows drooped over it. The bottom was good yellow sand. The water had the brown of the peat and was nowhere more than four feet deep. It was an idyllic place, had been an idyllic place until the day he had that crazy fight with Phil Loughran.

—He went to Australia, his cousin said. We hear he's doing well. The family, what's left of them, are still living here on my land.

Even to this day, and in the frosty air, he blushed to think of the lies he had told to Phil Loughran down there by the Black Stones—blushed all the more because, country boys being so much more cunning than towny boys, Phil almost certainly hadn't believed a word he said. Phil as he listened would have secretly laughed.

—So her name is Angela, he said.

Phil was a squat sallow-faced young fellow, dressed in rough corduroys and heavy nailed boots, his brown hair short-cropped, his eyes dark brown and close together. There was always a vague smell of peat smoke, or stables or something, from those corduroys.

—Angela the walking angel, he said.

They were dressing after a swim. Three other boys splashed and shouted in the pool. A fourth hung naked from a trailing willow, swinging like a pendulum, striking the water with his feet.

—So you tell us, Phil, you had the little man out of sight.

He made a sideways grab, as Angela had done on the wooded brambly slope above the pike-pool on the Drumragh. He was laughing. He said : Little man, you've had a busy day.

Then the two of them were rolling on the grass, swiping at each other, Phil still laughing, he sobbing, with temper, with the humiliation of having his tall tales of conquest made mockery of. Four naked dripping boys danced and laughed and shouted around them. It was the last day but one that he had been at the Black Stones. He had come second best out of that fight but he had a mean miserable sort of vengeance on his very last visit to the place.

Phil in his best corduroys—since it was Sunday—is crossing the water, stepping carefully from stone to stone, in his right hand the halter with which he is leading a love-stricken Claramore cow to keep her date with a bull on the farm on the far side of the river. So he calls to Phil to mind his Sunday-go-to-meeting suit and Phil, turning round to answer, is off his guard when the restive beast bolts. It is, fair enough, his turn to laugh, sharp, clear and cruel, as Phil, bravely holding on to the halter is dragged through the shallow muddy water below the stones. There are seventeen in Phil's family, and he is the eldest, and those corduroys will not be easily replaced.

Over the hard frosted fields his own laughter came back to him.

—I'm glad to hear he did well in Australia.

—They were a thrifty family, his cousin said. A sister of his might visit us this evening, the youngest of the breed, a god-daughter of mine.

The trail of the jet was curdling in the cold sky. The men had gone back to work. For penance he told his cousin and son and daughter how he had laughed on the day the cow dragged Phil through the muddy water. They stood by a huge sycamore a little down the slopes from the unfinished house. Icicles hung from bare branches. He said, nothing about how James had mocked his boasting.

—Weren't you the beast, dad, his daughter said.

—But it was funny, the son said.

—The young, his cousin said, can be thoughtless. Present company excepted.

For the daughter, the face of a good mimic distorted with mock fury, was dancing towards the cousin to stab him with an icicle broken from the sycamore.

—No, but seriously, he said when they had played out their pantomime of fury and terror : a grey man over sixty with a restful singing sort of voice and a pert little girl of sixteen.

—Seriously. Look at the sycamore. It was planted here more than a hundred years ago by an uncle of mine who was a priest. He died young, not long after ordination. He planted this tree on the day he was ordained, and blessed the earth and the sapling. You may recall, when you were young yourselves, some of his books were still about the house. Mostly Latin. Theology. Some novels. I told you about one of them and you rushed to get it. The *Lass of the Barns*, you thought I said. But, man alive, were you down in the mouth when you discovered it was the *Last of the Barons*.

—Oh dad, his daughter said.

—But I know the age of this tree by checking on the date on the priest's tombstone in Langfield churchyard. And my son says to me : We'll cut it down. It'll spoil the view from the new house. So I said : The house may fall, but this tree will stand while I do. The old have a feeling for each other.

—Lucky tree, the daughter said, that has somebody to stand up for it.

They went, laughing, back down the Barley Hill towards the warmth of the great kitchen of the farmhouse. Under the pall of the white frost it seemed as if nothing here would ever change : not the sycamore, not his cousin, nor the ancient sleeping land. Nothing would change, no matter how many airliners swept westwards up there, leaving nothing behind them but a curdling dissolving mark on the sky. All the ships that had carried all those people westwards, even so many sons and daughters of this house, and the ocean was still unmarked and the land here as it had been. It was elsewhere in the world the changes happened.

—But this fatal ship to her cold bosom folds them. Wherever she goes our fond hearts shall adore them. Our prayers and good wishes will still be before them, that their names be remembered and sung by the Strule.

The pond at the corner of the avenue was frozen over. He had fallen into it once, climbing the fence above and beyond it to chase a wandering bullock out of a field of young oats. The fence-post he had been holding on to had broken. The water, he had always imagined, had tasted of duck-dirt. But then how in hell would one be expected to know what duck-dirt tasted like? The fence-post, he noticed, was now made of iron, and that might be some indication, even here, of change. But not much.

The ash-grove to the left before you came to the stables—in that grove he had once criminally broken a young sapling to make a fishing rod—was now a solid wall of grown strong trees, a windbreak on days of south-westerly gales.

Would the horses in the stables be the same, with the same names, as they had been thirty years ago? He was afraid to ask, to be laughed at, to be told what he knew : that even here, even loved familiar farmhorses didn't live for ever. The dogs seemed the same—collies, with more sprawling pups under-foot than had ever seemed natural. The pattern of farming though, had changed somewhat, he had been told : more barley, more pigs fed on the barley, less oats, less root crops, more sucking calves bred in season on the open pasture, taken early from their mothers and sold to be fattened somewhere in con-finement, and slaughtered.

In the house ahead of them somebody was playing a melodeon, softly, slowly, and that was something that hadn't changed, because in the past in that house there had been great country dances to pipe, fiddle and melodeon. That was before so many of his cousins, all much older than himself, had gone to the States.

His mother had enjoyed herself. She was red in the face and moist-eyed from sitting by the open hearth with its high golden pyramid of blazing peat; from remembering, for the instruction of a younger generation, the comic figaries of her

247

dear departed dowager of a sister, Kate, who, as a widow in her thirties, had ruled not only Claramore but half the country-side; and from, let it be admitted, sipping at the bourbon. For while she was a great one to lecture about the dangers of drink, she was liable the next minute to take from her sideboard a bottle of brandy and a bottle of whiskey, to ask what you were having, and to join you herself, and she instinctively thought the worst of a man who neither smoked, drank, swore, nor rode horses.

—The young people, she said, are growing up well, God bless them. They haven't forgotten the old ways. That house was never without music and dancing.

The Claramore people had stood around the car, under a frosty moon, and sang Auld Lang Syne as their guests departed.

—That Loughran girl was a good hand at the melodeon. Did you all see her making up to the widow man, the returned American?

She poked him between the shoulder-blades as he drove slowly over the icy plateau.

—She sat on your knee, dad, the daughter said.

He could still feel the pressure of the underparts of the girl's thighs. She was conventionally slim and dark and handsome, with wide brown eyes; in appearance most unlike her eldest brother. She had sat on his knee in the dancing kitchen to tell him that Phil, in every letter he wrote from Australia, enquired about him. She stayed sitting there while his cousin sang : There was once a maid in a lonely garden when a well-dressed gentle-man came passing by.

—Was that story true granny, the son asked. The one about the lone bush.

—Would I tell it if it wasn't.

They descended into the first hazel glen. Over the rushing of its brook they could hear the roaring of another jet, out of Prestwick, bound for New York.

—They're lining up to get into America, the son said.

—To get out of it too, son.

Six hours or so to the bedlam of Kennedy airport : But now

our bold heroes are past all their dangers. On America's shores they won't be long strangers. They'll send back their love from famed Blessington's Rangers to comrades and friends and the fair maids of Strule.

People who travelled by jet left no shadows in old marketplaces. Generations would be born to whom the ache and loneliness in the old songs of exile would mean nothing.

—Jordan Taggart the cobbler, as I said, had his house on the road from Claramore to Carrickaness, and a small farm to boot. Against the advice of all, even against Father Gormley the priest that cured people, he cut down a whitethorn that grew alone in the middle of his meadow and, at nightfall, he dragged it home behind him for kindling. In the orchard before his house he saw two small children, dressed in white, and he spoke to them but they made no answer. So he told his wife and his three sons, who were also cobblers, that there were two shy children waiting, maybe for mended shoes in the orchard. But when two of the sons went out and searched they saw nothing. Then Jordan ate the supper of a healthy man and went to bed and died in his sleep.

—But he wasn't really dead, the son said.

—No, the white children took him. God between us and all harm.

In the darkness in the car she spat, but slightly and politely, and into her handkerchief.

The daughter said nothing.

They were back again in the meadow country where Angela had climbed the gate and, except for one last meeting, had climbed out of his life for ever. They bumped over the Drumquin crossing where there was no longer any railway to cross, no easy girl to call longingly after Tom Cunningham who was chasing girls in China and never wrote to enquire about anybody.

The daughter was alert again. She was giggling. She said: Dad, Granny wants to do something about the way you dress.

—I was only thinking about his own good, his mother said.

Although he was carefully driving the car over Clabber Brae, he knew by the way she talked that he was no longer there.

—But when I was by the seaside at Bundoran I saw these young fellows wearing loose coloured patterned shirts outside their trousers. I was told it was an American fashion, and I was sure that he would be wearing one of them when he came home.

He said : I'm no young fellow.

—What I thought was that it would cover his middle-aged spread.

As they descended by the military barracks into the town the daughter's giggles rocked the car.

—A maternity shirt, she said.

—For how could he expect anyone to look at him at his age and with a stomach like that.

Castle Street went up so steeply that it seemed as if it was trying to climb those dark grotesque spires.

—A young one, for instance, like that Loughran girl who sat on his knee because the chairs were scarce.

—That one, he said. All that I remember about the Loughrans is that her bare-footed elder brothers were always raiding Aunt Kate's cherry trees and blaming the depredation on the birds.

In the hotel bar only two of the commercial men were left. They said : What do you think now of your happy home town?

—How do you mean?

—Last night's tragic event, they said. Didn't you hear? Didn't you read the paper?

—I was in the country all day.

Back in the past where one didn't read the newspapers.

—A poor man murdered, they said. What your American friends would call a filling-station attendant.

—Robbed and shot, they said. Just when we were sitting here talking about murder.

The grandfather clock in the hallway chimed midnight.

—The New Year, he said. May it be quiet and happy.

In the ballroom in the far wing of the hotel the revellers were clasping hands and singing about old acquaintance.

—We should be there singing, he said.

—The second murder here this year, they said. The other was a queer case, two young men, a bit odd. Things like that usen't to happen. This town is getting to be as bad as Chicago.

—It isn't as big or as varied.

They laughed. They agreed that the town was still only in a small way of business. He asked them was the park called the Lovers' Retreat still where it had been.

—If that's the way you feel, it is.

More laughter.

—But it's gone to hell, they told him. It's not kept as it used to be. The young compulsory soldiers in national service wreck everything. They haven't the style of the old Indian army, when the empire was in its glory. Children's swings uprooted now. Benches broken. One of the two bridges over the millrace gone completely. The grass three feet long.

—Nothing improves, they said.

When they left him he sat on for a long time, drinking alone. Was it imagination, or could he really hear the sound of the Camowen waters falling over the salmon leap at the Lovers' Retreat? That place was one of the sights of the town when the salmon were running : the shining curving bodies rising from the water as if sprung from catapults—leaping and struggling upwards in white foam and froth. But one year the water was abnormally low, the salmon a sullen black mass in the pool below the falls—a temptation to a man with Tom Cunningham's enterprise. The water-bailiff and his two assistants and his three dogs came by night and caught Tom and his faithful companion with torch and gaff and one slaughtered salmon. But since the bailiff, a bandy-legged amiable man, was also the park-keeper he said not a word to the police on condition that the two criminals kept the grass in the park mowed for a period of six months.

—Hard labour, by God, boy. He has us by the hasp. The Big House with Wallace Beery. You be Mickey Rooney.

The bad news travelled and was comic to all except the two mowers. Then one day from the far side of the millrace that made one boundary to the park they heard the laughter of women, and saw Sadie and Angela, bending and pointing.

—Two men went to mow, they sang, went to mow the meadow.

—Grilled salmon for all, they called.

Tom crossed the millrace by leaping on to the trunk of a leaning tree that was rooted on the far bank. Sadie, laughing, screaming in mock terror, and Tom in pursuit, vanished into the bluebell woods. Tom's companion crossed the millrace prosaically by one of the wooden footbridges. Was it the one that the wild young resentful compulsory soldiers had destroyed? She didn't run. She wasn't laughing any more. Her brown hair no longer curled in little horns on her temples but was combed straight back. But the wide mouth, in spite of the black fusilier, was to him as inviting as ever. She said: You're a dab-hand at mowing. You've a future in cutting grass.

He said: I never see you any more.

—Little boys should take what's offered to them, when it's offered. Go back to your scythe.

—Go back to the fusilier, he said.

He went back to his scythe by climbing along the trunk of the leaning tree and leaping the millrace. The grass that fell before his scythe was crimson in colour and swathed in a sort of mist. The swing of the scythe moved with the rhythm of the falling water sweeping on to meet the Drumragh, to become the Strule, to absorb the Fairywater and the Derg and the Owenkillew, to become the Mourne, to absorb the Finn, to become the Foyle, to go down then by Derry to the ocean, taking with it the shadows of the woodsmen, the echoes of the brass and pipes and tramping feet of the army of a vanished empire, the stories of all who had ever lived in this valley.

He knew he was drunk when he heard the woman's voice speak respectfully to him and saw her through the crimson mist through which long ago he had seen the falling grass. She said: You wouldn't remember me, sir.

He didn't. She wore the black dress, white collar and cuffs of the hotel staff. She would be sixtyish. She said : We saw you on the teevee one night and I said to Francie who you were. But he said he didn't know you. He knew your elder brother better.

—My brother was well known.

—Francie's my brother. You might remember he used to ride racing bicycles. I saw you in the dining-room. I work in the kitchen. I knew it was you when I saw your son, and from the teevee.

—You're Sadie Law.

—I didn't like to intrude on you and the children.

He said there was no intrusion. They shook hands. He asked her how her brother was.

—He's in a chair all the time. He broke his back at the tomfool cycling. But he does woodcarving, and I work here. We manage. I never married.

Her face did not remind him of Sadie Law, but then he found that he could not remember what Sadie Law's face had looked like.

—Nobody, he said, could replace Tom Cunningham.

She neither smiled nor looked sorrowful. Her face remained the same. She said : Oh, Tom was a card. He went away.

Some revellers from the ballroom came in, drunk, singing, wearing paper hats. She said : I must be off.

—I'll see you in the morning.

—I'm off duty then. Because of the late dance tonight. But we hope you'll come back often to see the old places.

—Do you ever remember, he asked, a Fusilier Nixon, a wild fellow.

She thought : No. But there were so many fusiliers. A lot of them we'll never see again.

—We'll look out for you on the teevee, she said.

They shook hands again.

They said goodbye to his mother and drove away. His daughter said : Dad, this isn't the Dublin road.

—There's a place I want to see before we leave.

253

It was the place that Tom and himself used to go to when they considered that the mental strain of school was too much for them. For it was an odd thing that in all the comings and goings of that railway station nobody ever thought of asking a pair of truants what they were doing there. Everybody thought that everybody else was waiting for somebody else, and there were always porters and postmen who knew what you were at, but who kept the knowledge to themselves, and would share talk and cigarettes with runaway convicts, let alone reluctant schoolboys. No police hunted for drifters or loiterers as in American bus stations : and the sights were superb and you met the best people. They had spent several hours one day with Chief Abidu from southern Nigeria and his Irish wife and honey-coloured brood. He danced on broken glass and swallowed fire in a wooden booth in the Old Market, and, beating on his breast, made the most wonderful throaty noises; and came, most likely, from Liverpool.

—I understand, she had written, that the railway station is closed now. Only the ghosts of those who passed through it abide there. Some were gentle, some were violent men, morose or gay, ordinary or extraordinary. I had time to watch them passing by. It is pain that they died so young, so long ago.

The tracks were gone, the grass and weeds had grown high through the ballast. The old stone buildings had been turned into warehouses. Two men in dusty dungarees kept coming and going, carrying sacks of meal, at the far end of the platform. But if they spoke to each other they were too far away for their voices to be heard, and the cold wind moved as stealthily in grass and weeds as if it were blowing over some forlorn midland hillside. Where the bookstall had been there was just a scar on the granite wall, where she had stood, framed against coloured books and magazines, and watched the soldiers coming and going.

—The young English poet you mention, I knew briefly. He came to buy books. At first he had little to say, simply polite, that's all. Then one day he and another young man began to talk. They included me. But mostly I listened. It was fascinating. After that, when he came he talked about books. He asked questions about Ireland. He was uneasy there, considered it beautiful but alien, felt, I think, that the very earth of Ireland was hostile to him, the landscape had a brooding quality as though it waited.

—He was five or six months garrisoned in our town. They told me he could be very much one of the boys, but he could also be remote. He treated me kindly, teased me gently. But he and a brilliant bitter Welshman gave me books and talked to me. Sometimes they talked about the war.

—It was only after he was reported missing in Africa that I learned he was a poet. But I think I knew anyway.

—I never heard if the Welshman survived. I had several long letters from him and that was all.

Ghosts everywhere in this old town.

—Now I have a son who may pass through a railway station or an airport on his way to war.

He said to his daughter: That's where the bookstall was.

—Will you go to see her, dad? In the States, I mean.

—In a way I've seen her.

He was grateful that she didn't ask him what on earth he was talking about.

—As the song says, I'll look for her if I'm ever back that way.

The ghost of his father stood just here, waving farewell to him every time he went back after holidays to college in Dublin.

They walked through the cold deserted hall, where the ticket offices had been, and down the steps, grass-grown, cracked, to the Station Square, once lined with taxis, now empty except for some playing children and the truck into which the dusty men were loading the sacks. From the high steeple the noonday angelus rang.

—How high up is the bell? his son asked.

He told him, and also told him the height of the spire and of the surmounting cross, and why one spire was higher than the other, and how he had once climbed up there, and of the view over the valley, and of how he had almost fallen to doom on the way down, and of the vertigo, the fear of death, that followed.

255

—And a curious thing. Once, on top of the Eiffel Tower, that vertigo returned. And once over the Mojave desert when I thought the plane was going to crash. But I didn't see Paris or the Mojave desert. I saw that long straight ladder.

The bell ceased. The spires were outlined very clearly in the cold air, looked as formidable as precipices. Around them floated black specks, the unbanishable jackdaws.

—Once I got a job from the parish priest because I was a dab hand with a twenty-two. The job was to shoot the jackdaws, they were pests, off the spires. It was going fine until the police stopped me for using a firearm too close to a public highway. The sexton at the time was a tall man in a black robe down to his feet, more stately than a bishop. One day, when he was watching me at work, a bird I shot struck one of those protruding corner-stones and came soaring, dead, in a wide parabola, straight for the sexton. He backed away, looking in horror at the falling bird. But he tripped on his robe, and the bird, blood, feathers, beak and all got him fair in the face. At that time I thought it was the funniest thing I had ever seen.

—Grisly, his daughter said.

—But once upon a time I laughed easily. It was easy to laugh here then.

High Street, Market Street, the Dublin Road. A stop at the grave where the caretaker's men had already done their job. The weeds were gone, the sad hollow filled, new white stones laid.

Then on to Dublin, crossing the Drumragh at Lissan Bridge where, it was said, Red Hugh O'Donnell had passed on his way back from prison in Dublin Castle to princedom in Donegal and war with Elizabeth of England. The wintry land brooded waiting, as it had always done, and would do for ever.

He sang at the wheel: There was once a maid in a lovely garden.

—Oh dad, his daughter said.

So he thought the rest of it: Oh, do you see yon high high building? And do you see yon castle fine? And do you see yon ship on the ocean? They'll all be thine if thou wilt be mine.